A Taste of Sweetness

A Blossom Hills Romance, Volume 1

Kate Alexander

Published by Kate Alexander, 2020.

A TASTE OF SWEETNESS

First edition. July 28, 2020.

Written by Kate Alexander.

Sign up for Kate Alexander's Mailing List

This book is dedicated to my family and all of my friends who have become my family

Chapter 1

Zoey reached for her last Diet Coke and opened the bottle while driving the last leg of her journey to her new home, but as soon as the bottle hissed its warning from the screw-top lid, she knew she had made a mistake.

"No...oh no no no...oh shoot!" Zoey exclaimed and then silently started cursing herself. "Not now," she shouted, but it was too late. The carbonated fizz spewed over the top and sprayed her face and clothes. She carefully slowed her little Dodge Journey with her U-Haul trailer, moving to the side of the road. She glowered at the bottle and then began the frantic search for something to clean herself and the car from the sticky soda. All that could be found was one sad little napkin from her earlier drive thru dinner that day. Exasperatedly, she looked at her steering wheel and then down to her clothes. After a brief moment, she decided to clean the steering wheel instead of her shirt and jeans, which were a lost cause. "Okay, I need to find a rest area or something," she moaned to herself and then continued on her way.

About thirty-five minutes later, she finally found a rest area that she found suitable. Sure, there were a few gas stations along the way, but it was dark and they didn't look like the friendliest places to stop so she decided to find something a little less scary. By the time she pulled in, her clothes were sticky and starting to stiffen to the touch. She climbed out of the car and opened the back gate to the trailer where all her belongings now were packed solid. Taking a quick inventory of what was readily accessible, she thumped her forehead on the first box and started to quickly repeat the thumping. "Of course, my clothes are in the back."

She growled and sighed with the quick realization that the only clothes she would be able to quickly reach were from her small duffel bag in the car, and those were her pajamas from the night before. "Better than nothing, I suppose."

She reached into the car and pulled out her bag. As she did so, her cell phone went flying out of the car into the next parking space. She heard the crash on the ground and knew that sound all too well. To say that she wasn't graceful seemed to be an understatement, but at least most people thought it was part of her charm. She thought it was just annoying and expensive.

Dashing over to the ground, she went to pick up the phone, and the screen was destroyed in a horrible array of spider web cracks. Zoey looked up to the night stars and exclaimed, "God, I am trying to have a sense of humor about this, but now you are just being mean." She gathered up the phone and placed it back on the passenger seat and then made her way to the restrooms to clean up and change.

She later emerged from the restroom in her small tank top and pajama shorts cleaned from the sticky soda. Her tank top was white with purple lettering that said, "sprinkled with love" and tiny colorful sprinkles covering the top. Her bottoms were patterned with little cartoon cupcakes with pink and purple icing and sprinkles. She loved silly pajamas. They made her feel happy. The rest of her life was almost always such a mess. So, she felt, at least this way before she went to bed each night she could smile. As she got into the car, she began to have second thoughts about her attire. She was going to arrive to her new home at Blossom Hills and didn't want people judging her based on her choice of nightwear. She quickly disregarded that since it would be nearly 2 am by the time she arrived, and no one should be awake in a small sleepy town at that hour. Even her friend's bar would be closed by midnight since it was a Sunday. He promised to help unload the trailer when she arrived the next morning.

After what seemed like an endless drive she arrived and read the sign saying, "Welcome to Blossom Hills, where everything blooms to life." From what Derek had told her, it was originally founded on orchards. There were apple and cherry trees that the town built their foundations around with a few farms on the outskirts. Blossom Hills had found small success with tourism, being known for its seemingly magical ambiance and couples finding love. There were several bed and breakfasts thriving throughout the town and there was also a major festival for each season.

Zoey was not interested in finding love. Far from it. She had just left a string of bad relationships, and the last one left her weary of any seemingly well-intentioned man. She knew things were not ideal while she was in the relationship but didn't know just how bad it had gotten until her friend Derek had come to visit. He had come into town for his friend's wedding and made sure to have lunch with Zoey before he left. He took one look at her and frowned. Her light and her smile were too dim. When he first saw her come through the door, she had a big genuine smile that reached her eyes, but as the lunch went on and they were catching up, he saw her eyes grow a little vacant and the rest of her just seemed to fade.

"Zoe, what is going on?" he asked with a frown now on his face.

Zoey gave a small smile at Derek's use of her nickname. He was the only person who was allowed to use it. He'd earned it. "What do you mean?"

"I can't put my finger quite on it, but you just aren't yourself." He paused. "You seem off. The Zoey I know would have been laughing most of the time that we have been sitting here. You're smiling, but the meaning isn't there. Is this Shane guy treating you right? Are you hurt?"

Zoey's eyes got even rounder and her mouth parted to say something, but nothing came out for a brief moment. "No. I'm not hurt. He doesn't hurt me." She paused. "I can't believe that you would think I would stay with someone who would do that to me."

"Is he nice to you?"

Zoey hesitated for a brief moment and stared directly into Derek's eyes. She knew she couldn't lie to him but didn't need to have full disclosure that would make Shane or herself look bad. "Of course. We have our little fights and say things that we don't mean, but he does apologize when he crosses the line." If Zoey was honest with herself, she never crossed the line. She walked on eggshells and continually tried to please Shane. She knew that her average body wasn't what

men normally found attractive. She always felt less than perfect, like she should be grateful to have someone in her life.

Derek frowned and gave a slight growl. "It shouldn't ever
come to crossing a line."

"I promise I would never keep myself in a relationship
that is less than I deserve." The problem was that at that time
she didn't feel like she deserved much. Shane consistently
put her down about her looks, her value as a person and her
friends. Nearly all of her friends in town had deserted her because of her bad string of boyfriends, and Shane was the last
straw to alienate the few friends that she had left.

"Are you still baking?"

"I can't seem to stop myself. I want to open a bakery of
my own someday. I make money on the side making desserts
and cakes from referrals and friends. There are some weeks I
make more money doing those than I do with my adminis-
trative job."

"That would be amazing. I know you would have a long
line of customers every day."

Zoey beamed. "Thanks. I can't do anything about it now,
but maybe someday. Oh, I almost forgot. I brought you a
present." Zoey turned to her purse where she pulled a small
rectangular gift wrapped in University of Kentucky paper.

"Nice wrapping," Derek said with a sly grin as he began
to open the present.

"Thanks. I thought about the Scooby Doo paper, but figured you may have outgrown that by now."

Derek shook his head and gazed down at the present. It
was a picture of him, Zoey, and Zoey's ex-boyfriend Trevor.
Zoey stood in the middle with a flowing black and white

dress and wide hat with flowers around the brim. The two men flanked her sides in their button-down shirts and ties. When he brought his eyes up to hers, she could feel her tears gathering, ready to fall.

"Do you like it?"

"Zoe, I love it. I can't believe you still have this picture."

"Honestly, I had thought I lost it, but my brother brought me a box from mom's leftover stuff, and it was in a stack of papers. There were two copies. I kept one and thought you should get the other one."

Derek traced his fingers over the image of Zoey and then Trevor. Trevor was Zoey's college boyfriend who had died from an aneurism her junior year. "I remember this. This is from the Kentucky Derby, right?"

"Yes. The two of you were so excited that I won those tickets."

"it was amazing. I never laughed so hard when you and Trevor broke it to your roommates that they weren't getting the extra tickets."

"Good Lord. Those girls were horrid. I remember when we moved into that house and found out that a bunch of guys were renting the downstairs. They used to get all dressed up and try to flirt with all of you."

"Melissa should have known better. We all knew her, and she knew all too well we didn't like her. It didn't take long to figure out the others were just as bad. I remember trying to figure out where you came from because you were nothing like them."

"I never told you?"

"No."

"I only became their roommate because of the ad I answered on the board at school. Their third roommate got knocked up and dropped out of school to move home. They agreed to let me move in out of desperation. They only tolerated me because of my baking skills, and I stayed because the rent was cheap. Well, that and I loved the guys who lived downstairs."

Derek looked down at the picture again. "You still miss him, don't you?"

Zoey looked down and sighed. "Every day. Every day with my whole heart. It has been almost fifteen years now." She paused as she traced the design on the table. "Why is it every time I think about him, I am hurt and angry? I mean, I went through those stupid stages of death to acceptance, and there is still this whole in my heart that craves the love he gave me."

"And you don't have that with Shane?"

Zoey didn't answer. She simply tightened her lips and continued to trace the designs on the table, letting the silence give him her answer.

"It's okay, Zoe. I miss him too. He was a big part of our lives during college. He may have been your boyfriend, but he quickly became a good friend to me too."

"He was more your fan at first. He thought your game was damn near perfect."

Derek barked out a laugh. "Well, you certainly never had any issues telling me what I was doing wrong."

"Someone had to tell you when you sucked."

"You also had no problem telling me that I sucked at poker too."

Zoey laughed. "You all sucked. You guys were pathetic, but that money paid for all the groceries I needed to feed you monsters."

Derek nodded. "And my mother thanks you."

The lunch continued with pleasantries until nearly the end when Shane came bursting through the door and rushed up to their table. "I thought you were having lunch with a friend from college?" His face was scowling and provided an icy glare to Derek.

Derek looked amused. Shane, standing at 5'11" and a bit out of shape, was clearly no match for Derek. Derek would not be intimidated. He was a former athlete who still remained in shape, and at 6'4" would tower over Shane.

"I am her friend from college. Derek McKenna." Derek extended his hand to Shane, simply hoping to save Zoey from further discomfort.

"I thought your friend from college was a girl." By now Shane's voice was slightly cracking from temper and an immediate realization that he would quickly lose in an altercation with Derek.

"Sorry to disappoint your expectations. Should I put on a dress and wig to make you feel better?" Derek mused.

"No," Shane said and then turned to Zoey. "We need to go. We have to meet my family tonight. I am sure you simply forgot. It's okay." He gave a smile that was almost a sneer to Derek.

Zoey wasn't sure quite what to do. She wanted to stay with Derek but didn't want to have another fight with Shane. Had she forgotten about the family thing? She didn't think so. "I still need to pay for my lunch."

Shane pulled out his wallet and threw down two twenties. "There. Keep the change, Derek."

"I can pay for our lunch. I told her it was my treat," Derek growled.

"Fine. Pay and then go back to where you came from."

"Shane! That's enough." Zoey was angry. She had lost so many people in her life, and this was getting out of control. "Derek, I will call you later. I promise. Lunch was lovely." She gave Derek a hug and tilted her head to whisper in his ear. "I *will* call you later."

True to her word, four days later she did call. "I left Shane." She paused. "He just turned into the guy that made me feel hollow inside. He started out so nice, but then he started in with the name calling and comments about my body and friends. It hurt, and I felt so detached from everyone and everything, and he just didn't trust me. I didn't realize how bad it had gotten until our lunch, so I left. And I have you to thank."

"Are you okay now?"

"Yes. I got a short-term lease on a furnished apartment. I left most everything at Shane's except my baking supplies and personal things. Oh, and the 60-inch television that I paid for. I have to be able to watch my sports." She smiled big at this one. She knew Shane would be cursing her name when he found the large television gone.

"What you are going to do now? Are you going to stay there in Lexington?"

"I don't think so. There isn't anything keeping me here except being somewhat close to my brother, but still he is almost two hours away. Mom is in Florida now, and I have no real friendship ties here. I still want to open a bakery, but the market is so saturated here it wouldn't make sense."

"Well, let me know what you decide to do and where you go."

"I will."

Two months later, Derek called excitedly and told her that Estelle's Bakery in his hometown of Blossom Hills was closing. The owner, Estelle, decided to retire and go to Arizona. He had the landlord send Zoey the details of the leasing opportunity, and it was a perfect fit. The lease was reasonable and there was also an apartment just above the bakery that was fully furnished where she could live. It wouldn't be available for another three months, but this gave Zoey an opportunity to work overtime at her regular job and make additional money from baking on the side for needed expenses.

Excited about the new opportunity, Zoey cashed in her 401k and also received a grant from the Blossom Hills Chamber of Commerce for five thousand dollars to assist in opening the store. It could not have been more perfect.

This was a big risk, but she was confident in her baking skills and had earned a business degree in college. She knew she could do this. She hired movers to pack the U-Haul trailer and didn't even look in her rear-view mirror when she left town.

She pulled into the center of Blossom Hills where it looked like a picturesque movie. In the center of the town was a block of green grass with benches throughout and a large white gazebo in the center. This was surely the focus of every festival and town event. Her bakery was just on the other side of the street from the gazebo. Her front patio would be in direct view. *How perfect*, she thought. *I can put out a small table and chairs for people to enjoy in nice weather.* Small bubbles of happiness crept up from her stomach.

She turned down the small alley behind the bakery where there were a few dedicated parking spots. After grabbing her duffel bag and badly damaged phone, she pulled herself out of the car. She found the back door that went up to the apartment and suddenly realized just how tired she was.

Because of the email from her new landlord, Mrs. Glover, she knew that the key to the apartment was just under the fire extinguisher. She easily found the key and let herself in. It was a cozy apartment with a small kitchen with an island to the right of the entryway and then a small dining room and living room attached to make one great open space. Off to the left she saw another door that was mostly closed that she assumed was the bedroom. As tired as she was, she wanted to pull out her folder and go over some information before heading back to her new bed.

There in the front of the folder was the information for her bakery. She ran her fingers over the spiral writing that said, "Sweet Dreams Bakery." She sighed and whispered, "Finally." Then, realizing just how comfortable the couch was, she laid down and continued to read the papers. Before she knew what happened, she fell into a deep sleep.

Chapter 2

Tyler woke up lazily and turned to see his digital alarm clock. Groaning, he saw that it was only just after six. He looked around, slightly disoriented, and quickly remembered he was in his new apartment. It was a cozy little furnished place. He was in his hometown of Blossom Hills after moving back from Philadelphia. The company where he worked as a software developer had been sold and he was quickly displaced. The year before that, he had broken off his long-time relationship to Jane after finding out that she was cheating on him and had fallen in love with the guy. This sent Tyler on a destructive streak where he bedded any woman who would provide him with attention. Finding consenting women didn't seem to be any trouble for him. While he was a self-proclaimed computer geek, he was still a rather attractive man, standing at 6'1" with sandy blonde hair and green eyes. He did not have a chiseled chest like other men, but instead was slender with slight definition.

Deciding to make changes to his life after an evening of drinking too much and waking with a woman whose name he could barely remember, he realized he needed to get his life back together. His job was demanding, and he knew that he didn't give Jane the attention she needed, but he wished she would have addressed their issues with him before just going out to find someone else to warm her bed. When the company dissolved and Tyler received his generous severance package, he had decided it was time to become his own boss and freelanced with his computer services. Most days he consulted and designed software programs for large companies but was also filling his time with web and app designs for small businesses at a lower cost than most of his competitors. Somewhere inside of him, it eased his conscience by helping the small businesses.

Back now in Blossom Hills for a couple weeks, and in the new apartment for only two days, he felt good about reconnecting with friends and staying away from relationships with women that could let him fall back into self-destruction. He stared at the ceiling and debated with himself whether he should get up and start his day or try to go back to sleep. After all, he was his own boss and made his own schedule. As he considered going back to sleep, his stomach growled and made his decision for him. Wake up it was. He rolled out of the side of bed in his plaid boxers and made his way to the kitchen. His stomach rumbled again, and he thought to himself how much he missed Estelle's bakery. He had never been much for cereal or cooking his own breakfast. He thought no one should cook while they were still half asleep. He managed to grab a bagel and glass of orange juice and stood resting at the island. When he turned to look out the living room window, his breath caught in his chest.

There on his couch was a woman fast asleep. The juice glass made a loud thump as he set it down and rubbed his eyes. He must still be asleep because seriously, women didn't just show up and sleep on your couch like Goldilocks. He looked again and then mused that she could be Goldilocks, but instead of the blonde curls like the story she had strawberry blonde loose ringlets. A little more red than blonde, but cute as hell. Pausing, he thought he should panic more. After all, she was an intruder, but she looked so damned cute. Sweetness and charm surrounded her all the way from her hair cascading around her face to the nice curves around her hips and legs to those crazy pajamas. There were cupcakes on the bottoms that were giving him quite a peak of her upper legs and a tank top with sprinkles on it. There was writing on the top, but he couldn't figure out what it said because of how it crinkled while she was lying there.

After drinking her in for a minute, he started to think that he should at least wake her up and ask her what she thinks she is doing in his apartment. He should be outraged, but she looked so irresistible. Maybe she had a good reason. Still, having seen so many movies, he took his cell phone in his hand just in case he had to call the police when she woke up. Should he wake her up? She was out cold. He knew that he wasn't very quiet getting his breakfast, and he had even turned on the light.

He quietly walked into the living room and stood on the other side of the coffee table. Why wasn't he waking her up yet? He kept pondering this and decided that if he took any longer, it might border on creeper status, even if she was the one who broke into his apartment.

After clearing his throat, he said, "Good morning."

Nothing. Not even a slight stir from her. *Seriously?* he thought. He crouched down to get closer to her level and looked at her face. Wow, she was cute. "Hello...Good morning," he said, louder this time.

She stirred finally and then opened her eyes. Zoey shot up straight as an arrow as she gazed upon Tyler.

"Oh my God, what are you doing here?!? Get out! Get out!" Zoey quickly looked around for something to use as a defensive weapon and could only reach for the couch pillow. She rose to her feet and yielded it back, ready to throw it at Tyler if needed.

"Whoa there, sweetness. What are you going to do with that pillow? Fluff me to death?" He smiled at her and she frowned at him. He sighed and then said, "I live here. What are you doing here?"

"Sweetness?!? Really?? And you can't live here. I do. I signed the lease and paid for the place. This is mine."

"I think you are lost, or you got the wrong apartment. How much did you have to drink last night?"

Zoey gaped her mouth and launched the pillow. Tyler easily sidestepped the pillow's attack and smiled.

"All I had was diet coke and only about half a bottle at that since it exploded all over me!"

Tyler couldn't help but give a slight chuckle. He would have to ask for more details about that later, he thought. "Okay, this is 127A Cherry Street. What is the address you are supposed to be at?"

Zoey's face flushed in a show of her rising anger. "That is my address. I am going to call the police if you don't get out of my apartment now!" She grabbed for her obviously broken cell phone and gave a slight whimper.

Tyler raised an eyebrow at her. "You're seriously going to call the police on that phone?"

"Well, apparently not. I forgot it suffered from the great diet coke disaster."

"Oookaaay. How about I give you my cell phone to use and call the police if you want? And while you are at it, tell the sheriff that it is his turn to bring the beer for poker night."

Zoey's frown suddenly disappeared, and she quietly spoke, "You have a poker night?"

This time Tyler's laugh was much more audible. "Out of all that, the only part that got your attention was that we have a poker night?"

Zoey opened her mouth to start to say something and then closed it. She looked as if she didn't know how to respond. "Yes...well no. But now I know nothing is going to happen if you are buddies with the sheriff." She paused for a moment and then said, "Okay, look, I can prove that I live here. I have a copy of the lease right here in my folder."

She sat down on the couch and Tyler then took the chair on the other side. He couldn't help himself—he was drawn to her chest where her shirt now clearly said "Sprinkled with Love." The arch of the word "sprinkled" lined up perfectly with her breasts and just highlighted her curves all the more. Finally, Zoey's voice broke his gaze.

"Here. Look. This is my lease with this address."

Tyler took the papers and sure enough there was Mrs. Glover's signature and the lease with his address. *Well that isn't good,* he thought. He gazed down at her folder and saw the papers with her logo for the bakery and other papers that were clearly for the business just below him. Finally, he sighed and said, "Just a minute, I'll be back."

He left the living room and went to the second bedroom bringing back papers. "I just moved in here two days ago. I signed the lease three days before you did. I have it all here with Mr. Glover's signature." He handed the papers over and let her take time to read through them.

"How could this happen?" she said weakly. "I have to have a place to live. I can't sleep in the bakery." She sighed. "I need to call Derek." She then took a glimpse at her phone and tears began to well up.

"Mr. and Mrs. Glover have never been great with communication. They were probably both trying to rent the apartment and didn't tell the other that they found a tenant. This building is held in their trust and both of them are Trustees. There has always been a power play between the two of them as to who is responsible for all the duties of that trust." He just looked at her for a minute and then said, "You said that you need to call Derek. Is that Derek McKenna?"

She shot a quick look up at Tyler. "Yes. You know him?" Her smile brightened like the morning sky, and her blue eyes sparkled.

Tyler quickly felt disappointed. He didn't know that Derek had a girlfriend, and for some reason this created a pit in his stomach that he couldn't quite shake. "He is one of those poker buddies I mentioned earlier. You can use my phone to call him, but I would wait until at least 7:30. He isn't exactly a morning person."

Zoey laughed. "Believe me, I know."

Tyler sighed. Well, that settled it. She must be his girl-friend. Although it was strange that he never mentioned her before. "We need to call the Glovers and get this straight-ened out about the apartment. You didn't pay them already, did you?"

"Yes. I paid a check to Mrs. Glover that I overnighted to her for first and last month's rent."

"Well I suppose that Derek won't mind you staying with him until you find a place to live."

"That is a big assumption. Why would you say that?"

"I assume he is your boyfriend." Which still sounded strange to Tyler as he said it. Derek had been known as the town charmer and had racked up a longer line than Tyler did at his peak of self-destruction, but Tyler had been gone, so what did he know.

Zoey laughed again. "Derek? God, no. I mean don't get me wrong, I adore the man, but we have been friends since I was eighteen. He was the one who told me about the bakery closing so that I could move out here to open my shop."

That knot that was in Tyler's stomach suddenly started to release its grip from him. *Well, that is odd*, he thought. Why did that bother him so much? "Sorry. You just looked..." He stopped and drifted off. "Never mind."

Zoey appeared to be inspecting Tyler. Her eyes roamed his body and lingered on his chest and abs. She finally seemed to realized that she was staring at his body for a bit too long and quickly shot her eyes up to his and said, "So are you going to put some clothes on or are you always com-fortable walking around in your underwear around strange women?"

A smile crept through his face. "Well, it is my apartment, and this is how I am dressed in the morning until the mood strikes me to put more on."

Zoey's mouth dropped open and her eyes widened. "And at what time does your mood usually strike you?"

Tyler shrugged. "Hmm, ten-ish."

"Don't you have to go to work?"

"Sweetness, right now you are sitting on my office chair."

Her blue eyes grew icy, and she stared at him before saying, "What?"

"I work from home. I am a software developer and work on web and app designs. I have my own company, so I don't need to physically go anywhere else. As long as I have my computer and a Wi-Fi connection, I have the world at my fingertips."

"Oh," she finally said, relaxing a bit more on the couch.

"Look, let me finish my breakfast and get a shower. Then I promise to emerge a little more dressed. And what about you? Are you going to get a little more dressed?"

Shock appeared over Zoey's face. "Oh my god. I forgot." She gazed down at her tank and very short bottoms and proceeded to pull them down a little further. It didn't really help that much. "Last night my Diet Coke exploded all over my clothes that I was wearing. They are stiff and sticky. I was going to change into something else, but all of my clothes are packed in the back of the U-Haul trailer behind my baking supplies and other big stuff I couldn't get around last night. I just had this in my duffel bag from the night before." She grabbed the other pillow from the couch that she didn't launch at Tyler's head and attempted to cover herself.

"I don't think that pillow is going to hide much I haven't already seen. And don't worry, I didn't see much. I promise." Tyler's light heartedness and smile came through and Zoey relaxed the pillow. "Listen, grab your clothes from last night. I have a washer and dryer here in the apartment. You can throw them in with some clothes I was going to wash today. At least this way you won't be parading around town in the uh...cupcake shorts."

"Thank you. I appreciate that." She grabbed her bag and pulled out the offending clothes, handing them to Tyler. He quietly took them and disappeared around the corner of the hall. He then came back into the kitchen and started to finish his bagel from earlier.

Zoey was fidgeting on the couch and didn't seem to know quite what to do. Nervously, she picked up her paperwork and started taking notes in the margins of the documents on the coffee table.

"Okay. I am going to get my shower now sweetness, so don't go breaking into the bathroom to catch a peek."

Zoey's mouth gaped open and just a squeak came out and a hot red flush flooded her face. "I... I wouldn't... I... I am not that kind of girl." She stared at him and then said, "And stop calling me sweetness."

"I don't think I can. Besides, it was either that or Goldilocks, but with the cupcakes, sweetness just seemed a better fit."

"My name is Zoey," she said in a flat tone and her eyebrow arched.

"Alright then. Nice to meet you, Zoey."

She stared at him expectantly while he still stood in the doorway. "Aren't you going to tell me your name?"

"Honestly, I was waiting to see what pet name you would give me."

"That's not funny. And right now, I don't think that you would like the name that I would give you."

"Tyler."

"What?"

"Tyler, Tyler Ashford."

"Nice to meet you, Tyler."

"Thanks sweetness," he said as he turned and strode down the hallway to get his shower.

STUNNED, ZOEY COULD only just watch him walk away. Suddenly, Zoey realized just how hungry she was. She went into the kitchen and looked in the cabinets for something to have for breakfast. It was like Old Mother Hubbard in there. Besides some ramen noodles, spaghetti in a can and random opened chip bags, it was empty. She looked on top of the refrigerator and found a package of bagels. She pulled out one bagel and looked for some milk. Of course not. A carton of orange juice with just a swig left and beer. Not even a Diet Coke. Zoey sighed and grabbed a glass from the cabinet and filled it with tap water. She'd barely finished breakfast when Tyler returned in jeans and a T-shirt that said "No, I will not fix your computer". Zoey had to laugh. She bought that same shirt for her brother, Xander, who also worked with computers doing stuff she didn't even pretend to understand.

"Maybe I should have stuck with Goldilocks. You are eating what little I have of food."

"You can have your first three breakfasts for free once I open my bakery. That should make up for my sad bagel with no cream cheese and water. Seriously Tyler, what do you put on your bagels?"

"Nothing. They are fine the way they are. No fuss, no muss."

Zoey rolled her eyes. "I can't wait to feed you nice and proper. You will realize the error of your ways."

Tyler just shrugged. "Maybe. Anyway, I moved the clothes into the dryer. You can get a shower if you like. I put an extra towel on the sink for you."

"Thanks." She walked over to her bag and pulled out a small black and white polka dot travel case. "I will be right back."

SHE DISAPPEARED DOWN the hall and Tyler heard the shower start. He walked over to the coffee table where her papers were all spread out. He saw the lease and what appeared to be her business plan. He knew he shouldn't be reading any of this but couldn't seem to stop himself. He read about the products that she planned to put in the shop. He mused to himself how she named them each something cute like Devil May Care Puffs and Whole Lotta Panna Cotta. He then saw her plans to have a web page designed and what she needed to get that started. She had a small note in the margin that read "Beg Xander if necessary." *Xander...*he thought. *How many guys does she have in her life?* He started to feel bad about the apartment since it was just above the store front but he knew that he still had the right to be there since he signed the lease before she did.

Finally. he stood up and decided that he needed to stop snooping around in her stuff. He opened the window by the couch and stepped out onto the fire escape. This was his favorite place to be. This is why he loved the apartment. It had a small view of the town. The houses just behind it were just single level homes, so he was able to see out into the neighborhood and enjoy the quiet morning.

He climbed back inside after some time and went down the hallway to the dryer. He pulled out her jeans and shirt and started to walk down the hallway to drop off her clothes. As he reached the bathroom door, it swung open and there she was with wet hair and her body just wrapped in his towel.

"Uh...I was bringing you your clothes." He couldn't help it, his eyes started to gaze down at her chest and then downward to see just how much the bottom of the towel was covering. Her cheeks flushed red as she watched his eyes.

"Thanks...again." She grabbed the clothes and swiftly shut the bathroom door.

"Yup," he said to the closed door. He was starting to feel like an idiot teenager.

A short time later she emerged from the bathroom, still looking cute as ever. She walked into the living room and started to gather her things. "I think I should call Derek now."

"Right," Tyler said as he grabbed his phone. He dialed Derek's number and handed the phone over to Zoey.

THE PHONE PICKED UP after a few rings and a man's groggy voice came on the line. "Ty, this better be worth waking my ass up."

Zoey smiled. Yup, he still wasn't a morning person. "Not Tyler, Derek. It's Zoey." She heard the sound of quick rustling, like he was jumping out of bed.

"Zoe. Jesus. Where have you been? I had been trying to call you most of the night and I just kept getting voicemail. I was going to send Chase out after you if I didn't hear from you this morning. Wait. Why are you calling me from Ty's phone?"

"It is kind of a long story, but my phone got smashed beyond belief last night, and Tyler was nice enough to lend me his phone. And who is Chase?"

"Chase is our sheriff and friend of mine."

"Oh. The poker buddy?"

Derek paused. "How do you know about poker buddies already?"

"Tyler told me."

After a long pause, Derek said, "You still want my help this morning unloading the trailer?"

"Yes, please, that would be amazing. Most of the trailer holds my baking supplies so we just need to unload those into the bakery. As for my personal stuff...well, I have some things to figure out about that."

"What things? I thought we were moving you into the apartment upstairs."

"So did I. Like I said. It is a long story. Can I explain once you get over here. I will be waiting by the trailer in the back of the shop."

"Of course. Zoe, can you put Ty on the phone?"

Zoey shrugged and handed the phone to Tyler. "He wants to talk to you."

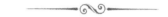

TYLER TOOK THE PHONE and cleared his throat. "Hey Derek, what's up?"

Derek's voice got low. "I should be asking you that. Seriously, you trying to hook up with my friend in the first two minutes she got into town?"

Tyler was shocked for a minute and took a second before answering. "That isn't how it happened."

"So, you moved in on her in the first hour?"

Tyler was starting to find this funny. "To be fair, I think she was in town for a few hours before..."

"Not funny," Derek interrupted. Tyler then moved into the bedroom to have the conversation be a little more private.

"I am not quite sure what is going on here, Derek. Is she your girl? Do you have feelings for her?" Tyler said while holding his breath. He wasn't sure why he was dreading the answer.

"No. She is my friend. Almost like a sister. I love her, but not like that. But she doesn't need your shit-show ways right now either. Her life has not been great lately, so don't try to charm her right now. She doesn't need it. If you want to sleep with random girls, go find another one."

Tyler gritted his teeth. Derek was his friend, and he didn't want to say the wrong thing. Tyler hadn't been with another girl in months and he was turning his life around. Sure, he bragged about his conquests from before with the guys, but he didn't feel the need to get all mushy with them and explain that he was over that scene now. "Look Derek, Zoey is a big girl and can make her own decisions, but I wasn't putting the moves on her." *Yet...* he thought. "When you come over, you will see what is going on. Nothing happened. I promise." As those words left him, he thought that all he could promise was that nothing had happened yet.

"Fine. Sorry. It's just that I look out for her, and I worry. A lot."

"No problem."

"Tell Zoey I will be there in twenty minutes."

"Okay. See ya later," and just like that Derek hung up the phone. Tyler checked his phone to make sure the call disconnected before going back out to Zoey.

"Derek said he will be here in twenty minutes."

"Okay, thanks." Zoey stared at Tyler for a few seconds. "Was it just me or did the testosterone level triple a few minutes ago?"

Tyler shrugged. "Derek seems to be a bit overprotective of you, and I just learned how much more he likes you than he does me." He smiled at her, and she relaxed and smiled back.

"I could see that."

"What? About his overprotectiveness or that he likes you more than me?"

Zoey laughed. "Both. Plus, he is addicted to my food."

Tyler thought for a few minutes and then said, "Do you want some help with the trailer?"

"No. Derek is coming and there really isn't that much." She gathered her papers, her shattered cell phone and bag and went to the door.

Tyler walked her to the door. "Okay, I guess I will see you around, swee..." He had to stop himself from calling her sweetness. "Zoey."

She looked at him like she was trying to figure something out. "Bye Ty." She paused for a second. "Nope can't do that as a pet name either. Bye Tyler." Then just like that, she was gone.

Tyler just stared at the door with a bewildered expression. *Shit,* he thought. *Not good.* Finally, he turned to go back to his computer and to get some work done for the day.

ZOEY REACHED THE BOTTOM of the stairs, then opened the back of the trailer and found the key that was hidden for her by the back door. She opened the shop and took a deep breath and spun around the room. Her smile was the brightest it had been in years. Her own shop. She quickly surveyed the equipment that was in the kitchen. Estelle took very good care of them. Everything was clean and appeared to be in good working order. She moved to the front of the shop where she knew that the most work would be needed. She had ordered specialty coffee machines that should arrive in a couple days and determined she may need to build more counter and working space. The display cases were a bit outdated, the floors were in desperate need of an update, the walls needed fresh paint and a redesign in the front. She had plank tile flooring that she traded for a wedding cake back in Lexington. She knew that she could lay the tile herself but may need additional help pulling the old tile from the floors. The tables and chairs were functional, but also needed a makeover or just to be replaced. After surveying the space, she realized that while this may be quite a bit of work, it should only take two or three weeks to get everything completed for her grand opening.

Then she heard a male voice in the back alley calling her name. *Derek,* she thought, and she rushed through the kitchen to the back where he stood next to the trailer. She smiled and ran to him giving him a tremendous hug. "It is so good to see you!" she exclaimed while still squeezing him tightly.

"Zoe. Breathe. I can't breathe." He was teasing her, and a smile came across his face.

"Oh please. I couldn't strangle you if I tried. That thick neck of yours is like an iron rod. The only time it bends is when you are snapping your head to check out some girl's ass."

"Hey. You're my friend and you're not supposed to tell me my flaws."

"I tell you your flaws because I am your friend," she said coyly.

"True enough, I guess. So, tell me what has happened in the past couple of days that I missed. Like why your phone is dead and why you were calling me early in the morning from Ty's phone."

She sighed and then told him about the Diet Coke, the pajamas, sleeping in Tyler's apartment and how she was homeless.

"Geez Zoe. If you were trying to make an entrance, I guess this is one way to do it. Where are you going to stay?"

"I don't know. For a minute I thought I would ask Tyler since we both signed a lease. I thought about guilting him a little."

Derek gave a slight growl. "No. Absolutely not. You can stay with me and Ariel."

"Aww...how is Ariel?" Ariel was Derek's younger sister and Zoey always liked her. She was sweet to the level that Zoey had never seen before. Ariel was a dreamer. She believed in true love, wishes and fairy tales. There wasn't a mean bone in her body, and men often took advantage of her sweet nature.

"Ariel is great. She owns the local gift shop. She opened it about eight months ago. Actually, it is the store right next to yours, so you will get to see her quite often."

Zoey's heart leaped inside of her. "You have no idea how happy that makes me. I was nervous about making friends out here. It will be nice to have her so close."

"Hey! You still have me."

"Of course, I do. So now I have two friends." Which was more than she had when she left Shane.

The two of them then finished moving the supplies into the shop. They talked about family, sports and their businesses. Derek's bar was thriving in the small town. He made sure to have events during the week when things would normally slow down like trivia night, karaoke or public service night where firemen and police received food at half price. He was proud of his bar and seemed to enjoy his life. Zoey asked about his dating life.

"Oh, I seem to do okay. Nothing special, but I am definitely not lonely." To be more specific, he dated a lot. Women just drifted to him and didn't seem to mind his no relationship rules.

"So, you haven't changed since college?" Zoey laughed.

"Sure, I have. Now the women are old enough to drink."

Zoey rolled her eyes.

Derek and Zoey's attention were drawn to the front door where an elderly couple were peering into the shop through the windows. Derek pulled himself away from the counter where he had been leaning. "That is Mr. and Mrs. Glover. They are probably here to check on you and hopefully fix your apartment situation." He opened the front door, and the couple walked in arm in arm and came directly over to Zoey.

Mrs. Glover spoke first. "You must be Zoey Carrington."

Zoey extended her hand and said, "Yes, and you are Mrs. Glover."

"Yes, and this is my husband Paul. First, I want to say how sorry we are about the apartment mix up. Tyler signed the lease first and my husband neglected to tell me that he had someone lined up for the place. But I think I have a solution that will help. We also own the building across the street where Daisy's Diner is. The apartment above the diner is also vacant. It is actually much nicer than the one above here. It is larger and has more updated furniture that our daughter-in-law picked out." She was beaming at the mention of her daughter-in-law. "Anyway, we are going to let you rent that place for the same rent we agreed upon before, and as a good will gesture I will knock off the first month's rent as well for the trouble." Mr. Glover paled a little and looked as if he wanted to say something, but Mrs. Glover put her hand on his shoulder. "We are both very sorry," and then she looked sternly at Mr. Glover daring him to contradict her.

"That is extremely generous of both of you. Thank you very much." Zoey couldn't help but feel relieved knowing that she would have her own place to sleep tonight.

"Terrific," Mrs. Glover said. "We will send over a new lease for you to sign this afternoon and just slide it under the door of the apartment." She dug out something from her purse and handed it over to Zoey. "Here are the keys. The address is 130A Apple Street. Parking is available in the rear just like here at the shop."

"Thank you again."

"Pish-Posh. Nothing to it. It was our fault. See you soon, and we are looking forward to having your pastries."

Then just as quickly as they breezed in, they walked out. Derek and Zoey just stood there looking at each other for a moment and then began to laugh.

Derek finally spoke first. "Well, I guess we are not done unpacking the trailer after all. Come on, let's go."

After a couple of hours all of Zoey's belongings had made it into the new apartment. Mrs. Glover was correct. This apartment was larger and more modern. The appliances were stainless steel and more updated with a larger kitchen. Zoey was thrilled. She began to unpack and take a mental inventory of what she needed from the store. She also needed to return the trailer and find a store to replace her shattered phone.

Okay, she thought, *Get the phone first then the store for food and other supplies and then dinner.* Her stomach grumbled loudly in complaint. She suddenly realized that she hadn't eaten since breakfast with that sad bagel and water. She found a fruit cup that she had from her meager supplies and quickly ate before heading out the door.

A few hours later she returned and parked behind the apartment exhausted from hunger and lack of sleep. She stopped into Daisy's Diner, took her dinner back up to her apartment and collapsed on the couch. In between bites of her greasy but delicious burger, she texted Derek her new phone number and thanked him for his help. While at the phone store she decided to get a local phone number to provide the customers in town. Having an out-of-state number always seemed to put off potential customers, so it just made sense. Plus, it gave the bonus of not being able to be reached by Shane or other past disasters. Zoey sent out other texts to Xander and her mom and a few other friends that she still wanted to have her information while finishing her dinner.

After dinner she cleaned up a bit and walked into her new bedroom. She was excited to try out her new queen-sized sleigh bed. As she laid down her thoughts drifted to the events from the past couple of days and smiled. Just before she fell into sleep, she saw Tyler's face and recalled his voice soothing her to sleep saying "Sweetness."

Chapter 3

The next morning Tyler again woke before his alarm clock. He could tell by the lack of sun peering through his curtains it was even earlier than yesterday. He groaned. "You have got to be kidding me." He didn't get much sleep. His mind kept wandering to a certain strawberry-blonde who smiled and wouldn't let him go. He shook his head at himself and rolled out of bed. In the kitchen, he grabbed his morning bagel and proceeded to head out the window and onto the fire escape. As he sat down, he could see light coming from below him to the back door of the open bakery. He heard what he thought was the radio. His body leaned forward as he strained to hear the song, but then realized it wasn't the radio.

Tyler crept down the stairs and bent around the railing just enough to peer inside. Then he saw her, and she was singing. The song was obscure, but Tyler knew it well. She was singing about packing her bags and never coming back. It only took a few verses for him to confirm it was *You Don't Treat Me No Good* by Sonia Dada. Not many people had heard of the song much less knew all the words the way Zoey did.

He stood and listened to the rest of the song as she danced and cleaned. *Jesus*, he thought. She was mesmerizing. He wondered what else was on her playlist. Then suddenly he saw her again and noticed she didn't have in any earbuds. She was just singing on her own. The whole damn song. Man, that was impressive. He liked the song, but even he didn't know all the words. Suddenly she stopped, as if she knew someone was listening. He stumbled his way backwards and hid back on the stairs. He wasn't sure why he was hiding, but he didn't want her to be self-conscious about it, or for that matter, stop. *Please don't stop singing*, he thought. For a brief moment he wondered why she chose that song. Was it just the last thing she heard, or was there something more? He was pretty certain it wasn't something that would have randomly played on the radio, at least not in this small town.

He shook his head and climbed his way back to his apartment. He really needed to get some work done today. Yesterday had been his least productive day. He kept thinking about Zoey, but knew he needed to heed Derek's warning. Not only could Derek twist him into a pretzel, but he still didn't have his stuff together, and trusting a woman right now just wasn't something he thought he could do. He wasn't sure if he ever would. Jane had told him that she loved him over and over again, but she still broke his heart. Actually, he was humiliated and then went all Alpha and decided to work his way through the women of Philadelphia. Sure, he still had needs, but he was trying to be the man his parents would be proud of. His drifting thoughts of Zoey more than proved that, but he sure couldn't love and trust again. Not with his complete heart—definitely not like that.

Tyler walked back up to the top of the fire escape, pulled out his laptop and went back to work on his latest code to write for his biggest client. The time mercifully passed quickly, and he felt better about his productivity for the day.

The days continued like this for the rest of the week. Every morning he found himself getting up early and going out on the fire escape, but now instead of enjoying the view he found himself climbing down to peer at Zoey and see what song she was singing. However, he found one thing peculiar. There were times that she was wearing earbuds and obviously not focusing on the song like before but was still singing along nonetheless. With earbuds it was usually more pop culture references such as Bruno Mars, Rolling Stones or Adele. However, without the earbuds it had much more feeling and thoughtfulness to her words while she sang and the songs she would choose were more in the same tone or thought. He tried hard not to think much more into this little eccentricity of hers and just enjoy the sound of her voice.

IT WAS FRIDAY AND ZOEY looked around the kitchen of the bakery. *It's perfect*, she thought. All of her supplies had been received and cleaned and prepared for the shop opening. She still had to paint and redo the floor in the front, but she felt confident that this could be finished by the end of the next week. Derek was also going to come Monday and Tuesday to assist with the front. Sometimes she would see the townsfolk walk by the shop and peer into the window to see progress or even catch a glimpse of their new baker. It amused Zoey. Coming from a larger city, no one would ever come up to the window of a closed shop. People kept to themselves and seemed to distance from anyone around. Not this small town. She had been greeted several times by locals while crossing the town square back to her apartment in the afternoons. Many people already knew her name, and it took her time to adjust to the fact that she wouldn't have to introduce herself but simply try to learn new names, since everyone already knew hers. Finally, she resigned to keeping a notebook with names and descriptions of the people she met so that when she did open her shop, she could address her customers by name. She wanted to impress the town and knew that getting to know them personally would be the quickest way to get this accomplished.

Suddenly she heard a soft voice from the back of the shop. "Zoey? Are you here?"

Zoey went to the back door and found Ariel. She looked like a small princess who just lost her tiara. She had blond shoulder length hair that was in a partial sweep with curls hanging down. She was still short at only 5'5". She had more of a classic 50s pin up body with a large chest and small waist. Every man found her stunning, and she had a sweet, almost naïve nature which made big brother Derek constantly in protective overdrive.

"Ariel! Oh, my goodness, it is so good to see you." Zoey wrapped her friend in a big hug and tears began to well in her eyes. "I missed you, and I am so sorry I haven't made it over to the shop yet to see you. I have been so busy trying to get this place in order, the week has just slipped away from me."

Ariel beamed at her friend and said, "Oh Zoey, it's okay. I've been busy too. But it is so great to have you here. And now your shop is next to mine. This is great." Ariel started looking around the shop and beamed back at her friend. "Wow, I am going to be on sugar overload all the time! I have missed all the stuff that Derek used to bring home to us while he was in college."

Zoey beamed with pride. "Well, you will have unlimited access now." Zoey turned to the kitchen and looked back to her friend. "Please come in, and I will show you around." Zoey gave Ariel the tour of the shop and talked for almost an hour about how the move to Blossom Hills came about starting with the breakup with Shane up to her awkward meeting with Tyler.

"Tyler Ashford?" asked Ariel.

"Yes. Do you know him?"

"He is Kyle's older brother." Ariel's cheeks flushed a bright pink at the mention of Kyle's name.

Zoey smiled knowingly, seeing Ariel's pinkened cheeks.

"I went to school with both of them but really know Kyle better. Kyle moved back from Philadelphia almost two years ago and is now working at the local paper. Tyler was also living there but only just moved back about a month or so ago."

"Why did they come back?"

"Oh, a couple reasons, I guess. Kyle was working for a large paper in the city and didn't really like the big city feel. Their dad had some heart troubles a couple of years ago. Kyle came back saying it was to help out his mom, but I know that he also hated the job out there. We had a nice chat about it one day." Ariel started to drift off and looked lost in her thoughts. "Anyway, Tyler stayed out there. He had a good job and a serious girlfriend, but then the girlfriend cheated on him and shortly afterwards he lost his job. Kyle said he came back here to work through some of his issues but didn't really tell me much more than that."

"Wow," said Zoey. "I had no idea all that was going on for him. Tyler seems so put together. Well at least for the short time I was with him."

"Guys are funny that way. You can see one thing but then there is so much more going on in the background."

Zoey's face dropped, and she thought of Shane and how he seemed like the perfect guy when they first met and then how he slowly changed into the man who made her feel like she had little to no worth. Then her thoughts drifted further back to the string of bad men who just got progressively worse. There had been none who made her feel light and complete since Trevor died.

"So, what about you?" Zoey asked, trying to smile at Ariel. "How is your dating life going?"

"I had a date on Wednesday. This guy named James. He works at the accounting firm on the outside of town. I met him from the guys poker night. He was..." Ariel's mind drifted off. "He was okay. No Prince Charming, but maybe he just needs a few more dates to get a little better."

"Maybe," Zoey said softly, but she was afraid that it wouldn't get much better and wouldn't crush her friends hopes.

Ariel smiled at her friend and then remembered, "Oh, I wanted to invite you to karaoke tonight at the bar. I will be there with some other friends. It will be a good way to get to know some people and have fun since you worked hard all week."

"I would love to. What time will you be there?"

"I get there around eight, but the singing won't start until nine."

"Okay, I will see you there probably closer to nine. Save me a seat please."

"Of course," Ariel said with a smile. "See you tonight." Then she turned and walked out the door with a little bounce in her step.

Zoey watched her friend leave and smiled as she thought how great it was that Ariel still seemed like the happiest person she ever met under any circumstances.

A few hours later Zoey was giving herself a final look over in the mirror. She was wearing a black and white top with lace up corset sides and a scoop neck that highlighted her cleavage from her newly purchased push-up bra. The tight black pants gave her more of an hour-glass figure then most of her other things she could find in her closet. She had put her curly hair partially up so a few curls could frame her face. She was always self-conscious about her figure. She felt that she could be pretty enough when she tried, but she had more curves than other women and wasn't blessed with the pin up curves like her friend Ariel.

"Well here goes nothing," she said as she gazed in the mirror one more time.

Zoey then started down the stairs and walked the two blocks to McKenna's Pub. As she walked in, it was a lively crowd. She could see people sitting in groups and then walking around to other tables talking to everyone like the whole room were old friends. This is such a different feeling then it was back home, she thought. When people went to bars back home, they stayed to their own tables unless they were trying to pick up a date for the night. Zoey smiled and felt a sense of warmth growing inside her as she continued to look for Ariel.

She finally caught sight of her friend at the back-corner booth. It was a larger booth than all the others in a giant U-shape that appeared to be able to sit almost ten people. Ideal for conversations among friends. Ariel caught sight of her and waved her over. She was sitting there with two other women and three men who appeared to all be in their thirties. Then the closer she got, she realized one of the men was Tyler. She gasped and stopped walking for a minute. *Oh, God. He's here. Not good.* Then from behind her she heard a deep gruff voice, "Are you going to go over there or let my sister's arm fall off waiving you down."

Zoey smiled and turned around to see Derek standing there. "I am going...geez give me a minute."

Derek smiled and gave her a slight nudge towards the booth.

Tyler locked his eyes with Zoey's. He stopped talking and didn't move as she approached the booth. His eyes glazed over as he dropped them down to her cleavage and then down to her hips and legs. After his obvious intake of her body he moved his eyes from her legs up to her face. After a longer moment, he began to rise from the booth so that Zoey could slide in between him and Ariel.

Zoey sat down and smiled warmly at Tyler. "Hi Tyler, good to see you." She was desperately trying to not show him how much he affected her. She didn't need to get involved with yet another guy. Ariel was right. They seem fine at first, but you never know what is going on in the background. Her past string of men was plenty of proof of that.

"Hi Zoey, you look nice."

Zoey cocked her head and then smiled and said, "Thank you." She wasn't used to men complimenting her so openly, or if they did, it was only until they got what they wanted and then things changed.

Zoey greeted Ariel and looked around the booth at the others. Ariel began introductions. "Zoey, this is Dixie. She is the owner of Essence Studios and a brilliant photographer." Dixie gave a smile and greeted her with a wave. Ariel then turned to the next girl and said, "This is Josie. I never quite understand what she does," Ariel laughed a little, "but she is also brilliant and could organize anyone's life, oh, and she lives in the same building as you."

Josie, who looked professionally polished still in her blouse and jeans, coolly reached out her hand to Zoey. "It is nice to meet you. Ariel has been chatting our ears off about your pastries. I think I speak for all of us when I say that we are very much looking forward to your bakery opening." Zoey was struck with how smooth and evenly toned her voice was when speaking to her. Even in the loud bar she was level and clear. She seemed like the type of person who could either command everyone's attention or strike fear with just a narrowed gaze of her eyes.

"The pleasure is all mine," Zoey said politely trying to match Josie's formality and tone.

Then on the other side of Ariel was an attractive man who had blonde hair and facial features similar to Tyler's only instead of Tyler's green eyes they were a bright steely blue. "This is Kyle, he is Tyler's brother." Again, Ariel's face reddened, and she stared in his eyes while he extended his hand out to Zoey.

"Welcome to Blossom Hills. You may not remember, but we met once when you and Derek were in college. I came out to visit him one weekend during one of their parties. And I have heard all about you from Derek and Tyler," Kyle said.

"Have you? I am almost afraid to ask what they said," Zoey said laughingly while glancing over at Tyler who seemed to narrow his eyes at Kyle.

"All good things, I promise. Well at least after Ty got past the whole breaking and entering part of the story."

Tyler cleared his throat and Zoey's face flushed even more with embarrassment.

Finally, Ariel turned to the last man in the booth who had been smiling at the exchanges between Tyler and Zoey. "And this is Chase. He is the sheriff here."

"Hey, Zoey. I am also Tyler's best friend, so just be warned I have been told all about you as well." His smile was huge and bright and seemed to take pleasure in embarrassing his friend. A thump could be felt as Tyler obviously kicked his friend under the table to get him to shut up. Tyler followed that up with an obvious face that was telling Chase to shut up.

Zoey's head was spinning. There were so many new people and she wasn't used to being thrown into a group and feeling welcomed so quickly. Normally when she would go out with people after work or be introduced to mutual friends, she always felt out of place and would be counting down the minutes before she could make a graceful exit. As the evening went on and the karaoke festivities began, she found that she was engaged in the conversations and had a great time. Derek would occasionally stop by with drinks for the table, never needing to take orders. He knew his friends, what they liked and if they wanted refills. Zoey didn't even have to give Derek any order. He was her college bartender, and he was always testing out his new cocktail recipes on her that the guys had declared as girly drinks. Zoey was always happy to give him any feedback. Zoey loved most of the fruit drinks blended with vodka, rum or other mysterious liquors that he would never tell her about, saying it was his secret. Tonight, it was no different.

About an hour into the evening, the girls had decided to be brave and sing. Zoey felt a slight panic. She didn't want to sing. Sure, she loved to sing, but that was in private. She didn't want others to hear her. She could hear Shane's voice booming in the back of her head, *Nobody wants to hear your shrieking in the morning. Enough with the singing.* Then she heard Tyler's voice, "Zoey?"

"Huh? Sorry what did you say?"

"Are you going to pick a song?"

"Oh. No," she said, hoping that would be the end of it. Tyler just sat there looking at her confused. "I think I want to enjoy everyone else tonight. Besides, nobody would ever want to hear me sing. It's a disaster." She gave a forced smile to Tyler, who still looked puzzled.

Tyler kept looking at Zoey with brows drawn down. It was making her fidget in her seat. Finally, he tried to smile and said, "I am sure you would be good. Besides, this isn't a concert hall. You heard old Edgar over there try to belt out Aerosmith earlier. That man could have called all the cats into the bar with that voice."

"True. I wish I had a fraction of his confidence."

Tyler turned to look Zoey in the face and his hand brushed along her side. An electric jolt passed through them and he withdrew his hand quickly. They looked into each other's eyes and didn't say anything for a moment.

From the other side of the booth, the others seemed to take notice of the weird moment between Tyler and Zoey and started to watch them. Zoey was the first to break the gaze and turned to the girls and said, "So, what are you ladies going to sing?"

Josie said, "I want something loud and angsty but Little Miss Sunshine over there keeps picking out these sappy songs. We need girl power not mush."

Ariel shrugged. "So sue me. I love love. Everyone else should too."

Groans came out from around the table and everyone laughed. The girls went to put in their song selection and then came back to the table. Josie looked at Zoey and said. "Come on girl, bathroom break."

Zoey giggled and looked at the guys and said, "Sorry, guess I am going too, you know that girls travel in packs thing." And with that she left the table and followed them down the hall.

DEREK CAME BACK TO the table and slid into the booth where the girls had just vacated. "Man, we are busy tonight. How are things going over here?"

"Good, we were just talking about song selections, and the girls went to the bathroom," Kyle said.

Derek rolled his eyes. "So we have at least fifteen minutes before they get back then."

The boys just laughed. After a moment Tyler said, "Hey, I tried to get Zoey to pick a song to sing but she won't go up there. What gives?"

Derek frowned. "Let it go, Tyler. Believe me, I know what a good singer she is, but If she doesn't want to sing, she doesn't have to. There is a lot you don't know about, and if she isn't ready leave it alone."

Tyler's radar went up immediately. He saw Derek's protective tone kick in. He started to protest and thought about saying he had heard her sing and also knew just how incredible she was. Quickly he realized that it would sound a little creepy and stalker-ish and he thought better of it and backed down. "I know, I just thought she might have fun with it."

"This is her first night out since coming to town. Give her some time before making her come out of her shell. It is a lot to meet all of us at once."

Chase finally spoke up. "Hey speak for yourself, I am a damn delightful person."

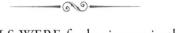

ALL THE GIRLS WERE freshening up in the bathroom mirror, except Zoey. She always had the philosophy that she was only getting ready once, and after that the hair and makeup were on their own. Josie finished first and turned to Zoey. "What is up with you and Tyler?"

Well that was direct, Zoey thought. "Nothing," she said with a slight panic in her voice. She realized that she needed to work on hiding her thoughts better.

"Uh-huh. Then why does he look at you like you are his last meal?"

Zoey gaffed. "No, he doesn't," but she wished that he did.

"He does," piped up Ariel, and she was starting to get that wide-eyed dreamy look in her eyes.

For a minute Zoey thought about calling out how Ariel was so obviously infatuated with Kyle, but she didn't want to embarrass her friend. "No, he doesn't. He is just being friendly. He lives above my shop and he is just being nice. Besides, even if he did, men are not even on my radar. Men seem like a great idea but then you get squished like a grape."

"Amen, sister," said Dixie. She looked at Zoey for a minute and finally said, "Just be careful. Tyler has been known to go through women quickly. Chase is hopeful that he is turning back into the old Tyler, but you just never know."

"Right, you never know," agreed Josie.

"Okay, thanks," said Zoey.

Ariel then came forward and tried to wrap them all in a hug. "Aww...look at us bonding already. I am so happy to have you guys."

Zoey just had to laugh as she looked at Dixie who smiled and Josie just rolled her eyes, but they still let Ariel squeeze them into the hug.

"Alright, let's get back to the boys before they get into too much trouble," said Josie.

With that they went back and joined the boys. Nearly everyone sang except for Zoey and Chase. When Zoey questioned him, he just gave a sideways glance and said, "I don't sing." And with that commanding calm voice, Zoey knew better than to ask. Josie, Dixie and Chase were the first to leave. This left just Kyle, Ariel and Tyler in the booth. Derek was able to stop by more frequently as the night went on and more customers left to go home.

Zoey could see the good relationship between Tyler and Kyle. This just made her miss her brother, Xander. She realized she would need to call and invite him over to see her shop and new apartment. She found herself bonding with the boys, talking about sports and what others would call *guy* movies. She never really fit in with the super feminine girls and always drifted towards having closer male friends like Derek.

Finally, during last call, Zoey realized that she needed to go home and get some rest. She still had so much work to do and wow, the bar was starting to spin. Just how many drinks had Derek brought over to her? Five, six...no wait seven. Oh god, she was going to hate life tomorrow morning.

She looked at the others and said, "OOOkaayyyy, I tink I have to go home now. There are too many of you."

Tyler and Kyle smiled at her and then she saw two Tylers. Yup. Time to go home. She started to gather her purse and gave Ariel a hug and whispered in her ear, "I see you to-mor-oooww."

Ariel giggled and said, "Okay, sweetie."

Zoey felt a sudden pang of frustration. "Hey, why aren't you as drunk as I am."

Then she heard Derek behind her. "Because I switch her to virgin drinks after half the night. Geez Zoe, you have turned into a lightweight."

Zoey straightened. "Well...this is the first drink I have had in a while."

"A while?"

Zoey started giggling again. "A year-ish, and you pour heavy."

"God, Zoe you should have told me." Derek looked worried as Zoey started bouncing back and forth. "Look, stay here with Ariel while I close down, and I will walk you home."

"No! I only live a couple blocks from here. I can walk." She started poking his chest.

Tyler came up behind her. "I will make sure she gets home." Derek gave him a sideways glance and Tyler continued. "The right home. Geez, McKenna, calm down."

"Fine. You good with that, Zoe?"

Zoey put out a pouty lip. "No choice, right?"

"No," both men said at the same time.

"Fine then."

With that, Tyler and Zoey left McKenna's and headed out to the dimly lit street. Tyler was the first to speak. "Did you have a good time tonight Zoey?"

Zoey looked up at him and started to wobble. He quickly put an arm around her to steady her as she walked. Finally, she said, "Yes, I did. The girls seem great. I have always loved Ariel, but for me to like the other girls too, that says something." She was thinking that she was starting to sober up a little and then stumbled again. *Dang it.*

Zoey paused on the sidewalk and tried to regain more balance. She loved the feeling of Tyler's arm around her. She found herself burying her head into his chest. Tyler bent his head down to rest on top of hers and gave her a squeeze. Zoey felt herself wanting more from him. She wanted to say something but couldn't find the words to start. Tyler brought his other hand to the back of her neck as she looked up at him.

Zoey spoke and broke the tension of the moment. "I am good now. We can keep walking. What was I saying?"

"That you don't normally get along with girls."

"Oh yeah. Well, I don't like a lot of the girly things, except for my baking. Then I am all flowers and lace. I don't know why."

"It is just part of your charm. Part of a lot of things I like about you."

They continued on in silence with his arm around her until they got to the access door to her apartment.

"Here I am. You can go now," she said.

"Oh no."

"No?" She looked at him, confused. "Did I go to the wrong apartment again?"

Tyler laughed. "No sweetness. I am just not dropping you off until we get you up the stairs safely and into your apartment. If you fell and got hurt walking up those stairs, Derek would kill me."

"Pfffft. No, he wouldn't."

"Wow, you don't know him like you think you do. He has been giving me all kinds of death stares since you came to town, and I have no doubt he wouldn't hesitate to kill me."

"Fine. Let's go."

Zoey started up the stairs and turned back to see if Tyler was following her a few times before finally ending up at the front door of her apartment. She grabbed her keys from her purse and turned to look at him again. "Okay, I am home."

"Unlock the door and go inside Zoey," Tyler said with his eyes lowered on hers.

She looked up and felt her face flush and couldn't stop herself from saying, "You want to eat me."

Tyler's mouth opened and his eyes widened at her. "What?"

Zoey gasped. "Oh God. I didn't mean to say that you...Oh god...I gotta...I mean...I gotta go." And with that, she opened the door and slammed it in Tyler's face. Mortified, she leaned against the door and took a deep breath. "Good one Zoey. This is what you get for hanging with girls," she said to herself.

She nearly fell to the ground when she heard Tyler's voice come from the other side of the door. "Zoey are you okay?"

She clasped her hands over her mouth and then breathlessly said, "Uh-huh."

"Sweetness?"

She removed her hands and cleared her throat. "Yes... I am okay. Going to bed now. Night Tyler."

She still didn't hear him leave the hallway, and suddenly heard him say, "Just so you know, I don't want to eat you. Maybe just nibble on a part or two."

"Oh God," Zoey breathed out.

"Goodnight sweetness."

Zoey finally pulled herself up from the door and walked down the hall and laid down with her mind racing with thoughts of Tyler, his voice, and of how his touch was making her melt to her core. *Not good,* she thought.

TYLER LEFT ZOEY'S APARTMENT and cut across the town square past the gazebo to the other side where his apartment was waiting for him. Once he got home, he made his way to his bedroom and undressed for bed. He then looked out his window where he quickly realized he could see into Zoey's bedroom just across the square. Her light was still on. He stood there waiting for a few minutes, waiting for her light to turn off. Then almost on command the room went dark, and he moved from his window to his bed and drifted off to sleep where his dreams of a certain sweet baker were waiting for him to devour her.

Chapter 4

Zoey woke the next day to a pounding in her head. *Bang, Bang. Bang.* She sat up, opened her eyes and tried to focus. *Bang. Bang. Bang. Oh God, it is getting louder* she thought. Then she heard a deep voice, "Zoey? Are you in there?"

Surprised, she got up from her bed and stumbled to the door. *Too much noise. Too much movement. I am going to kill Derek for poisoning me.* "Coming. Hang on."

She made her way to the door and opened to find Tyler looking way too good for the morning after drunken frivolity. No, wait...that was just her. He was mostly sober last night. Tyler stood with a wide smile in a Superman shirt and jeans. He was holding a couple of carryout boxes and two drinks. Finally, after a few seconds, he said, "I brought breakfast. Thought you could use some help getting going this morning."

Zoey groaned. "You are way to peppy for me. And what are you doing over here so early? I am still dying."

Tyler gave a soft laugh. "It's ten-thirty Sweetness. I thought you would...or should be up by now. And I thought you might not feel like cooking, so I brought food to you."

"I would have been happier if you brought me some Tylenol."

"I have that too. It is in my pocket."

"God bless you."

Zoey stepped aside to let him in. Tyler set the food in the kitchen and searched the drawers for some silverware. He looked over at her as she went to sit on the stool by the island and said, "I didn't know if you liked coffee so, I brought orange juice and coffee."

"I will take the OJ, and that Tylenol."

Tyler smiled, pulled out the bottle and handed it to her with the orange juice. "Ariel said to tell you hello. I passed her on the way over here."

"That was sweet. I just love her."

"Yeah, I think everyone does. She was worried about how you were doing, but she was busy with the store and couldn't stop over."

"I'll go see her later and let her know I survived." Zoey started to eat the breakfast that Tyler brought over. "Derek is right though. I really am a lightweight now. I can't be drinking like I am still in college anymore." She smiled weakly at Tyler. Suddenly she gasped with the realization that she wasn't even dressed yet. She looked down to see what she was wearing and was mortified to see yet another small tank top and high-rise boxers this time with smiling rainbow unicorns. "Oh God," she sighed. "I will be right back. I need to change."

"Why? I love your pajamas."

"This is embarrassing. Why is it every time I see you, I am half dressed?"

"I am just lucky I guess." Tyler smiled and continued, "I could help you lose that half if you want."

Zoey's face grew hot and her face flushed a bright red. Her mouth opened to say something, but nothing came out but a quick little squeak. Tyler set down his food and walked closer over to her. She held her breath. Her heart began to race, and she kept thinking she should move and go get dressed. Yup. Moving now would be a good idea. Then he was standing right next to her. His eyes gazed into hers and he said in almost a whisper, "Zoey."

"Yeah."

His hands traveled up her bare arms to her shoulders. Shivers ran throughout her body and her eyes widened. His hands slowed, grazing higher to hold her head through her hair. They started to lean in towards each other and were so close that Zoey could feel his warm breath on her face.

BANG. BANG. BANG. The loud knocking on the door broke the moment, and Zoey jumped away from Tyler. She walked over to the door and opened to find Derek on the other side standing in his cargo pants and blue polo shirt. "Hey Zoe. I came over to check on you."

Zoey smiled, gave him a quick hug, and moved aside to let yet another man in her apartment. Derek came over to the kitchen where he saw Tyler standing there looking quite at home. Tyler's head drooped a little in what seemed like disappointment. Zoey looked between the two men and waited for one of them to acknowledge the other. Finally, Tyler looked over at Derek and gave a slightly gruff, "Hey, Derek."

"Ty." Then the two men just stared at each other for a few seconds and Zoey felt the level of testosterone rise to an unbearable level.

She looked at Derek quizzically. What was his problem with Tyler? She knew he wasn't jealous, and he was Tyler's friend. She could feel tensions rise and decided that she needed to be the one to speak next. "Tyler was nice enough to bring me breakfast this morning. Wasn't that nice of him, Derek?"

"Yeah. Nice."

"Okay, look, you boys play nice with each other for a couple of minutes. I am going to go and change clothes and be right back." *And the quicker the better,* she thought. She almost sprinted down the hallway and disappeared into her bedroom.

DEREK WAS THE FIRST to speak after Zoey left the room. "Have you lost your goddamned mind Tyler?"

"What? What is your problem? I brought the girl some food." Tyler was getting more frustrated by the second. He had been told repeatedly that there wasn't anything between Derek and Zoey, but he was acting like a possessive boyfriend.

"You slept with Zoey when she was too drunk to think straight! I know you like to move quick on your conquests, but not with her." Tyler could tell that Derek's voice was straining to keep his voice low enough for Zoey not to hear.

"I didn't sleep with her," Tyler said through gritted teeth. "Jesus, Derek. You know I am not a complete asshole, or at least I thought you did. Look, I brought her home like we told you last night. I dropped her off at her front door and then I went home. I thought she could use some food to work on her hangover and brought her some Tylenol. That's it." *Well, that and I almost kissed her before you interrupted us.*

"Really? That's it."

"Yes. Look, I like her. I am not going to lie to you about it, but you need to stop treating me like I am the enemy here." He paused for a moment and dreaded the answer to the next question. "Am I stepping in the middle of something with you and Zoey that I should know about?"

Derek stopped and stared at his friend for what seemed like forever. "No. Not like that, but she does mean a lot to me. She has been through a lot and she is just getting her feet back under her. Don't try to rush her into anything she isn't ready for."

"What happened to her?"

Derek shook his head. "Not my story to tell. You have to talk to her about it."

"Alright then."

"Just don't do something that is going to make me want to kill you."

"Okay, I got it."

Then Zoey's bedroom door swung open, and she came down the hall. Tyler looked at her and let a small smile drift across his face. She was wearing black leggings with a purple asymmetrical shirt that bared her left shoulder. Tyler thought she looked adorable and wanted to kiss her shoulder and work his way down. As he started to get lost in his thoughts, he felt a slight shove from Derek. Tyler grinned.

"Okay boys. Did you play nice or do I need to kick some-one's ass?"

Derek exaggerated a knife wound to his chest. "Ouch, that hurts Zoe. I always play nice."

Zoey narrowed her eyes at her friend and said, "Uh-huh. So, what did you stop by for Derek?"

"What, I can't just swing by and check on my friend?"

"Yes, but you look like you had something on your mind."

"Fine, I do. Mom is giving me grief about you stopping by. She wanted me to ask you to come over for lunch today."

Zoey's smile got wide and she said, "I would love to see her today. You going to be there too?"

"Nah, I have some things to get done at the bar before rush tonight, but Ariel will be there."

"Okay. Sounds good. What is her address?"

"Don't worry about that. Ariel said she will pick you up after she leaves the shop around eleven-thirty and take you."

"Wow, that doesn't leave me much time. I kind of over-slept this morning."

"I have seen you throw yourself together in fifteen min-utes before," Derek said laughing. "I think you can manage in about an hour."

"I'm no cute college kid anymore. It takes time to look fabulous now."

"You're fine. You could show up in your pajamas and she would think you still walk on water."

"True."

"Anyway, I have to get going. Have fun with mom and give me a call later."

"I will. Bye Derek."

With that, Derek took one last hard look at Tyler and gave Zoey a hug and walked out the door. Zoey went back to the kitchen and stood on the other side of the island from Tyler.

"So...I want to thank you for breakfast and the Tylenol, but I really should get ready to see Amanda. I have been meaning to get over there and just haven't had a chance yet."

Tyler's face dropped, and he gazed straight into Zoey's eyes. "It was my pleasure. I just wanted to make sure you were okay after last night."

"I am. Thank you."

"Right. So, I guess I will leave you to it then." He grabbed his coffee and started to walk to the door with Zoey right behind him. "Anyway, if you need anything you know where I live. Just come over anytime."

"Okay, I will. Thanks." As they stood in the open doorway, he kept getting closer into her space. Tyler looked a bit pensive. Zoey tried to read his thoughts. Was he going to lean in to get that kiss that had been stolen from them earlier? Was he going to give her a hug? Just as the moment was starting to get intimate again, they heard the soft musical tone of Star Wars in the background. Tyler broke his gaze and looked behind her. She turned around and said, "My cell phone. I need to get that. I will see you later, Tyler."

She turned around to go answer her phone while Tyler closed the door and left her apartment.

Zoey turned, answered the phone and said, "Hi mom."

"Hello Zoey. How are things going? Are you getting out and meeting people?"

Zoey sighed. "Yes mom. You would be so proud, and I am going to have lunch with Ariel and her mom today." Zoey and her mom, Cassie, had always had an odd relationship. Cassie loved her daughter but was always baffled why she wasn't more like her. Zoey loved sports and hung out with men more than women. Cassie was very feminine and never understood why her daughter could have so many men around her, but not one of them in a romantic role. Cassie always told Zoey she wasn't trying hard enough with her appearance and needed to do more to marry the right man and give her grandchildren.

Cassie asked her daughter how the work was going on the bakery and how her new apartment was. Zoey didn't feel the need to explain about the mix up on the apartments or go into great details. She simply told her mother that the town was great and that she was happy with how things were shaping up with the shop. Cassie quickly asked if Zoey had any dates yet. Zoey drifted her thoughts to Tyler, but she wasn't going to get her mom started on a lecture on how she should behave to win him over.

"No, mom. No dates yet. I have to concentrate on the bakery right now. I am on a tight schedule and want to open as quickly as possible."

"Well of course you do honey. Just don't be close minded to any new opportunities that may come your way. You are not getting any younger you know."

"I know Mom. If I fall madly in love with someone, I promise I will call and let you know."

"Don't be sarcastic Zoey."

"Who me?" Zoey said dripping with sarcasm.

"Funny Zoey."

"I thought so. Anyway, Mom I really have to go. Ariel will be picking me up soon."

"Well that is nice dear. Is Derek going to be there?"

"No, he has some things to do for the bar."

"He was always such a nice boy Zoey."

"Mom. Stop."

"Fine, honey. I will talk to you later."

"Bye Mom." Zoey disconnected the phone and sighed heavily. It always took a lot of energy talking to her mom. She loved her, but just wished she wouldn't try to put so much pressure on her about her appearance, marriage and kids. She left the living room and finally was able to get a shower and get ready for her lunch.

Ariel knocked on Zoey's door right at 11:30 and Zoey greeted her friend with a great big hug. Zoey grabbed a bottle of wine from the top of her refrigerator and her purse and they went down to Ariel's car.

"Mom is excited to see you," Ariel said, looking over at her friend.

"I am too. Your Mom is one of the sweetest people I have ever met."

"I know. Derek and I have been lucky. She is great. Dad really blew it with her." Ariel's Dad, Jeremy, was married to Amanda for twenty years. Derek and Amanda thought they had ideal parents, but then their father was caught cheating on his wife with a twenty-something blonde who worked in his office. He tried to apologize and told Amanda that it was a onetime thing and would never happen again.

Amanda loved her husband and wanted to keep their marriage intact, so she forgave him. Then only three months later, another woman knocked on their front door to tell Amanda that she was sleeping with Jeremy and that he loved her. Amanda calmly looked at the woman and just said, "Thank you. I understand." Then with that she closed the door on the woman and promptly went up the stairs to pack his suitcase so he could walk right back out that door when he got home. Jeremy had protested and tried to tell his wife that he loved her and not some other woman. Amanda refused to listen to anything further and told him to walk away now or he would learn to regret that choice. He wisely left the house, and a few months later they were divorced.

"Do you still talk to your dad?" Zoey asked, knowing the whole story since Derek had told her while they were in college and she also knew that Derek refused to speak to his dad since he left.

"Of course, I do. He is my Daddy. I hate what he did to Mom, but still I know he loves me. He is a terrible husband, but a good dad."

"That is good at least," Zoey said with a wistful tone. Her father had walked out on her and her mom when she was only three. He tried to maintain a relationship with Zoey until she was about eight and then just stopped calling and showing up. Shortly after that, he moved and just didn't bother to give Cassie any forwarding information to contact him. Cassie was just as happy to never see him again, but Zoey still had wished she had a relationship with her father. Zoey did have a good stepfather though. He was kind and tolerant of Cassie's sometimes overpowering personality. He loved her and doted on her every whim, and Zoey never quite understood their relationship but was grateful for him all the same.

"I saw that Tyler came over to see you this morning," Ariel said with a bright smile.

"Yes, he did. He brought breakfast and Tylenol. I think that was the sweetest thing anyone has done for me in forever. I was completely out of it this morning."

"You seem to be spending a lot of time with him lately." Ariel's voice was lifting in a sing-song manner that Zoey knew all too well. Ariel believed in true love and romanticized everything. Zoey thought this seemed to give her more trouble than she deserved with men.

"I wouldn't say a lot of time. I only saw him about half an hour this morning, and half of that time your brother was there too."

"What happened last night after you left the bar with Tyler? Did he kiss you?"

"No," Zoey said honestly, and she flashed back to her embarrassing moment at the end of the night. "He walked me home and to my door, but I was so drunk I made a fool of myself."

"Why, what did you do?"

Zoey groaned. "I told him that he wanted to eat me."

"What?!?!" Ariel snapped her head around to look at her friend and started to swerve the car.

"I got nervous. He was getting close to me and just kept looking at me and I was thinking about what you guys said to me in the bathroom and it just came out. I just blurted it like some raving lunatic. I was mortified, so I just hurried back inside the apartment and closed the door on his face."

Ariel was laughing. "Oh no. I am so sorry, sweetie. But seriously, it couldn't have been that bad since he still brought you breakfast the next day."

"I know. Weird, huh? I keep embarrassing myself in front of him and he just keeps on coming back for more."

"He likes you, and I promise he is a good guy. He just went through a phase before."

"You mean where he was sleeping with everything that walks?"

"Yeah. He doesn't seem to do that now. I have seen him turn down a few women at the bar who were very pretty. He just didn't seem interested, but he does seem interested in you."

"I am not sure if that is a good thing or bad."

"I think it is a good thing. You should give love a try again. I promise not all the guys are idiots. And hey, if it ends up that he is an idiot we'll just have Derek kill him," Ariel said with the sweetest smile.

Zoey laughed and said, "I think Derek is already all over that."

"Of course, he is. He loves you."

"I know."

The girls finally arrived at Amanda's house. It was a cute Victorian two-story home with a patio garden in back. When they arrived, Amanda greeted Zoey like she was her long-lost daughter.

"We sure have missed you," Amanda said.

"I have missed all of you too. I treasured your visits while we were in college. You always make me feel like family."

"You are sweetheart. You looked out for my Derek and kept him fed properly. He would have lived on fast food and ramen noodles if it wasn't for you."

"Yeah, I am afraid I am responsible for his freshmen fifteen."

Ariel laughed and said, "And his sophomore ten."

"True," Zoey said.

"Well come on girls, lets head to the patio. I already have lunch waiting."

The three women went through the house and into the back yard. Zoey was delighted to see that Amanda looked so happy and healthy. Amanda stood at the same height as her daughter and had a youthful energy with her skin glowing a natural shade of pink. Her blonde layered hair caught the sun that almost created an almost natural halo effect. She carried herself with grace and charm that could catch any man's eye, but she no longer had any interest in finding love. She felt that she had her great love, and it didn't work out so there was no need to try again.

The girls chatted about the bakery and Ariel's shop. Amanda talked about her work at the senior center where she was the activities counselor. She loved her work and the seniors that she helped each day. She felt that she was lucky to be paid to plan bingo nights, art classes and events where groups could come to entertain like the high school choir. Then Amanda's face turned serious and looked toward Zoey. "I heard things didn't go very well with the last boyfriend."

Zoey shifted in her seat. "No. He wasn't very nice to me very much after we were together for a while. He never physically hurt me or anything like that, but he was angry most of the time. I was constantly walking around trying to make sure I didn't make him angry over something stupid. It wasn't until I had lunch with Derek and Shane interrupted us, that I realized just how bad it had gotten."

"Oh sweetie," Amanda said. "How did it go when you left?"

"Not well, but I didn't really give him an option about the outcome." Zoey felt a stinging in her chest recalling just how not well it really went. She told him that she didn't love him anymore, and that she was moving out. He lost his temper and began shouting at her and aiming for her biggest insecurities, and the words ran through her mind. *You will never find someone better than me. No one could love a fat whore like you.* Zoey had tried to stay calm and not let him know just how much he was hurting her. *Stupid bitch. You will never amount to anything.* As he continued to hurl insults at her, she had tears falling down her face and she realized that she just had to leave quickly. She grabbed her last bag that she hadn't packed in her car earlier that day, walked out the door and listened to the crashing sounds of things being thrown against the walls.

"Zoey?" Ariel asked while softly looking at her friend.

"Sorry. I'm okay. It just wasn't good, and it still hurts to think about sometimes."

"Well of course it does dear, bad breakups and bad men do that. But what is important now is that you are here, and we love you." Amanda was smiling at Zoey, with just as much love and affection for her as she had for her own children. Zoey knew that Amanda had known about her past from the loss of Trevor, her strained relationship with her mom and her bad relationships since college. Derek had told Zoey that his mom always asked about her and Zoey had given him permission to tell her what was going on before she moved to Blossom Hills. Derek told Zoey that his mom was proud of her for being brave enough to leave and start over somewhere new where she would always have love and support.

"Thanks. I love you guys too," Zoey said beaming at her friends.

As they were leaving, Zoey gave Amanda a huge hug and knew she had made the right decision by moving to Blossom Hills. Once they were in the car, Ariel turned to her friend with a serious look across her face and said, "Shane was really horrible to you, wasn't he?"

"Let's just say that I am a little worse for the wear. I thought Derek told you everything," Zoey said with a little confusion in her voice.

"Well he gave me the 'Disneyfied' version. He does that. He tries to protect me from all the bad stuff. That gets annoying sometimes, but then I am also grateful for that sometimes too. I still believe in love at first sight, soul mates and happily ever after is possible, even though I can't seem to find mine yet. I know it will happen; I can just feel it."

"I don't believe in any of that anymore. I just can't."

"Just give your heart over to the right guy."

"At this point I have only a small piece of my heart left and giving it to anyone terrifies me." Tears welled up in Zoey's eyes. She didn't want to get lost in a relationship again. How could she risk another man breaking her into a million pieces and shattering what small amount of self-esteem she was able to walk away with?

"I know it does. Just give it some time and you will know when it is right. I promise."

Zoey didn't feel like it would ever be right but she still loved Ariel's passion for all things possible, and she wouldn't be the one to shatter Ariel's view of the world. Finally, she looked at Ariel and said, "I hope you are right."

"I am, and maybe I am going out with my Prince Charming tonight."

"You have a date tonight?"

"Yes, I do," Ariel said excitedly. "I am going out with James again, that poker buddy guy I told you about, the accountant. He dresses incredibly well and has always been very nice to me."

"Well, good for you. Where are you guys going?"

"We are going to Casperelli's. I love the food there, but it is definitely one of the special occasion restaurants. Too rich for this little shop girl."

The two of them continued talking about her upcoming date until they arrived back to Zoey's apartment. After they said their goodbyes, Zoey made her way up the stairs. She debated on working more at the bakery for the remodel but decided that rest sounded like a much better option. Tomorrow, she could start on the remodel for the front of the shop.

Chapter 5

The next morning Tyler woke up to his phone pinging a series of text messages from Chase.

Chase: Wake up.

Chase: Get your ass out here.

Chase: You better not be standing me up again.

Chase: Don't make me come up there.

Tyler groaned. He had been putting off his run with Chase for a few days. The two men used to run three times a week, but since Zoey came to town Tyler had been canceling in lieu of hoping to be able to catch a glimpse of Zoey and hearing her sing. Tyler knew that he needed to drag himself down there or Chase would definitely make good on his threats.

Tyler: I am on my way.

Tyler got dressed and made his way down the stairs to start his run with his friend. He wasn't in the mood to talk, and normally Chase would prefer the silent run, but apparently getting stood up a few times had made him a little chatty today.

"So, what's with the brush off this week? You keep skipping out on me. You're going to get fat."

"Shut up."

"You can't eat all those wings and drink beer and still look as pretty as me if you are going to be lazy."

"Wow, aren't you full of it today?"

"Tell me what is going on and I will stop."

"I just needed a break and have a large project I am working on."

"Is that project a certain pretty little baker?"

"What?"

"Don't make me explain it to you," Chase said, almost laughing at Tyler.

"Zoey doesn't have anything to do with this," Tyler said as he quickened his pace to avoid the topic. Chase easily kept pace with his adjusted speed.

"It is a sad day when you try to lie to your cop best friend, and by the way, you can't lie for shit."

"Thanks. Can we just run now, or do you still want to act like a girl and talk about feelings?"

Chase slapped his friend on his shoulder and just shook his head. "Okay. Race you home and loser buys lunch." The two men picked up the pace and raced down the road. Tyler bought lunch.

ZOEY WAS RIPPING OUT the linoleum from the front of the shop so she could lay the tile. She was proud of the progress she had made since this morning. She painted the trim by the front windows, washed down the walls inside to prep for paint and was now halfway done with pulling out the old flooring. She was listening to her playlist on Spotify and singing along when she suddenly saw a pair of Lug boots standing in front of her. She jumped back and looked up to find Derek standing before her with a wide grin.

"Hey Zoey. How is it going?"

"Good. I still have to pull the rest of this flooring so I can lay the tile, but I am making good progress."

"Want some help?"

"Actually, I would love that."

The two of them worked for a few hours and were taking a break at the small table by the front window when Derek said, "Hey, we are short a person tonight for poker night. One of our guys isn't able to come. If you still like to play, I would love to have you over. Buy-in is fifty dollars and its Texas Hold 'Em."

"Are you kidding me? I would love that. I haven't played in years." Zoey started to giggle and feel like an excited teenager. "Is your group any good?"

"Well you know how I play."

"Yes, I do. You suck."

"Only because you can read me so well. Normally I kick their asses. They can't read people for shit. Well, except Chase and his damn cop instincts, but he has shit for luck on the draw of cards."

"I will be there. What time?"

"We start at eight."

"Okay should I bring anything?"

"Oh baby, you know what I like," Derek said with a devilish grin.

"Yes, I do, you sad sad little man. You need to get a woman."

"I did last night."

"What? Wow! Who is she? What is her name? When are you going to see her again? Is she nice?"

"Slow down there, Zoe. Her name is Shonda and I will never see her again. And she was *very* nice."

"Ew... you are such a man. Why won't you see her again?"

Derek gave a small shrug and said, "She is a tourist. She was only here for a couple days and I caught her on her last day."

Zoey shook her head. "So glad to see some things haven't changed. You need a good woman in your life."

Derek gave her a side hug and said, "I have three good women in my life. Mom, Ariel and you. I am good with that."

"I think you need and deserve more, but I will let it go for now."

"Thanks Zoe." The two of them continued to work for a couple more hours and then Derek left to get ready for poker night and Zoey shortly followed as well.

TYLER WAS SITTING AT Derek's table with a stack of chips in front of him, laughing with his friends as they talked about sports, women and work. Then a small knock came at Derek's door, and Derek went to answer.

"Since when does James knock for poker night?" asked Chase.

Derek's face grew stern and said, "James got uninvited."

Kyle leaned over to Chase and whispered, "James went on a date with Ariel and it didn't end well. I wouldn't ask Derek about it."

"Okay, then. He is dumber than I thought," Chase said, shaking his head.

Derek opened the door and there stood Zoey. Tyler peered around the corner and saw that she was wearing an R2-D2 shirt with a sweeping neck and a nice pair of jeans that curved with her hips to give her an amazing hour-glass shape. *I will take this over James any day*, he thought. He was frozen just looking at her. Not only could she sing and bake but oh my god she likes Star Wars too. Then he noticed a large plastic container in her hands. Derek took it from her and went into the kitchen. Zoey followed to the area where the kitchen flowed directly into the dining room where the boys were sitting ready to play.

"Hello boys!" Zoey said with a bright beaming smile. The men greeted Zoey, then looked longingly at the container she had brought. She followed their gazes and said, "Oh yeah, I brought treats. Anyone want one?"

All the men hopped from the table like a bunch of six-year-olds and gathered around the counter. She opened the container and there were several small cakes. All of them were in the shapes of diamonds, spades, clubs and hearts. There were two flavors, chocolate and red velvet. Kyle was the first to grab one and dig in.

"Oh my God Zoey. This is amazing."

Derek laughed and said, "I was lucky to have this all through college. Now you know why I practically begged her to move here."

Chase was the next to taste Zoey's perfect sweet confections. "Wow." He looked at her and batted his eyelashes her way and said, "Will you marry me?"

Tyler shot Chase a look and elbowed him in the gut. Had it been anyone else it would have knocked the wind out of them, but Chase just gave a slight ouch, looked at Tyler and said under his breath, "Or maybe not."

The men all grabbed more snacks and drinks and sat down to the table. Zoey gave her buy-in and found her seat between Tyler and Derek. Kyle looked at her and said, "Zoey, do you know how to play poker? Do we need to give you a cheat sheet?"

"Oh, I think I understand a little and what beats what.... It is kind of like the order of what beats what in Yahtzee right?" She gave an innocent smile to Kyle and tried to look as naïve as possible.

Tyler remembered how her face lit up when he talked about the poker game the first night they met. That was the face of someone who knew the rules of the game and liked to play.

Kyle had a big grin on his face and said, "Don't worry hon, we will help you as needed."

Tyler looked at Derek as he was obviously holding back a laugh and then to Zoey. These idiots don't know what is going to hit them. Sure enough, as the evening went on Chase was the first one out. Derek was right, he had zero luck with cards, but he figured out quickly that Zoey was well experienced with playing the game. Kyle was the second one out losing to Zoey because he kept on misreading her tells. Derek went out shortly afterwards on a bad beat on the river to Tyler. This left just Tyler and Zoey for the heads-up play.

Zoey kept chipping away at Tyler's pile hand after hand. He kept on thinking that he figured out her tells. One time he thought it was her pulling at her curls, another was when she was spinning her thumb ring. His final attempt was when he saw her playing with her chips in certain different ways, but each time he thought he had her figured out he was wrong. Zoey seemed to have had him figured out within the first ten hands of the night. He was amazed that he made it to heads up play, but he had several lucky hands that kept him alive throughout the night.

On the final hand, Tyler seemed happy with his hand and had just a slightly smaller stack than Zoey. It was getting late and he could feel Zoey wanting to go in for the kill, but he knew he had a good hand and needed to hook her in. Surprisingly, Zoey made a large bet that would commit Tyler, but not enough to scare him off the hand. He contemplatively played with his chips and she smiled. He studied her again for quite some time.

"Make a move already," bellowed Kyle from the kitchen.

"I am thinking," growled Tyler. Tyler and Zoey had their eyes locked on each other, and Zoey's smile deepened. Derek was standing by the table between just on the other side of Tyler. Tyler could feel Derek studying him.

"She has a tell, but you will never see it at a poker table," Derek whispered to Tyler.

Tyler took a minute to think about what Derek said. Then an inspired idea hit him. "I am all in but raising the stakes. If I win this hand, I get free breakfast for a month."

The guys all snapped their heads to Zoey. Chase was the first to break the silence. "Nobody told me we could bet food. I want back in." He then promptly shoved another of Zoey's cakes into his mouth and smiled.

"Shut it," Tyler said.

Zoey thought for a moment. "Well, I have more chips than you do, so my call will involve a higher stake from you than my simple breakfasts. You in?"

"Anything," Tyler said a little too quickly.

"Bad move dude," Derek said from his side. Derek smiled as he knew all too well how many chores he had to do for Zoey in college because he was dumb enough to take her bets. "She is punishing with manual labor."

"I feel good about my chances. Name your bet Zoey."

Zoey tilted her head to the left, smiled and said, "You build my website for the bakery. I tried earlier this week and failed miserably. It ended with me cursing out the laptop and stress baking."

Tyler felt like he won the lottery. He was planning on offering his help to her with a website anyway to be able to spend more time with her. Even if he lost his free food, he was still getting what he wanted. "Done," he said. So, with that, they both pushed their chips to the middle and showed their cards.

Laughter erupted from the boys as Zoey showed her winning hand. Tyler shook his head and looked at her and said, "Nice hand Zoey."

"Yes, I love it when I have the nuts," she said laughingly. Derek shook his head and laughed, and Chase nearly choked on his beer.

Kyle looked on and grabbed his brother by his shoulders and started to shove them out the door. "I am going to take this poor dejected boy home now. You broke his spirit Zoey."

"He'll live," Zoey responded.

Kyle started to leave with Tyler, then turned back to Zoey again and said, "Hey, I was thinking I would like to write an article for the paper about your bakery and its upcoming opening. It would just be a quick interview and some pictures that Dixie would take of you and the shop."

"That would be great. I could use the publicity for the opening. When do you think you would want to come by?"

"I could stop by tomorrow or Tuesday if you would like. I want to get it in Wednesday's edition."

"Sure, that would be great. Just let me know which day is better for the both of you."

"I will. Thanks Zoey," said Kyle as he walked through the door.

TYLER STOOD LOOKING at Zoey. He was mesmerized. Zoey was amazingly adorable. She felt comfortable around the guys as if she were always there and just fit. Her smile brightened the whole night, and she was letting her guard down a little more each day. Now she was standing there arching a brow, waiting for him to say something. He realized that he had stood there too long and needed to say or do something. He reached for his wallet and said, "Let me know when you want to work on the website." He drew out his business card and took her hand to place it in her palm. Her breath caught and eyes fluttered. Tyler could feel the electricity running between them again. "This is my card. My cell number is on the bottom. Call me anytime. For anything at all."

"Okay," Zoey said breathlessly. "Thank you. Would tomorrow be too soon?"

Tyler couldn't help but to feel a little jump in his heart. "No, not all."

"Come on Ty," came Kyle's voice from outside.

Tyler gave a crooked smile. "I have to go. I will stop by the shop tomorrow morning around nine."

"See you then." Then they both realized that their hands were still held to each other, and Tyler released hers and went out the door.

FROM THE OTHER ROOM, Chase and Derek watched the exchange with Tyler and Zoey in great interest. Then in voices low but still high enough so that Zoey could hear, Chase turned to Derek and said, "Is your best friend going to break my best friend's heart?"

Derek took just a second and looked at Chase and said, "Is yours?" Both men shook their heads and went back to the kitchen for more beer and snacks. Zoey stayed long enough to help Derek with clean up and collect her winnings, that would be sure to help her pay for more bakery supplies. Smiling, she thought about how she was able to get Tyler to take care of the website and found herself excitedly looking forward to the next day.

Chapter 6

The next morning Zoey got up early and headed for the bakery. She could see by the lack of lights above the bakery that Tyler still wasn't up yet. She didn't think he would get up much earlier than just before their appointment at nine since he never seemed like a morning person. She noticed the town wasn't much for mornings either, but she assumed that was just how it was in small town life. The only other lights that seemed to stir before dawn was that from Josie's apartment. She worked as a project manager and had crazy hours depending who she had for a conference call that day.

Zoey started working on some cinnamon rolls for her and Tyler to have for breakfast. She knew the value of the assistance Tyler was giving her and didn't want to take advantage. The least she could do was feed him. She pulled out her retro style black and white damask apron and started to work. She was kneading the dough and singing along to her playlist. She was quickly able to prepare the dough and slice into large rolls. She placed them in the oven and then began to make the icing. She dropped the softened butter into the bowl, added the powdered sugar, milk and vanilla beans. She was diligently mixing when she heard a low voice from be-hind her at the back door.

"Good morning," Tyler said, leaning on the door frame.

She immediately stopped singing and made a quick movement with the hand that was mixing the icing, causing some to fling back up on her face. She turned to see him still there, still leaning calmly on the doorframe and laughing.

"Tyler, I...I wasn't expecting you for at least another hour."

"I know, but I was upstairs and then started smelling that incredible aroma of your baking and just had to come down."

"Oh. Well, uh...thanks," Zoey said sheepishly. Then quickly she realized that she was singing just before Tyler came down. "So, how long were you standing there?"

"Not long."

Zoey's face began to heat up and she could feel herself start to blush. "Long enough to hear me sing," she said with a wince. *No one wants to hear your shrieking voice.* She heard Shane's voice in the back of her head.

"Just a little," he said as a half-truth. If he was being hon-est, he listened to her for about three songs before he came down. "It was nice though."

"Oh. Sorry, I just do it when I bake or clean. It keeps me focused. I don't know why."

He started to walk over to her with an intent gaze and said, "Don't be sorry, I liked it."

"I don't sing that well." Zoey was embarrassed. Only those closest to her ever heard her sing.

"Yes, you do."

Zoey shifted awkwardly. She had never done very well with taking compliments. With a bit of effort, she gave an awkward smile and said, "Thank you."

By now Tyler was standing next to her and said, "Sweetness, you are a mess."

"What?"

"You have icing on your face," and he took his finger and quickly swiped away one area that had a glop just below her eye. "Let me help."

"You don't need to..." but before she could say anything else, he picked her up and sat her on the counter to have her more at his eye level. She was surprised and forgot what she was going to say. He reached behind her for a towel that was on the counter and started to wipe other places where the icing had fallen on her face.

Zoey was still looking at him wide eyed and said in a soft voice, "All better now?"

Tyler shook his head. "No. There is still one place left."

Zoey raised her hand to her face and asked, "Where?"

Tyler took her hand and removed it from her face, bowing his head until his forehead met hers and they were staring into each other eyes. Zoey found that she could no longer stop herself from wanting this. Wanting him. He cupped her head into his hands and brought his lips to hers and kissed her. At first it was soft and testing. It was as if he was making sure she was feeling what he was. Her blood was rushing through her body heating her from the inside out. Her heart sped to an alarming rate. She wrapped her arms around his neck and parted her lips, giving a warm invitation to her mouth. The kiss continued as he ran his hands down the back of her spine and traveled back up her hair where he tangled his fingers in to deepen the kiss.

Zoey felt her stomach turning around and around inside as she felt Tyler's warm body pushed up against her, tensing from desire and need. Their kiss finally broke as they breathlessly looked at each other, touching foreheads.

Tyler was the first to speak, "God, Zoey. I..."

Then before he could finish, they both heard a voice from the alley way by the back door, "Zoey, are you there?"

Tyler took a couple of steps back just as Ariel appeared in the doorway. "Hey Zoey." She looked in the bakery and then noticed Tyler staring at her as well. "Oh, hey Tyler."

Zoey did her best at gaining some composure. "Hi Ariel. You are here early." She had seen Ariel coming into work several times since she moved to town to open her shop next door and thought it was unusual to see her here at this hour.

"Yeah, I know. I was hoping to catch you before I opened the shop. I wanted to talk to you about my date."

"Oh yeah. James. What happened?" Zoey had known from poker night that he had been uninvited with the boys, so she knew that it couldn't be good.

Tyler stepped behind Zoey and said, "Derek is going to kill him."

"It was so embarrassing," Ariel said with tears beginning to well up in her eyes. "I was coming back from the restroom and James was on his cell phone with his back to me and I heard him talking. I heard him say, 'Don't worry it's in the bag. I'll have Cinderella screaming my name by midnight.'"

"What?" Zoey said in disbelief.

"Yeah. Turns out he just wanted to sleep with me and thought he would get his way on our second date. Then when I confronted him about it, he got all self-righteous and said, 'Come on I took you to Casperelli's,' like I am just supposed to give it up based on that."

"What an asshole," Zoey said. "Please tell me you slapped him."

"No, but I did knee him in the balls," Ariel said proudly while straightening her spine. Tyler involuntarily shifted to behind the counter, seemingly to protect his manhood. The girls laughed and continued to catch up for a few minutes until the cinnamon rolls were ready.

The three ate breakfast and Ariel said her goodbyes to open up her shop. Tyler turned to Zoey and said, "So, where were we?" He placed his hands on her hips and pulled her in close.

Zoey caught her breath and said, "We were going to build my website."

"I thought we were doing something else," Tyler said not hiding the disappointment in his voice.

Zoey sighed, wanting to give in to her desires, but she knew she just wasn't ready. She didn't trust men. In her experiences, they either left her or broke her heart and spirit. "We were, but for now I just need my website built." They both looked into each other's eyes. It seemed as if Tyler could see the fear in her eyes and took a small step back while holding her eyes to his. Zoey's voice broke his gaze again. "Tyler...please. I..."

"It's okay. You don't have to explain." He raised his hands up to her face, caressed her cheek and brought her in for an embrace. At first she was rigid, but then he tightened his hug and rubbed his hands down her back. She melted into his arms, wrapping her arms around him, and felt the tears going down her face.

He pulled her back and saw a tear rolling down and he wiped it away. "Don't cry. I get it. I am here if you need anything. You can talk to me too you know."

"I know," she said weakly. "I appreciate it."

"Come on. Show me what you have in mind for the website," Tyler said, hoping that the change of direction would ease that look on Zoey's face. The two of them diligently worked together and got the basic structure of the site complete with the exception of the pictures of the bakery and products that she would be selling.

"You should talk to Dixie about taking pictures for the website when she is here for the interview with Kyle. That would be the best time since she will be here anyway."

"That is a good idea. I will call her today. Do you have her number?"

"Sure, give me your phone." Zoey handed her phone to Tyler and he took his out to get Dixie's information and entered the number on Zoey's phone. "I put my number in there too so if you need anything just call me." Then he smiled and said, "Or just yell up the fire escape."

"I will. Thanks Tyler, for everything." She gave Tyler a hug, and he wrapped his arms around her and gave her a kiss on top of her head.

"Like I said, anytime." Then with that he turned out the back door, up the fire escape and through his window.

After Tyler left, Zoey let out a long breath she didn't know she was holding. "Oh God, I am in trouble," she said walking back into the bakery shaking her head.

THE NEXT DAY KYLE CAME over with Dixie to complete the interview. Zoey had gotten up early to bake several pastries for the pictures and had cleaned an area in the front of the bakery that already had finished tile and the back wall painted. The remodel was coming along, but she still had to finish about half of the tile in the front of the store and put some finishing touches by the display cases. Kyle and Dixie were eating some bear claw clusters and croissants while Zoey said she needed to freshen up a little for the pictures. She went to the back bathroom and tried to fix her hair. She was getting frustrated and was feeling a little overwhelmed when Dixie appeared from around the corner.

"Sweetie, are you okay? Do you need some help?"

"I hate my hair, and my makeup is a melting from baking all morning," Zoey said with a pout.

"Ah...I see. Let me call in reinforcements."

"That is not necessary..." Zoey said but by now Dixie was already on the phone and put her hand up to Zoey.

"Hey girl," Dixie said into the phone. "We are having a hair and make-up emergency over here at the bakery for Zoey's interview." Then after a brief pause from the response on the other line, Dixie said thanks and hung up her phone.

About five minutes later, Josie came speeding through the bakery with a large case in her hands and corralled Zoey back to the bathroom. Zoey looked at Josie and said, "You didn't have to rush over. I know you must have been busy to-day."

"Nonsense. You are our friend and needed help. That is the end of it," Josie smiled at Zoey and went to work on her make-up and hair. She moved quickly and efficiently. Before Zoey knew it, she looked in the mirror and gasped.

"Oh my God, Josie. I look...well, great."

Josie looked clearly at Zoey in the mirror. "You always look great Zoey. You are beautiful. Don't let anyone ever convince you otherwise."

Zoey's mouth opened a little to say something, but she wasn't sure quite what to say and tears started to well in her eyes.

Josie turned Zoey around and said, "None of that. You are not going to mess up my artwork. Now off with you. Go give an amazing interview."

Zoey quickly reached for Josie and gave her a huge hug. Josie laughed and said, "Oh, okay, you're a hugger."

"I am. Deal with it," Zoey said, embraced her new friend a little harder, and turned to leave for her interview.

Dixie quickly took pictures of Zoey and the shop. Zoey couldn't believe just how quick and efficient Dixie was at getting the right shots. Dixie did whatever it took to frame the picture at the best angle. She was standing on chairs, crouching in weird positions and even laying on the ground. At one point Dixie seemed to have trouble with her right hip as she was attempting to rise from a crouch. Kyle rushed over to her side and helped her back to a standing position. Dixie looked a little embarrassed and thanked Kyle.

Zoey looked questioning at Dixie, who averted her gaze and then to Josie. Finally, Josie spoke in a soft tone. "She was in a bad car accident when she was in high school. From what others have told me, it was horrible. She still has trouble with her hip and leg sometimes. Nobody talks about it much."

Zoey wanted to ask more, but she could feel that it was not the right time. Kyle approached her and asked if she was ready to start. He turned on his tape recorder and sat next to Zoey.

After a few brief introductory questions, he got to the heart of what would be his article.

"What brought you to Blossom Hills?"

"I had an old college friend who grew up here and told me about the opportunity with Estelle's Bakery closing. I had been working as an office manager in Lexington and had always dreamed of opening my own bakery. There were things going on in my life that made it seem like the right time to change my path. So, when I heard about the opportunity here, I knew that it was meant to be."

"How long have you been baking?"

"I have been creating my own recipes since I was a teenager and I find joy in creating pastries and cakes. People always bond over food and I love being a part of that."

"What is your favorite thing to create?"

"The daily special. It is usually based on my mood. I never have one thing that I love to create on a constant basis. Baking is about creativity and heart. I want to make something special each day that shows how much I love what I do."

"What will the special be for opening day?"

"I am not sure yet. I never know until the night before, so we will all be surprised."

"When is opening day?"

"Opening day will be next Wednesday, but I will be holding an open house Tuesday night from six to nine that will feature after dinner desserts."

"Well I think I speak for everyone when I say that we are all looking forward to it."

"Thanks, Kyle." He reached over to the tape recorder and turned it off.

"That was great Zoey. I really appreciate your time."

"No, thank you Kyle. This will be great exposure for my shop."

Zoey then turned to Dixie and asked, "Can you email me those pictures you took today, and I can pay you for them to use for the website?"

"Of course. Here is my card. Just email me and I will send you the pictures and we can work out the rest."

"Thanks."

"Are you going to the Ides of March party at McKenna's on Saturday?"

"I hadn't heard about it. What is it?"

"Kind of a grown-up version of a toga party. Drinks are half price if you dress up and the best costume gets one hundred dollars."

Kyle chimed in, "I always win. I look amazing in a toga."

Zoey and Dixie laughed, and Kyle made a pouty face and said, "Hey, I am hot."

Dixie patted him on his chest and said, "Of course you are sweetie. We just know you well enough to not be charmed by you."

Well, except for Ariel, Zoey thought.

A short time later her new friends left, and Zoey went back to working on the shop to prepare for its opening. At the end of the day she determined that she was going to need help and would need to hire one or two part-time workers to assist her with daily operations. Before she left, she created a help wanted sign and placed it in the front window hoping that she could find someone who could be ready to work within the next couple days.

The next day she hired two people to assist with the store. The first was Dana, a tall, average built woman in her late thirties with two children in elementary school. She wanted something that could work around the hours when the children were in school, and she seemed to be an ideal fit to assist in the mornings. The second was a seventeen-year-old high school senior named Phil. He used to work with his dad on construction sites doing manual labor, but now he was looking for something else, so he didn't have to work with his dad.

"Don't get me wrong," Phil said. "I love my Dad. He is a great guy, but if I have to keep working with him, we will drive each other insane before the end of the month."

"No problem. So, would you be immediately available to help me finish with the remodel instead of waiting to start after opening the store?"

"That would be great. Would I sound too eager if I asked if I could start tonight?"

Zoey brightened and felt like he was going to be a great fit. "No, not at all. Actually, that would be perfect, thank you."

They worked out a schedule and his pay over the next couple of minutes and he immediately went to work on finishing the tile work in the front of the store. He was done with the floors by the end of the night.

"Wow, Phil. That is amazing. It was taking me forever to get this done. I can't believe you did that so quickly."

"I do tile work all the time for my dad, so this was nothing. Normally, I have a whole house to tile."

"Well tell your dad that I said you are amazing and thanks for letting you work with me."

"I'll tell him, thanks."

ON WEDNESDAY, AS PROMISED, the article about the bakery was on the front page of Blossom Hills Press and on their website. Zoey was so proud. The pictures looked great and the article that Kyle wrote put her and the bakery in an even better light than she could have hoped for. For the first time in years she felt positive about the direction her life was taking and felt as if she was building a solid life in her new town. She also forwarded the picture files to Tyler for the website. About ten minutes later, she heard her phone ping with a text.

Tyler: *I got the pictures. They look amazing. You looked amazing.*

Zoey: *Thanks. It was all Dixie and Josie working their magic.*

Tyler: No, it is your magic. Trust me.

Zoey thought about those words, "trust me." She wanted to trust him. He seemed so genuine. She had been warned about his past and how he went through so many women, but he didn't seem that way now. Then her mind kept betraying her, *but you are a horrible judge of character with men.* She thought for another minute and texted back to him.

Zoey: Can I?

Tyler: Can you what?

Zoey: Trust you?

Zoey held her breath as she saw the three dots that showed Tyler typing and prayed for a yes. Then she jumped at the ping coming through.

Tyler: Yes. I would never hurt you.

Zoey: I want to believe you.

Tyler: I want the chance to prove it to you.

Zoey: I am working on it. I promise.

Tyler: Have you had dinner yet? Are you hungry?

Zoey hadn't really thought about eating and realized that she hadn't eaten since breakfast around six that morning.

Zoey: Yes. Starving.

Tyler: Want to go with me to Daisy's for dinner?

Zoey: Yes. Sounds good. See you in ten minutes?

Tyler: I will be right down.

Zoey went to the bathroom to make sure she didn't look like a disaster from working all day and washed her face off. She looked in the mirror and thought it would just have to do. Then as she left the bathroom and went around the corner, she found that Tyler was already standing in the door-way.

"Hello, Sweetness."

Damn, he looked good. Zoey couldn't look away from him. He was dressed in khaki's and a tight-fitting blue polo shirt. No man should look this adorable all the time. It just wasn't fair. How was a girl supposed to make good judgments when her hormones just wanted to jump into his arms? She let out a small breath and said, "Hey. You didn't have to dress up just for me."

Tyler looked a little confused and looked down at his clothes. "I have been wearing this all day. I had a meeting with a client this afternoon about a new project."

"Oh, do you need to get work done? We could go another time if you need to work."

"No, I am good. I wouldn't have invited you if it was a bad time."

"Right. Sorry."

"Don't apologize Zoey. It's okay. Are you ready?"

"Yes. Let's go." Then Zoey gathered her purse and phone and directed Tyler out the back door and locked up to leave. She turned and without even thinking linked her arm in Tyler's and headed to Daisy's.

As they walked across the square, she realized just how comfortable she was walking with her arm wrapped around his. He had a natural ease about him, a peace that she hadn't found with the men she had been dating. She wanted to trust him, but she was still so weary and was doubting her judgment. Tyler couldn't be that bad of a guy if he was friends with Derek, but James was a friend of Derek's too and look what he did to poor Ariel. She needed more time—just a little more time to figure out if what he was saying was true, that she could trust him.

They reached Daisy's Diner, and he opened the door for her and led her in, placing his hand on the small of her back. It took her by surprise. No man had done that for her, at least not since Trevor and that was about fifteen years ago. Zoey's heart was doing a happy dance in her chest and she looked adoringly at Tyler as they made their way to their booth.

"What did I do to deserve that look from you?" Tyler asked as they sat down.

"Just for being you. I needed this break. Thank you."

"You're welcome. I wanted to see you, so I feel like I am getting the better side of this deal."

The two began an easy conversation about how their week was going. Tyler talked about his job and some new projects he was working on. He talked about Kyle and how they both lived in Philadelphia. He explained that Kyle was working for the major paper in Philadelphia and just got burned out on doing stories on the horrors of the city. He decided that he much more preferred the small-town life and reporting on the stories within the town.

"So, he is happier now?" Zoey asked.

"Yes, much happier, but the scars are still there from what he saw while he was in the city. He was reporting on the murders, rapes and violent crimes. He had to be at so many of the crime scenes to do the reporting, it just wore him down. When he found out that Mr. Patterson was retiring and selling the paper, he jumped at the chance to come back home and be near the family and maintain the paper."

"That is great. So, what about you? What made you come back to Blossom Hills?"

Tyler winced. He took a deep breath and said, "Okay. I am going to be upfront and honest with you. I want you to trust me, but I am not going to look like a good guy in this story. Also, I don't want you to hear about it from someone else." He grabbed her hand and continued, "But please hear all of my story and know I am in a good place now."

Zoey pulled her hand back, mentally braced herself and said, "Alright. Go on."

"I was engaged to a woman named Jane back in Philly. I think she loved me in the beginning, but then as time went on, I got busier with my job and couldn't focus my energy on her as much as I should have. Then at some point she began sleeping with another guy. She fell in love with him and we broke up. She ended up marrying the guy. I was angry. I then started being with just about any woman who would have me and then left their lives just as quickly as I came. After a while I realized that I hated the person that I had turned into. I knew I had to turn my life around. So, I stopped my dating with a vengeance thing, decided to concentrate on myself and going back to the person I used to be before Jane. Then my company dissolved, and I lost my job. So, I decided to become a contractor and work for myself. This meant I didn't have to stay in the city I had grown to hate, and I could be back here to be close to my family and friends."

Zoey sat quietly in the booth with her hands folded on the table across from him. She was listening intently. He took her hands in his and continued, "I can't tell what you are thinking, but I want you to know I am not that person anymore. I am a better man now. I know the kind of guy I want to be. The kind of guy that I used to be before things happened with Jane. And I promise if you let me in, I will stay by your side."

Zoey looked lost in thought as her hands were still held in his. As she looked in his eyes, she could see his honesty. His openness and hopefulness were plainly displayed on his face.

"Zoey," he said.

She blinked. "How many?"

"What?"

"How many women did you sleep with after Jane?"

Tyler looked into her eyes. He hesitated before saying, "Does it matter how many?"

"Yes." She paused. "Yes. I don't know, but if I don't ask, I will always wonder, and I think I need to know. Is it over a hundred?"

Tyler took a breath and seemed to stop a laugh. "No. Definitely less than a hundred."

He was watching for Zoey's reaction, and she took a breath of relief. It wasn't nearly as bad as she was thinking. Zoey was still digesting the information and finally asked again, "How many then?"

Tyler took a minute to think and finally said, "Over my entire life, I don't have an exact number. Jane was my fifth, but it was after her that the number got out of control." Zoey was still waiting and didn't seem to want to ask again. "I would say somewhere between thirty to forty after Jane."

Zoey sat thinking. Shane was her tenth lover overall, and she was about the same age as him. He was more chaste than she was before Jane. He said that he wanted to be the man he was before Jane and she wanted to believe him, but she wasn't going to just hand over her heart again. She had to learn something from her past relationships. But she couldn't deny her attraction to this man. He was having an effect on her that no man had had for a very long time.

Tyler finally broke the silence. "Zoey? Are you okay? Please say something."

She blinked several times and appeared as if she was returning from her thoughts. Making a decision, she said, "I am okay. The number is actually better than what I had built up in my head, but I still have more questions if that is alright."

The relief could be seen on Tyler's face. "Ask me anything. I won't lie to you Zoey."

Zoey nodded. "I think this is more important than the number of women. How did you get these women into your bed?"

Tyler looked confused for a minute before she clarified. "Sorry, what I mean is did you try to romance them and give promises that you didn't intend to keep, or were you upfront about your intentions?"

"I was upfront, always. However, that doesn't mean there weren't a few women who thought they could try to change my mind to make it more permanent."

"What happened to them?"

"I tried to be as direct as I could and make it clear that I wasn't interested in anything more."

"I can appreciate that. I can't look you in the face and say that I never slept with a man without knowing I didn't want something more. It would be naïve of me to think that a man has never done the same."

The tension on Tyler's face dissolved as he looked at Zoey. She wasn't looking at him with contempt or judgement, just a soft thoughtfulness that also looked apprehensive. He rose and moved to the other side of the booth to be closer to her. He slid one arm behind her back and used his other to tilt her face towards his. "Let me make this clear. I want more from you Zoey. I won't hurt you, and I won't leave. I can wait if you're not ready, but I know what I want and can see how good you are for me."

Zoey wanted to cry. He was saying everything she wanted to hear. This gorgeous man was interested in her. It didn't seem possible. She knew she had an average body and what she thought was a little more than average looks. His hand on her back was bringing sensations alive deep inside her that had been dormant for so many years. There was a tenderness and protectiveness that she didn't feel with Shane or any of the last boyfriends she had. "I believe you, but I can't just jump into this. I need more time...please."

A WARM SMILE BEGAN to form on Tyler's lips. He was just so grateful she didn't say she hated him after hearing about his past that he had been so ashamed of. He wanted to know more about her past and what was holding her back, but there was time for all of that. He brought her closer to him where she melted into his body and rested her head on his chest. He kissed the top of her head and they finished their dinner in a quiet contentment.

BACK IN LEXINGTON, Shane received an email from a mutual friend of his and Zoey's. He opened it, curious after reading the title of the email, '*Did you see this?*' In the body of the email was just a link. Intrigued, he clicked on it and it opened to the article about Zoey from Blossom Hills Press. His anger grew with each line he read. Then he came to one line and read it several times, *Zoey Carrington learned about our small town from local football legend and college friend Derek McKenna.* He felt a surge of self-righteous anger and as the next few minutes melted into another, it just continued to grow.

"Just a friend my ass, that fucking whore." Then with a surge of temper he threw the tablet across the room and hit the far wall where the screen shattered into cracks over the picture of Zoey in her new bakery.

Chapter 7

The next few days moved quickly as Zoey, Phil and Dana worked diligently on the bakery. They were desperately trying to make sure it was ready for the open house on Tuesday. Others had visited frequently during the remaining renovations. Derek would occasionally stop by with lunch for them, and in exchange Zoey consistently fed his cravings for the sweet morning pastries. Tyler was in and out often checking with Zoey on details for the website and the two sometimes would walk together back to Zoey's apartment once she closed. He was giving her the time she had asked for. He wasn't pushing to kiss her much more than the occasional kiss on the forehead or holding her hand as they walked. He never asked to come into her apartment, and she didn't offer, but she welcomed his embraces as he left and was growing more comfortable with him each day.

Josie, Dixie and Ariel stopped by Zoey's apartment Friday to have a girl's night. They had ordered pizza and were drinking wine and catching up on the gossip of the town. Zoey quickly realized that there were no secrets in Blossom Hills. She learned about the scandals, such as whose husband was cheating on whose wife, which teenager was causing havoc by partying in the woods bordering the orchards and more embarrassing stories about the boys growing up.

"Okay, enough about all this, let's get to the juiciest gossip in town," said Dixie with a wide smile at Zoey.

"Oooo, what's that?" Zoey said with excitement.

"Darling," Josie said with a swirl of her wine glass. "Sunshine over there is talking about you."

Wide eyed, Zoey gasped. "Me?!? Why? I am boring."

"HA!" said Dixie. "Catching the heart of the local hottie is not boring. So, spill it. What's going on with you and Tyler? It isn't like you guys have been trying too hard to hide it."

Zoey didn't think they were hiding anything. "There is nothing going on beyond what you have seen."

Then the sweet soft voice of Ariel came from the far side of the couch. "Really, then why did Kyle tell me that Tyler kissed you in the bakery."

Blushing Zoey said, "Well yes there was that, but that is all we have done so far. Kissing."

Josie looked over at Zoey coolly and said, "You do realize these two love starved girls are not going to let you get away with just that, right?"

"I am getting that thanks," Zoey said and then continued with resignation. "Alright, so Tyler and I talked about us a little over dinner one night. He told me about his past. He was up front and honest about it. I appreciated that. He isn't perfect."

"Honey, no man is," said Josie with a calm gruff.

"Right. Well, he told me he wants more with us. I told him I wanted more time. I mean, I just moved here. The bakery isn't even open yet and my last relationship could go in the record books for disasters. I don't want to repeat mistakes. I can't."

"Well, I think you and Tyler would be great. Yeah, he went through an asshole phase, but even his asshole phase was mild compared to most of the other men I have known," Dixie said as she leaned over for another slice of pizza, her fourth that night. Zoey felt a twinge of jealousy. That girl could eat and still look fabulous. *Some things just weren't fair*, she thought.

"I have to admit I was expecting worse when he explained it to me," Zoey said.

"Blossom Hills standards are much different from what you and I are used to," Josie said dryly. Zoey knew that. Zoey was from Lexington, and while it wasn't a major metropolis like New York City, it was a far cry from what most people thought of when it came to it. Lexington was a thriving city with nightlife, an art scene and a party atmosphere by the University of Kentucky. People were loose with dating and no one really knew anyone else's business. Josie had also come from Atlanta but loved the smaller life here in Blossom Hills.

"Hey! We are modern here too," said Ariel with a tone of offense.

Josie patted her friend on her face in a motherly manner and said, "That is so sweet you think so, honey."

Ariel pouted and the girls all laughed. Then Josie turned to Zoey and said in all seriousness, "Zoey, just make sure you don't make the poor boy wait too long. We see how he looks at you, and I think we could all agree that we wish someone looked at us the way he does at you."

A small chorus of "Yeah" came from Ariel and Dixie.

"I know. I am working on it. I promise," Zoey said leveling her gaze at her friends.

The night continued and the girls finished dinner and the two bottles of wine. They were all saying their goodbye's as Josie turned to Zoey and said, "I wanted to let you know you can use my toga for tomorrow's party. I have to go out of town for work tomorrow morning and can't go now. Would you like for me to bring it to you tomorrow?"

"Oh, I don't think it would fit me."

"Trust me sweetie it will fit. The thing is like a circus tent and I just belt it at the waist. I made it out of a bedsheet."

"Okay then, thank you."

THE NEXT DAY JUST AS Josie had promised she dropped off the toga before catching her flight. Zoey tried it on, and Josie had been right. It fit just fine; in fact, it was big even on her. *Josie must drown in this thing,* she thought. Zoey grabbed some gold glittered accents she had in the back of her shop from a canceled order and used those as shoulder accents. They were shaped like golden leaves much like the Romans had worn. She was satisfied that the toga would work just fine and put it back on the hanger in her office so she could easily change before they all left for McKenna's that night.

Phil had come to help with finishing touches on the bakery. Zoey had grown fond of the teenager. He seemed mature for his age, and very respectful of others. She also noticed several times when teenaged girls would walk by the bakery window to catch a glimpse of him working in his tank top. He didn't seem to notice or care about the attention he appeared to be drawing from the girls, he just kept diligently working. It was because of that hard work that the bakery was ready ahead of schedule. Zoey realized that she could take the next day off completely. Then she thought about Tyler. Maybe she would see what he was doing and if he wanted to spend their Sunday together.

Phil took a look around the bakery and asked, "Is there anything else you need for me to complete before I go home?"

"No. You have been amazing. I never would have completed this early or even on time if it wasn't for your help. Are you still able to work Tuesday night for Open House?"

"Are you kidding me? I am looking forward to it. I plan to eat at least one of everything that night."

"Well you have definitely earned it. Now go home."

"Yes, ma'am."

Phil was walking out the back door just as Tyler and Ariel popped in, both in their respective togas. Ariel looked adorable in her mini-skirt toga and Tyler's broad shoulders were highlighted with the draping of the sheet he wrapped himself in. Clearly, he had grabbed it from his closet and just fastened it any way he could around his body.

Ariel was the first to speak. "Ready?"

"Almost. Just let me change into the toga and put up my hair. I will be right back."

Zoey disappeared into the office to retrieve her toga and went to the bathroom where she did a partial updo with her curls and left a portion down framing her face and neck. Satisfied, she returned to her friends.

"Ready. The bakery is finished. You guys want a peek around?"

"Absolutely!" Ariel exclaimed.

Ariel went first through to the front followed by Zoey and then Tyler who walked behind her with his hand on her back. It was a small touch that Zoey was becoming accustomed to with him and when they were together, she needed to get used to his touch wherever it might be. It could be with his arm around her shoulders, his hand on her back or their arms linked with each other. She knew Josie was right—he wouldn't wait forever. She needed to let him in soon, but she was realizing he was already there just waiting for her to give the nod to move forward.

Then Ariel gasped in awe. "Zoey, this is amazing! You have done so much work. I don't even recognize this as the same place as Estelle's."

Ariel was right. The old wallpaper was gone, and the room was bright and airy. Zoey had taken the back wall behind the counter and painted it a sky blue with a white mist echoing the background. At the top was the menu with scrolled letters and descriptions. The cases had been lovingly restored and the racks replaced with new trays of blue and white. The tables had also been refinished with the wood details showing through. Zoey had placed blue glass vases with white beads lining the bottoms, then a smaller standing sign with the logo of the bakery and words outlining the top saying daily special.

Zoey had stopped in the middle of the front of the store and Tyler had wrapped both his arms around her waist from behind her. "Thanks, I couldn't have done it without all the help I have gotten from everyone. I am even done early and can take tomorrow completely off."

She felt Tyler lean down and whisper into her ear, "Does that mean I can steal you away tomorrow?"

She tilted her head up, looked into his eyes and whispered back, "Yes." His arms tightened around her. She felt a shiver go up her spine and found herself starting to give her heart away.

They realized that Ariel was looking at them both with wide eyed happiness and then she said, "Awww, don't mind me. Carry on."

Zoey shook her head and said, "I think we should go now." She looked back at Tyler and said, "Can you lock the back door and we will all go out the front." He turned and disappeared to the back and Zoey went to grab her purse from the counter. She smiled at her friend and said, "Don't start."

"What?" Ariel said with feigned innocence. "I have no idea what you are talking about," and then she started to giggle.

Tyler came back to the front of the shop and met up with the girls. "Okay, we are all locked up. Let's go." The three friends walked out the front door and to the end of the square to McKenna's with Zoey in the middle and one arm around each of them feeling more at home than she had ever felt before.

ACROSS THE SQUARE IN the shadows of the gazebo stood Shane who was glaring at the trio as they walked down the street to McKenna's. His rage flowed through his veins in a red-hot flame. He watched as Zoey smiled up at Tyler and he gave a sadistic snort at them. He couldn't believe what he was seeing. She left him for her college friend and now she was flaunting around with yet another guy. She ruined his life by cheating on him and acting as if she was the innocent one. He was the one who was placed on suspension at his job because of her. His boss had seen him at the restaurant when he found her with Derek, and he heard the heated exchange between him and Zoey in the parking lot afterwards. Shane was on the fast track for a promotion and he nearly lost his job for what his boss called an ethics violation. She was going to pay for her betrayal, for her selfishness and her slutty ways. She would know that there were consequences to her behavior. With that thought screaming through his mind he made his way to her bakery to have his own piece of vengeance.

Chapter 8

The Ides of March celebration was a complete success. Derek was busy all night and barely had time to talk to his friends. Kyle was true to his word and again won the one hundred dollar prize for best toga. This year he added a fake knife in his back with a small sign that said "Et Tu Brute?" Dixie and Ariel had Zoey dancing and laughing throughout the night and things couldn't have been better. By the end of the night Chase, Tyler, and Zoey were the only ones remaining. The three of them had decided to stay back and help Derek with the cleanup so he could get home at a reasonable hour. Chase's cell phone rang, and he excused himself to answer since it was coming from the station. His face darkened as he hung up with a grave look and walked over to Zoey.

"Zoey, you need to come with me to the bakery. Tyler you should come too."

Zoey's face grew concerned and she looked at him and asked, "Why? What's going on?"

"There was a break in."

"Oh my God," Zoey exclaimed and went to grab her purse. At that point Derek walked in from the back room and had a questioning look on his face.

Tyler quickly turned to him and said, "The bakery was broken into. Chase just got the call. We're leaving right now." Without a second thought, Derek grabbed his keys and turned to follow everyone to the bakery.

When they walked up, there was already an officer standing outside, obviously waiting for Chase to arrive. Zoey was behind Chase with Tyler holding her shaky hand. The two windows of the store front were smashed in with glass everywhere. The front door looked as if a battering ram was used to open it and was hanging on by one hinge. Zoey carefully stepped inside and began to look around. The tables and chairs had been upheaved. The beautiful blue vases were shattered on the new tile floor. There were holes in the drywall where some object had been used to smash them in. Her display cases were destroyed and left in writhing pieces of wood and metal with the shattered glass. Her portable sign that was to read the daily special had the word "whore" written across the middle. It was all too much to take in. She felt a flood of fear, anger and anxiety taking over and her knees were beginning to give out.

Her emotions were coming up to the surface and she began to sway while she was surveying the damage. Tyler quickly stepped in behind her to give her support before she fell to the floor. Zoey's weight leaned against him as she weakly said, "Who would do this? Who would do this to me?" The tears were freely starting to fall. She realized that Chase was surveying the damage and he started to go into the back of the shop to see if there was additional damage there.

Zoey then heard Derek's voice from behind her. "Son of a bitch." She watched Derek turning in circles and finding more damage with each additional look.

TYLER DIDN'T MOVE. By this time, he had Zoey wrapped in his arms in a protective embrace and was hoping that he could help provide her with a sense of security. She was shaking and crying. Tyler couldn't believe that someone could hate Zoey this much. Zoey was the sweetest and kindest person he had known. She was genuine in her care for others. He had seen it with Derek and the girls she welcomed so openly.

Chase came out from the back and asked Zoey to come with him to look at something. She followed with Tyler and Derek close behind. The kitchen was just as damaged as the front of the store, but the single thing that stood out with the most attention was a piece of paper with the word "bitch" written across it that had been stabbed into the wall with a kitchen knife.

Zoey's emotions were completely taking over and she was freely sobbing now. Tyler thought about how hard she had worked to prepare the store to open, and it had all been ruined within one short night. Someone clearly hated her. Tyler moved her to the stool so she wouldn't collapse to the ground and kept his arms around her. Derek had started to move to the note that was knifed into the wall and was going to take it down, but Chase moved in front of him and said, "Don't. It is evidence. Don't touch it."

Scowling, Derek nodded and walked away.

"Zoey, do you know of anyone who may have a grudge against you?"

Zoey looked shocked. "I barely know anyone here. Really, the only people I have interacted with are you guys. I mean, I have met people here and there at Daisy's or in the square, but not enough for anyone to want to do this. I just don't understand."

"I think I have a pretty good idea of who did this," said Derek with a growl.

The three of them quickly turned their heads to look at Derek. "Come on Zoe. Don't you think this is something Shane would do?"

She looked surprised and took a few seconds to answer. "No. Not like this. And besides, he is in Lexington. I never told him where I was going. I don't even talk to any of our old friends over there."

Tyler looked down at Zoey with great concern. If someone was willing to travel from Kentucky to North Carolina to cause this kind of damage, she could be in more danger than she may want to be willing to admit. He was not going to let her stay alone tonight, no matter how much she protested.

"I think he is capable of this," said Derek.

Chase nodded and took a step closer to Zoey. "I am all too familiar with domestic abuse cases and just how bad things can get." He nodded to Derek and continued, "We will check him out. I will have the Lexington police talk to him." He turned to Zoey and said, "I am going to need you to give me his contact information and details. I also have some questions I will need to ask you to fill out the report. I know this is a bit much, so we can do it here inside the shop or we can step outside if you want."

"Here is fine Chase. Just let me go into the office and I will get you Shane's contact information."

After Zoey left the room to go to her office, Derek walked over to Tyler and said, "She can't be alone. Not now."

Tyler looked at Derek with a set determination on his face and replied, "Believe me, I am already ahead of you. There is no way I am letting her stay at her place alone. I will give her a choice of my place or hers."

Derek nodded and said, "If she doesn't feel comfortable with you, send her to my place. The creep who did this, whether it be Shane or someone else, is still out there and I don't want anything to happen to her."

"Agreed."

Chase walked over to Derek and said, "What about this Shane guy? Was he physically abusive to her before when they were together?"

"Zoey said no, but she did admit to some extreme verbal abuse and that she would do her best to not set him off for fear of what he might do or say."

"So, it was starting to escalate to physical when she left?"

"I think so, yes. If it hadn't already and she is too ashamed to tell me. Has she said anything to you about it, Ty?"

"No, we have talked quite a bit about my past, but she has been pretty tight lipped about her life before moving here. This is the first I am hearing about all of this."

Zoey reappeared in the room with a paper in her hand and gave it to Chase. "This is Shane's address, phone number and email address, but I still don't think he would drive all the way over here to do this to me. We have been over for months. It doesn't make sense."

"You never know. We just need to be careful, Zoey," Chase said in a calming tone.

It was always strange for Tyler to see Chase in cop mode. He had been living in Philadelphia for most of Chase's career. He could see why he was so respected in the town as an authoritative figure.

Chase then proceeded to fill out the report with Zoey and asked all the appropriate questions. It was quicker than Tyler expected, but there wasn't much for Zoey to say since as Chase knew she was at McKenna's during the break in and wouldn't have any information to provide as to what happened. Chase explained that his team would be doing an investigation throughout the night and again in the morning. Zoey may not have access to the shop until late Sunday or Monday. She grew a little pale and was trembling in Tyler's arms.

Chase gave Zoey his card and the report number that she could file a claim with her insurance and told her to go home and try to get some rest.

Derek nodded to Tyler and said, "I am going to go back to the bar but let me know if she needs anything."

Tyler nodded and then turned his focus back to Zoey. He put his arm around her and whispered in her ear. "Come on, follow me. We need to leave here." As they turned to leave, they found Dixie and Kyle running up to the bakery. Dixie had her camera strapped around her neck and Kyle looked tussled.

Dixie was the first to speak. "Chase had me come to take pictures for the police report. God Zoey, I am so sorry. It'll be okay. I promise. Let me know if you need the pictures for your insurance, okay?"

Zoey nodded and just remained leaning on Tyler for support. Kyle looked at the two of them with concern and asked, "Do we know who did this?"

Tyler growled at his brother, "No comment."

Kyle looked taken aback and then said, "Geez Ty, I was asking as a friend, not a reporter. I'm not a complete asshole."

Tyler's tension eased for a minute and said, "I think you should talk to Chase for details about the break in. Zoey is in no shape to talk to anyone right now."

Zoey looked as if she was going to protest, but she gave a shaky sigh and leaned back into Tyler. Her voice quivered as she said, "I am sorry, Kyle. Maybe later, okay?"

Kyle nodded and turned to Tyler. "Let me know if there is anything I can do to help. At least call me in the morning, okay?"

Tyler nodded and then took Zoey up the stairs to his apartment. He walked her to the couch and sat her down. "Stay here. I will be right back in just a couple of minutes."

"I want to go home Tyler, please."

"You are Sweetness, but I am packing a bag. I am staying with you. There is no way I am going to let you stay there on your own tonight."

Zoey was still shaking as she was sitting on the couch. Tyler couldn't clear his head. There was so much obvious hate in the destruction downstairs. He waited for Zoey to object or question him more, but when she didn't Tyler took it as her consent and proceeded to go to his bedroom and pack his bag.

Within a few short minutes, Tyler was walking Zoey back to the other side of the square to her apartment. He took the keys from her hands, unlocked the door and escorted her inside. Tyler put his bag down on the couch and walked her back to her bedroom. She was still wearing the toga and had glitter from the accent pieces on her face and chest. It pained Tyler to see her looking so beautiful and haunted at the same time. She wasn't moving from the bed, and she appeared to still be in shock. Tyler looked through her dresser drawers and found a set of pajamas and set them on the bed next to her. "Get changed out of that toga. How about a drink? Do you want something?"

Zoey nodded.

"What would you like?"

Zoey shrugged her shoulders. "Anything is fine."

Tyler disappeared and went into the kitchen. While he was gone Zoey had changed into her pajama pants and matching tank top. She was sitting back on the bed and dazedly looking around her room. Tyler could hear her talking to herself. "All that hard work, just gone. I don't know if I can do..." She stopped, noticing that Tyler had walked into the room just as tears began to roll down her cheeks.

Tyler stood to the side with two oversized mugs. "Hot chocolate," he said as he passed her one of the mugs.

"You are amazing," Zoey said quietly.

Tyler sat down on the bed next to her and wrapped his free arm around her. "It is going to be okay. You will see.

We will get the bakery back up and running in no time. I promise."

Zoey nodded against his chest. He kissed her head and whispered, "I am going to change really quick. I will be right back." He set his mug on her nightstand and went to the bathroom with his duffel bag. He stared into the mirror and took a deep breath. He couldn't believe someone could do this to her. He also believed Derek was right about Shane being the one who destroyed the bakery. This was too personal of an attack to be just some random kid causing havoc. He had so many questions for Zoey about what happened to her before, but he knew he couldn't push her, and he especially couldn't ask anything of her tonight. He changed into a t-shirt and athletic shorts and went back to Zoey's bedroom to check on her.

She was still sitting on her bed drinking the last of her hot chocolate. She looked exhausted and her eyes were swollen and red. Tyler's heart was breaking for her. "Hey Sweetness, you doing a little better?"

"Yeah. It is just a lot to process."

"Of course. Get some sleep and lets just figure out next steps tomorrow. You need some rest okay?" He walked over to her and kissed the top of her head and started to turn and walk out of the bedroom but was stopped by her hand on his arm.

"Can you stay in here? I am a little freaked out and don't want to be alone."

"Yes. I just didn't want to overwhelm you by staying in here with you." Tyler knew how skittish she was about the two of them and didn't want to risk the progress they had made by doing something she wasn't ready for.

"It won't be. Please stay."

Tyler nodded and as Zoey laid down, he took the other side of the bed and laid beside her so that her back fit inside the front of his body. He took a deep breath to control how his heart was pounding being this close to her. His heart stopped as she started to shake from what he thought was her getting chilled. "You cold?" he asked as he wrapped his arm securely around her waist.

"No, I just..." Then she began to cry again.

"It's okay. You're safe here with me. Nothing is going to happen. Please Zoey get some rest. I will be here all night."

"Okay." Then only about ten minutes later he felt her breathing even its pace and she drifted off to deep sleep.

The next morning Tyler woke up laying on his back with Zoey's head on his chest and she was still fast asleep. He started to gently rub her back in small circles. She started to wake up and turned her head to look in his eyes. He smiled down at her and said, "Good morning."

"Good morning."

"You hungry?"

"Yeah, I am."

"Okay, get dressed. We are going out."

"I can cook breakfast."

Tyler shook his head. "No way. Pretty soon you will be making breakfast for the entire town almost every day. We are going to enjoy you not working in the kitchen."

She started to protest, but he rolled her over and brought his mouth down to hers to stop any argument.

"Tyler, I can..."

Then he kissed her again.

When he finally released her from the kiss, he said, "No. I am in control of today. Got it?"

Zoey saw the determination in his eyes and finally said, "Okay. You're the boss, but only for today, and I need a shower first." And with that, Zoey slid out of bed and started gathering things to get ready for the day.

While Zoey was in the shower, Tyler heard her cell phone ring. He went over to the phone and saw that it was coming from Chase's number. He picked up the phone and answered, "Hey Chase, It's Tyler."

"Hey Tyler. I am glad you are still there."

"Yeah, I am not going anywhere. At least, not until we know more about what happened. Can Zoey go back to the bakery yet?"

"We are wrapping things up this morning, but she can't go back to clean up until probably around two."

"Take your time. I am taking her out today to get her mind off things."

"Good idea. I reached out to Lexington PD about this Shane guy. Once they have a chat with him, I will know more. If it isn't him, I will need to talk to Zoey again. I don't think anyone here would have done such a personal attack like this. This is someone she knows."

"Yeah, I know. That is what worries me the most."

"Well give her my best and let her know she can come back to the bakery this afternoon."

"Will do. Talk to you later."

Tyler then made a few phone calls of his own to make some arrangements for the day. Then he heard the shower turn off a few minutes later and walked down the hallway towards the bathroom to check on Zoey. She was fixing her hair and already dressed in jeans and a black V-neck shirt that flared at her hips to show her great curves. Tyler couldn't stop thinking just how irresistible she looked and walked up behind her and wrapped his arms around her. "Do you know how beautiful you are?"

Zoey's face flushed and she looked down. "No, Tyler I am not..."

Tyler spun her around and took his hands and brought her head up so her eyes could look directly into his and said, "I want you to listen to me. You are beautiful. Every piece of you. From these crazy curls that smell like strawberries and vanilla to the soft curves of your body. And that is just some of what is on the outside, which pales to the person you are inside." He paused and smiled down at her and continued, "You...are...beautiful."

"And you are amazing," Zoey said breathlessly. She then reached her arms around his back and started to trace her fingers up the hollow of his spine. Tyler's muscles stiffened and reacted to her touch. He bent down and kissed her, lightly at first. He was barely touching her lips and then kissed her again with a little more force. He wanted her. Her lips parted for him to allow his tongue to meet hers in a ferocious dance. He slowly moved his hands down to her hips and lifted her up onto the bathroom counter. Their heads were more even, and their mouths were greedily taking in each other. Zoey's hands moved down his chest, feeling his

muscles and then resting on his heart where it pounded wild-
ly. She gazed at him and said, "Your heart...Tyler...it..."

"It is what you do to me. I can't make it stop." He then
started moving his mouth to her neck where he peppered her
with more lingering kisses. Zoey's head tilted back to give
him better access and her legs spread apart to allow him to
step in between her. He could feel his arousal through his
pants rubbing between her thighs. She gave a deep sigh of
contentment. Then he felt another pulse of his erection re-
acting to her sounds of delight. "Zoey..." Tyler said in a deep
throaty tone.

She brought her head back to meet his and their foreheads touched as she was arching her back so that her breasts
were meeting his chest. Their breathing was heavy, and he
could see the flickers of desire in Zoey's eyes. Just then,
pounding came from the other room.

They just looked at each other for a minute. BANG
BANG BANG. Then Tyler whispered, "Shit. I need to get
that."

Zoey looked down at Tyler's obvious signs of arousal and
said with a weak smile, "I think I should get that. You may
want to take a minute."

Tyler sheepishly grinned and said, "You can answer but I
am coming with you."

Zoey got to the door as Tyler strategically stood behind
the kitchen counter. She shook her head and laughed as she
opened the door. Standing there was Kyle, looking a little
worse for the wear. His hair was a little disheveled, and he
had dark circles under his eyes. Still, he smiled at Zoey and
said, "Good morning Zoey. Where is my idiot brother?"

"In here," Tyler called from the kitchen.

Kyle walked inside and went over to where Tyler was standing and handed him a set of keys. "She is all ready like you asked."

"Thanks," Tyler said while studying his brother. "You look like crap."

Kyle gave Tyler a sideways glace and said, "Well, I was working all night for the paper and slept at the office for a whole two hours before SOMEONE called and woke my ass up."

Tyler laughed and said, "Sorry about that."

Kyle just grunted back at his brother. "Can you give me the keys to your crappy car so if I need to leave, I have something?"

Tyler nodded and handed him another set of keys. Kyle then turned and looked at Tyler and said, "I have the project to work on, so I will call you later."

Tyler nodded and Kyle walked out the door. Zoey turned to Tyler and asked, "Why do we need Kyle's car? And what project is he working on?"

"We need Kyle's truck, and who knows about his projects. It's always boring newspaper stuff I kind of glaze over when he drolls on about it."

"Oh, you mean like he does to you when you talk about coding and programming?"

"Exactly," Tyler said with a grin. "Now we need to get going." Zoey went to the living room to grab her purse and phone and stopped by the window. She looked across the square at the bakery where she still saw the police car parked out front. She made a deep sigh and Tyler could see the tears start to gather in her eyes.

Tyler crossed the room and wrapped his arms around her. "Hey, none of that for now. We will worry about that later. I just want you to clear your mind and come with me." He kissed her on top of her head as she leaned into his warm chest.

They left the apartment and got into Kyle's truck. Inside there was a bag on the console containing bacon, egg and cheese croissants and in the cup holders were two bottles of orange juice. "Kyle did this for us?" Zoey asked.

"Yup. But believe me, he still owes me a million more favors. He was kind of a mess as a kid and got into his share of trouble in Philly."

"Oh, you have to tell me about it."

"He would be mortified if I told you about some of his escapades."

"It is only fair. I am sure Derek has told him some of my mortifying highlights from college."

Tyler turned to her with a serious look in his eyes, "He didn't tell us much about your history. I mean we all knew he had a close friend from college that was a girl that he would talk to and visit sometimes, but when we would grill him about it, he clammed up. Kyle knew a little more than I did, but not by much. To be honest, for the longest time we thought maybe you two had a thing going on and he just didn't want to tell us."

"There has never been anything between us," Zoey said a little guardedly. "Not like that."

"I know that now, and I believe you."

Zoey nodded and looked out the passenger window as they drove through the streets out of the town. Tyler reached over and grabbed her hand and squeezed. Zoey smiled and leaned back in a quiet satisfaction until they reached their destination.

Zoey stepped out of the truck to find that they were at a cliff that overlooked the town. Tyler grabbed a quilt from the back seat and the breakfast and set up an area by the overlook for them to sit. He gave Zoey a grin and said, "I even have Diet Coke in the cooler for later."

Zoey laughed. "You are the perfect man."

They ate their breakfast and talked about Blossom Hills and their childhoods. After breakfast, they sat on the quilt with Zoey's back nestled on Tyler's chest. They were able to look over the cliff together with Tyler's head resting by hers so that he could occasionally kiss her hair and speak into her ear so that his breath was warm and calming to Zoey. Tyler explained how he felt that he had a pretty charmed childhood. His mom and dad loved each other very much and were good parents. Hannah and Mark met when they were twenty-one when Mark moved to town and volunteered at the high school with troubled teens. Hannah was the high school's English teacher, and it was love at first sight. Mark had asked Hannah out several times before she finally agreed to the first date. She thought him handsome and most likely a player, so he had to convince her that when it came to her heart he wasn't playing around. They married five months later and if it had been up to Mark, he would have married her after the first date.

"They are great examples of what life is supposed to be like. Sometimes that comes with an unspoken pressure to live up to what they have," Tyler said while looking out over the town.

"I think they would just want you to be happy. No expectations."

"Now you sound like my mom."

"Good, she seems like a smart lady."

"She is. She retired from teaching but never stops trying to teach me and Kyle."

"Your dad retired too?"

A tight grim line was now formed on his lips. "Yes. He had a bad heart attack a couple of years ago. Mom focuses on hovering over him. He has had to change his diet and take it a little easier, but Mom is driving him a bit crazy. He thinks he is still invincible."

"That has to be hard."

Tyler nodded. "What about you and your family?"

Zoey explained how her dad had walked out on her when she was only a toddler and how he had at first tried to continue visits but just seemed to lose interest after a couple years and stopped seeing her and even stopped calling. She hadn't talked to him since she was eight. Her mother, Cassie, remarried when she was only four to a nice man, David, who doted all over her. Zoey explained that while her mother loved her, she had a hard time not being critical of her. Cassie and David had a son, Xander, when Zoey was six. Zoey spoke fondly of Xander. He was also a computer software developer who was living in Cincinnati.

"Xander wanted to stay close to mom and me, but the job market for technology is much better in Cincinnati than it is in Lexington and it is only a little less than two hours from Lexington so he moved there."

"You miss him?"

"Very much. He says that he is going to come visit me here soon, but he hasn't said when yet. I wanted him to come for the bakery opening, but he had a project rollout at work and couldn't come this week." Zoey sighed. "I guess it was for the best."

Tyler could see she was starting to get upset again, and he desperately wanted to make her feel better. "The bakery will be okay. You will get it back in shape in no time."

"I hope so." She squeezed his hand that was holding hers and asked, "Do you really think it was my ex who did this?"

"I do. Zoey this was too personal of an attack. Is Shane your only ex who had the temperament to do this?"

"I wish I could say that he was, but he is the most recent. The men I have dated since college have just been a long line of men who treated me badly." Zoey took in a deep breath. "Shane was the worst, though."

Tyler's heart was breaking. He couldn't understand how someone could hurt her. She was sweet, kind-hearted and just amazing. He was surprised that she remained the person that she was if she had been going through years of men treating her this way. "You said since college these were the kind of men you have dated. What about in college?"

Zoey's body tensed up and Tyler almost immediately regretted asking her. He thought he may have pushed her too much. "When Derek met me, I was with a guy named

Trevor. Trevor was great. He used to tell me all the time that I was pretty and how much he loved me. We went to different colleges, but we still tried to spend as much time together as we could. He even became good friends with Derek and the guys Derek lived with."

Tyler waited for her to continue her story and when she didn't, he asked, "And you guys broke up?" He was starting to feel a pang of jealousy about a guy who obviously meant so much to her.

Zoey shook her head. "No. My junior year he was walking the quad of his campus and had a brain aneurism and died."

"Oh, God Zoey. How long were you together?"

"Three years. We began dating the summer before my first year of college."

"So, you started dating guys who treated you badly after that?"

"I didn't date anyone for over a year. I had Derek and the guys. I don't know what I would have done without them. They took care of me. They made sure that I didn't get hurt, just like a bunch of big brothers. Derek was upset about Trevor too. I hadn't realized how close they had gotten until he died."

Tyler started looking back around that time and remembered when Derek came home for that spring break and had told him and Kyle about a friend that died. He didn't go into details about how he knew him or connected him to the girl he talked about all the time.

"I see why you and Derek never crossed over that friendship line then."

"I never had eyes for anyone but Trevor, but even if Trevor hadn't been there, we never would have gone down that path. Derek charmed the pants off any woman he came across. I was immune to that kind of charm." Zoey snuggled closer into Tyler and continued. "Anyway, after college I was a bit lost. I lost everyone that I had close to me. My friends were my support. Derek moved back here and the other guys kind of scattered across the US and got married. I didn't seem to fit anywhere. Being close to girls never seemed to be my thing, and when I would find guy friends to build friendships with their wives or girlfriends didn't trust our friendship and I would get pushed away. It was lonely. I started gaining weight and then just dated anyone who would pay any attention to me. This meant settling for guys who were less than perfect...far from perfect. They would start out nice enough, but then they would just get a little worse. They would start with little digs about my weight, or hair or any other small thing. I would get fed up and leave, but then the next guy would be almost the same, but just a little worse. By the time Shane rolled around, I had almost no confidence. Then Derek and I had that lunch and he helped to open my eyes to see that things had to change."

"Zoey, I am so sorry you went through all this. I wish you would have seen Derek sooner."

Zoey shrugged. "I think the timing was perfect. If someone had tried to tell me before that, I am not sure I would have listened."

"Xander never tried to step in before this?"

"Xander doesn't know how bad it was. I tried to keep him separate from the guys I dated. The one he got the most exposure to was Shane, and even Shane could keep his behavior in check in front of my family. However, I don't think Xander liked him, but he never said anything."

Tyler wanted to turn her around and tell her just how amazing and beautiful she was. He wanted to make love to her and wipe all her bad memories from her mind, but he knew now was not the time. He knew that she was going to need some time, and he could wait. She was worth it.

Just before lunch they packed up the truck and began their return trip home. They stopped at a drive-through and ate lunch on the way back. Once they almost reached the city limits, Tyler got a call on his cell phone. He had a quick conversation and said, "Okay, we are headed back to town now. See you soon."

"Who was that?" Zoey asked.

"Chase. He said that we can go back to the bakery now."

"Good, I want to get started."

Zoey looked like she was starting to feel better. Tyler hoped that by talking about her past it helped them to take steps forward. He wanted her no matter what challenges she may be facing. He was beginning to hope that she could open her heart completely. He didn't want her to face a future fearing what may happen. He wanted her to know that together they could do anything.

Chapter 9

Tyler pulled in front of the bakery and as Zoey stepped out of the truck, she found several people waiting inside for her. The glass from the front windows had all been swept up and cleared. She saw Derek's mom, Amanda, sweeping up the inside of the front of the bakery. Dixie and Ariel were unwrapping new vases for the tables. Phil and his dad were busy patching the drywall from the holes in the wall. The hateful word, whore, had been wiped clean from the portable sign. The mangled mess of display cases had been removed leaving open spaces ready for new displays. Zoey's eyes filled with tears and a huge smile and she whispered, "Oh my God. I can't believe you guys did this for me. I can't..."

Ariel ran to her friend and gave her a big hug. "Sweetie don't cry. We all love you. And this was all Kyle and Tyler's doing."

Just then Kyle came from the back of the shop with paint brushes and paint cans. Zoey ran up to him and gave him a giant hug. She was squeezing him with all her might in an embrace and was crying into his shirt. "Geez Zoey. You are crushing me."

Zoey continued to hug him and cry into his shirt. She looked up at him as he didn't seem to know what to do looking helplessly at Tyler. Tyler walked over and put his hand on her shoulder. She released Kyle and looked sheepishly at the brothers.

"What did you guys do? How did you get this together?"

Tyler spoke up first, "I had Kyle write an article about the break in for the paper. He posted it on the website and all their social media."

Kyle looked a little easier and continued. "We were flooded with people asking how they could assist. We had tons of volunteers and all the supplies were donated. People have been impressed with you Zoey, and they wanted to help."

Zoey wiped her cheeks and said, "I can't thank you both enough."

Just then Chase came out from the kitchen with paint stains on his t-shirt and jokingly said, "Well, you could feed us."

Derek came out right behind him and gave him a slight shove. "Is that all you do? Think about food?"

"I am sure she doesn't want to hear about the other things I think about."

"Oh my god, Chase!" Dixie gasped from behind Zoey.

Chase looked at Dixie and smirked. "You want to hear about my other things Dixie?"

Dixie dropped her mouth open while Chase laughed at her.

The group continued to work through the rest of the day. As Chase suggested, Zoey baked cupcakes and coconut crème pie for the group. By the end of the day the only thing that needed to still be repaired or replaced were the display cases, which had been ordered and expected for next day delivery, and the glass front windows that were also going to be installed on Monday. Derek, Tyler and Zoey were the last ones to remain at the bakery. The three were in the kitchen enjoying the last of the baked goodies. Zoey was sitting on her prep counter with Tyler standing next to her with his arm around her waist.

Derek was sitting on a stool enjoying the last cupcake. He started licking his fingers and said, "You are going to make everyone in this town gain twenty pounds."

Tyler's eyes sparkled and said, "I think more like forty for Chase."

Zoey started remembering all her time with Chase and had to agree. "He is always eating. What is with that?"

Tyler looked at Derek and said, "He hasn't been with a woman in forever, so he is substituting."

Derek nodded.

Zoey said, "You boys are terrible. Poor Chase."

"Don't feel sorry for him. He says worse about us all the time," said Tyler recalling just how much grief Chase was giving him about Tyler being "lovesick" with Zoey.

"It's a guy thing Zoe," Derek confirmed.

"So, if we are going to pick on each other like a bunch of dumb guys, what are you doing with your love life?" Zoey said looking at Derek.

Tyler laughed at Derek when he started to squirm under Zoey's gaze.

"Geez Zoe, you know me. I love women. They love me. I just don't love for them to stick around."

"Yeah, I know. I remember that crap philosophy from college. I just thought you might want to change your mind."

"Nah. This is way too much fun," he said waggling his eyebrows. As he started to walk past Tyler he said, "Besides I don't ever want to look like this poor sap."

"Hey!" Tyler said in a mocking offended voice. "One day my friend you can be sappy *and* happy too."

"Alright you two, I have had enough of this for one night." Derek went over to Zoey and gave her a hug. "Give me a call later and don't make it too easy for this guy."

"What happened to guy solidarity?" asked Tyler.

"Zoey will always outrank your dumb ass," Derek said.

Zoey straightened up with pride and said, "Ah, thanks."

Derek walked out of the bakery and towards the bar. Tyler and Zoey finished cleaning up the last few dishes and left for her apartment. Tyler walked her inside and she looked questioningly at him.

"Staying again?" Zoey asked with a slight hopeful tone.

"Sweetness, I would stay every night if you would let me."

Zoey felt chills shiver from her feet up to her head. She was feeling lightheaded and was craving his lips on hers.

Tyler looked at her and continued. "I really don't want to leave you alone right now. Whoever did this is still out there, and you shouldn't be here by yourself."

"Oh," Zoey said disappointedly.

Tyler tilted her chin so she was looking him in the eyes and he said, "But believe me when I say that is the smallest reason that I want to stay. I am drawn to you. You have this power over me that I can't explain, and I can't stop thinking about you." He drew her closer to him so the front of their bodies were touching. "I want you; can you feel that?"

She could feel it. She could feel it from his heart racing to the hardness of his erection against her body. She saw it in his eyes half draped as he looked down at her. She kissed him and he lifted her up off her feet. She wrapped her arms around his neck and continued to devour his mouth. She couldn't get enough of him and wanted more. Tyler slid her back down to the floor so she could stand next to him. She gazed up at him and said softly, "I want you too. I need to feel you all over me."

Tyler groaned and began lifting the bottom of her shirt and felt the initial shock of her bare midriff in his hands. She tilted her head back at the warmth of his touch. Just as his hands began to rise up to reach the underside of her breast, the tune of the Star Wars Imperial March could be heard in the background. It was Zoey's cell phone. "Ignore it," she said.

He continued to move his hands up and down her stomach and reaching slightly higher to the cleft of her breasts. Then the cell phone started to ring again. Zoey shook her head and said, "I am not answering that."

It stopped ringing and Tyler moved his mouth down Zoey's neck to her collarbone and lightly licked where it met and traced down to her shoulders. Then almost instantly the sound of Star Wars began again.

"I am beginning to hate Star Wars," Tyler said.

Zoey sighed and said, "I think I better get that."

Tyler nodded while Zoey answered the phone.

"Hello."

"What the hell Zoey," said a male voice from the other line.

"Xander...hi."

"Don't 'Xander hi' me. You barely move to a new town; the bakery gets broken into and you don't call me? I'm your brother, Zoey. You are supposed to call me when big things happen, and don't you dare try to brush this off either."

"I wasn't trying to brush it off Xander. I just didn't get a chance to call you yet. Anyway, how did you find out already?"

"I saw the article online from Blossom Hills Press about the break in. I started following the page after you told me about your article." Zoey could hear Xander's frustration, worry and repetitive thumping. He always bounced his fist on the table when he was frustrated or thinking. "What kind of town is this, anyway? I thought you were moving to a nice small town."

Zoey started to feel defensive. "It is a nice town Xander. They don't think that anyone from town did this."

"What do you mean, no one from the town?"

Zoey sighed. "Can I start from the beginning without you interrupting me?"

Xander sounded frustrated but she could hear the worry in his voice. "Yes, and Zoey are you okay?"

"Yes, I am okay." She went to the couch to sit down. Tyler seemed to know that this conversation may take some time, so he bent down and whispered in her ear that he was going to take a shower. She nodded and continued with Xander. She explained the details of the break in and the damage that was done including the nasty words that were a personal attack against her. She also explained how they think that Shane may have been the one who did this to her.

"God Zoey. Do you really think he's that messed up? I mean you guys ended months ago."

"I don't know, maybe. It was just so directed towards me and I really don't know anyone here enough to have them want to do something like this."

"Yeah, I guess so. So, they are going to question him?"

"Yes. Chase said that they were contacting the Lexington PD to follow up, but I haven't heard anything else."

"I hate you being up there alone. Can you stay at Derek's until we know more? I don't know what I would do if something happened to you."

"I am not staying at Derek's, but I am not alone either."

"Oh. With Ariel?"

"No. Tyler is staying here with me."

"Who is Tyler?"

"Do you remember me telling you about the guy who lives above the bakery and works in software development?"

Xander paused for a minute. "Yeah. And you know him well enough to have him staying with you instead of Derek?"

Zoey loved her brother but really didn't want to get into details about her personal life with him. She really liked Tyler a lot. He had been direct and honest with her. She didn't doubt where she stood with him, but she was still holding back a little. She didn't want to get hurt again or put herself in a situation where she put blinders on about a guy's true nature. She believed that Tyler wouldn't hurt her, but she hadn't been the best judge of character since college. "Yes, Xan. I know him well enough."

Xander groaned. "Please tell me that you aren't sleeping with him already. Zoey you need time still."

"Do you really want details of my sex life?"

"Ewww. No, not really. Does Derek know this guy?"

"Yes. He is part of the group of friends that he hangs out with, and Tyler's brother is Derek's best friend too."

"Alright, I guess. Just please be careful Zoey. I love you, and you are so far away that I just worry."

"Well try not to worry. I am going to bed now okay?"

"Yeah. Just make sure to call mom and tell her before she finds out from somewhere else like I did."

"Okay, I promise. Night Xander. I love you."

"Night. Love you too."

Zoey hung up and could still hear the water running in the shower, so she went into the bedroom and laid down to wait for Tyler.

TYLER CAME OUT OF THE bathroom after taking an exceptionally long shower. He had been tense from worry and from the desire. He had continual images of taking Zoey in his arms and making love to her while she whispered his name. The memories of earlier were still running rampant through his mind, and he felt his arousal start again. Damn, he was acting like a horny teenager. He needed to get a grip. He walked into the bedroom and found Zoey already asleep in bed. She looked adorable. Her long lashes made cute lines around her eyes and her hair cascaded around her face. She was sleeping on her side, hugging a pillow to her chest and stomach. He didn't want to wake her up, so he went to the other side and laid down beside her. He grabbed the blanket and pulled it over the two of them, snuggled up from behind her and wrapped his arm around her waist.

Zoey began to stir and wrapped her arm around his and softly said, "Mmm...Tyler." She looked as if she was trying to say a little more, but all that came out was another soft mumble and sigh of contentment.

"Shh...get some sleep. I'm right here." He moved even closer to her so she could feel the back of her body completely covered protectively by his.

"Right where you belong," she said. Then she stiffened in his arms and held her breath.

Tyler smiled into her shoulder and gave her a light kiss. "Yes. This is where I belong. Now get some rest."

She slowed her breathing, closed her eyes and said, "Okay."

Tyler looked down at her as she drifted off to a much more peaceful sleep than she had the previous night. His breath calmed to match her rhythmic breathing as they seemed to melt into each other.

THE NEXT MORNING ZOEY awoke to her alarm going off at 5 a.m. She looked over at Tyler who was still dead to the world on the other side of the bed. She got ready and then went to the kitchen and started to cook breakfast. She made an omelet with hash browns and sausage. She knew Tyler wasn't much for cooking breakfast and wanted to do something nice for him. As the sausage was cooking, he came into the kitchen with a bright smile.

"It smells amazing," he said. "But you didn't have to cook for me."

"Yes, I did. Now get out of my kitchen. Breakfast is almost ready," she said as she swatted a towel on his perfect ass.

Tyler laughed and went to the small dining room table.

Zoey quickly moved around in the kitchen. She always felt at home while she was cooking. She was graceful and efficient. No move was wasted, and everything was done with a purpose. While some people may try to stir too often or fuss with the cooking process too much, she knew instinctively what was needed to complete the meal.

They sat together and ate their breakfast while talking about their plans for the day. Zoey was expecting the shipment of display cases and front windows. She believed that she would have the bakery ready for the open house on Tuesday. Tyler had work to do that day as well. He had a conference call at eight to update a client of the new software project that would hold customers' information and inventory. He also had a few consultations for new prospective clients and some coding to write for another project. They cleaned up from breakfast and Tyler packed his bag to take back to his place and exchange for new clothes for the next night.

"You don't have to keep staying with me."

Tyler frowned. "Are you trying to get rid of me?"

Zoey sheepishly looked down and said, "No. I just don't want you to feel obligated to stay with me. I can always stay with Derek, Ariel or—"

Tyler bent down and tilted her chin up to make her stop mid-sentence. "Do you really think that I stay here because I feel obligated?"

"No...I don't know."

He was now cupping her face in his hands and said, "I want to stay here. I want you to fall asleep in my arms every night. Granted this wasn't how I originally planned to have it happen, but it is what I want."

Zoey tilted her head in his hands and her eyes dilated with desire.

Tyler looked back into her eyes and continued. "Is this what you want? Because if it is too much I can back off and let you—"

Zoey gasped and quickly covered his mouth with her hand to stop him from talking. "No, this is what I want. I want you here too." Zoey searched his face for a reaction and slowly dropped her hand.

"Okay then," he said as he wrapped his arms around her thighs and lifted her up to him. Her feet dangled again as she wrapped her arms around him and kissed him enthusiastically.

Zoey loved it when he picked her up to kiss her. This man made her feel light and heady and when he lifted her there was something about the weightlessness and letting go that brought warm and fluttering sensations through her chest to her stomach.

Their kiss ended as their foreheads rested on each other. Zoey finally said, "We have to go to work now."

Reluctantly Tyler brought her back to her feet and thoroughly kissed her again. "Okay. I just wanted to get that in."

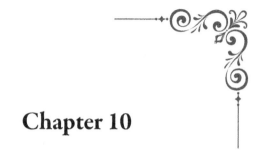

Chapter 10

Shane was feeling pretty good about himself. He had taught that smug ex of his what happens when you lie and whore around on him. He had driven back to Lexington that night. His anger and smug self-satisfaction had given him enough energy to keep him awake all night. Once he got home, he even managed a surprise visit to his new girlfriend, Roberta. They had sex while he recalled how satisfied he felt destroying the bakery. There was a certain feeling of power and gratification in fulfilling what he felt was a justified revenge. He amplified his thrusts and grip on Roberta with each satisfying memory of destruction.

Monday, he called into work saying that he wouldn't be coming in until the afternoon since he wasn't feeling well. He was still exhausted from his trip and his adrenaline was still coursing through his body each time he recalled the sight of shattering glass and obliteration of Zoey's dream.

Around 3:45 that day his secretary came to his office and nervously informed him that there were two gentlemen from the LPD who were up front wanting to speak to him. His eyes widened and he gruffly told his secretary to have them wait for five minutes and then send them on back. He couldn't believe it. How could the police be here? And that quickly? He had just left Blossom Hills Saturday night. He was fairly certain that there wouldn't be any prints. He had worn gloves that night and there were not any surveillance cameras that he could see around the building or even the town square. He had to calm down. Zoey had probably just thrown out his name and they were just fishing.

A few minutes later the two men were escorted in by the secretary and they greeted Shane. Both men were well built and over six feet tall. Shane felt himself straighten his posture in an attempt to match their physique.

"Hello, I am Detective Buxton, and this is my partner Detective Morris."

With a quickening pulse Shane nodded at the men and asked, "How can I help you both today?"

"We just need to ask you some questions about a break in that happened Saturday night."

Holding his breath, he attempted a calm tone and said, "What break in?"

"Do you know a Zoey Carrington?"

"Yes, she is my ex-girlfriend," Shane said knowing that he couldn't lie about their past.

"Well her bakery was broken into and vandalized Saturday night."

"Wow, that is terrible," Shane said in such an unconcerned flat tone that made Detective Morris look at him with more pointed interest.

Detective Buxton continued. "Yes, well your name was provided as a possible suspect. So, I need to ask about your whereabouts Saturday night."

Shane leaned back, folded his arms across his chest and said defensively, "Wait, you think I did this?"

"I didn't say that you did sir, but we still have to check all possibilities."

"Well, I was with my girlfriend all night," Shane said confidently. He knew that Roberta would be more than happy to provide him an alibi. She knew how lucky she was to have him and wouldn't risk losing him.

Detective Morris arched a brow at him and said, "We are going to need her number so we can talk to her."

Shane got even more defensive. "Look guys, I haven't seen or talked to Zoey in months. She left me and we haven't had contact. She moved out of town and I have moved on."

Detective Morris leaned in closer to Shane and said, "If you haven't seen or talked to Zoey in months, how do you know that she moved out of town?"

"What?" Shane said blinking in surprise.

Detective Morris calmly repeated while having a knowing look at Shane, "I said if you haven't seen or talked to Zoey in months how did you know that she moved out of town?"

Shane was trying to wrap his head around what he just said and started to panic in the pit of his stomach. "Well, I just heard about it; you know, through friends."

"Of course," said Detective Buxton. "Well, like we said we are going to need your girlfriend's number to follow up."

Shane nodded and took a post-it note, wrote down her name and telephone number and handed it to Detective Buxton. When Shane turned to look at him Detective Morris saw a cut on his neck about half an inch long.

"That is a nasty cut there. How did that happen?"

Shane absently grabbed at his neck. He had gotten it when the glass from the display cases had flown around in the air and a piece had gotten lodged in his neck. He directly looked at Detective Morris and said, "Oh you know how it is. Got it this morning shaving."

The two detectives stood up and Morris said, "Right. You have to be careful with new razors."

Shane looked at him with a narrowed gaze and said, "Right. Well if you will excuse me gentlemen, I have a lot of work to finish today."

"Yes, I am sure you do," said Detective Buxton. "Well, if we have any further questions, we will let you know." Then the two men left his office. Shane shut the door behind him and quickly made a phone call to Roberta to give her clear instructions. He was not going to go to jail over his bitch of an ex.

THE TWO DETECTIVES had a small chat with the receptionist who answered their questions in a kind hushed tone. Morris noticed how she kept nervously looking back at Shane's door which was still closed. She confirmed that he was out of the office for half the day saying that he was sick. When asked if he ever had gotten into trouble at work about his temper or mistreatment of clients, she did mention that he was suspended a number of months ago but that she didn't know the details of what happened to cause the suspension. When asked if she was ever mistreated by Shane, she simply stated that he never made threats to her but that he could be difficult to work with.

The men thanked her for her time and walked out of the office.

"He is full of shit. You know that, right?" said Morris.

"Not a doubt in my mind. He did it. Did you see that he didn't even wait for us to leave the building before making a phone call," said Buxton.

"Yeah, where is your money going? The new girlfriend, or an attorney?"

"Girlfriend. Definitely."

"Well let's talk to her first and when Shane's boss comes back from his conference next week, let's see what we can find out about that suspension."

Buxton nodded and said, "Sounds good. And make sure to call that sheriff and let him know what's going on. Maybe he has some of that blood from the cut on Shane's neck at the scene."

A few hours later the two detectives were able to speak with Roberta who did in fact confirm that Shane had spent the entire night with her. While she spoke to them Morris noticed that she kept pulling her long sleeves further down her arms trying to cover her hands. He could see that she was trying to cover something up.

"You know that you are not helping anyone if you are covering for him, right?" Morris asked.

She shook her head and looked at the other detective and said, "Of course not. But he was with me that night. He couldn't have done this." By now she was covering her two arms across her stomach and appeared more frightened by the direction of this conversation.

Knowing that she wasn't ready to tell the truth yet, Morris took his business card out and went to hand it to Roberta. He placed the card in one hand while he gently placed his other hand on her arm to brace it while he put the card there. She winced when his hand touched her arm, and he knew immediately what she was hiding. He said in a low tone while looking into her eyes, "If you ever need to talk to us about anything, you give me a call."

She accepted the card and placed it into the zipper pocket of her purse. She said thank you and walked the two men out the door.

Morris looked at his partner after they got into their car and said, "Did you catch that?"

"Yeah. Her arm is injured."

"Didn't the sheriff say he was confident that he wasn't physically abusive before with Ms. Carrington?"

"Yeah. Sounds like he is escalating."

"Yes, it does. I am going to call him and let him know of the situation and to be on the lookout until we can get more evidence."

ABOUT AN HOUR LATER, Tyler watched Chase answer his phone with a firm set to his jaw. They were just about to leave for their run when the call came in and Chase's mood quickly changed. Tyler watched as Chase paced the floor listening to the caller. Tyler was growing more concerned the longer Chase was on the phone.

"Right. Well, I appreciate the update. Let me know when you have more information," Chase said and then put his cell phone back in his pocket.

Chase looked at Tyler and said, "That was the Lexington PD. They talked to Shane. I am not going to go into specifics, but we are going to look into him some more. Did the alarm get installed this afternoon?"

"Yeah, Mrs. Glover had it installed today for the bakery, my apartment and Zoey's across the street. It even has a silent alarm with a panic button in the front and back of the bakery. My alarm up here goes off as well with that strobe if the panic button or regular alarm goes off since we are in the same building."

"That's good," said Chase feeling a little better about Zoey being down there alone tonight. He then continued, "You still staying with her?"

Tyler nodded and grinned, "Just try to keep me away."

"God, you're such a sap."

"Your time will come my friend." Finally, the two men left the apartment to go on their run.

DOWNSTAIRS IN THE BAKERY Zoey was prepping large amounts of cookie dough to freeze and bake throughout the week. There were certain desserts where you could freeze the dough to make it easier during the week to keep the shop stocked and cookies were one of them. Dixie and Ariel were on stools in the kitchen with her catching up on gossip and drinking wine.

"Josie comes back tomorrow. She is going to be pissed she missed all the action," said Dixie.

"Wish I could have missed the action," said Zoey as she dumped confectioners' sugar into a stainless-steel bowl.

Ariel ran over to her friend and gave her a hug, "I know sweetie, but we are here for you."

Zoey hugged her friend back and said, "I know, and I can't tell you how much I appreciate that. You guys are great."

"Of course we are darling," Dixie said in her best Josie impression.

"Oooo, you're lucky Josie isn't here to kick your ass for that," Ariel said with a giggle.

Dixie sat up and looked at them and said, "I am not afraid of her." Both girls looked at her in disbelief. "... well maybe a little."

The girls all laughed as Dixie slouched back down a bit further in her seat.

"So how are you and Tyler doing?" Dixie asked looking at Zoey.

"Great. He is great," Zoey said.

"That's it? That is all you are going to say? Please don't make me pry it out of you. Chase has been teaching me interrogation techniques. I can make you talk," said Dixie.

"What more can I say?" asked Zoey.

"Is he a good kisser?" asked Ariel.

"Screw that, is he great in bed?" Dixie asked.

"Oh my God, Dixie," Ariel said with a gasp.

Zoey looked at her two friends and finally said, "Yes he is a good kisser. Amazing, actually. And as for you," she said looking at Dixie, "I don't know how he is in bed. I mean, nothing more than how he sleeps, anyway."

"Are you kidding me? You haven't had sex with him yet? What are you waiting on?"

"I don't know. It just hasn't been the right moment yet. Things have been a little crazy," Zoey said reaching into the oven to pull out the small batch of cookies she made for the girls. Then she could hear Tyler's voice from the previous night, *I want you.* She shook her head to clear it and looked at Dixie. "What about you?"

"Oh, you know me, busy with visiting Grams and Gramps and with the studio, but I did have an internet date last week."

"How was that?" Ariel asked.

Dixie grabbed a cookie and took a bite. "Oh my God Zoey, this is amazing."

"Dixie," Ariel said impatiently.

"Oh right, the date. It was just coffee. He seems somewhat normal. But we won't be going out again."

"Why not?" Ariel asked disappointedly.

"He kissed like a Saint Bernard. Drooly and all over the place. It was disgusting."

Then from behind her Chase leaned over her and took a big bite out of the cookie she was holding and said mumbling with a mouthful of food, "That is because you weren't kissing the right guy."

She glared at him over her shoulder and said, "Well when someone kisses you, they are just going to get a mouthful of food."

"Well, I am delicious," he said smiling down at her.

"Hush, you're disgusting," Dixie said as she shoved the remaining part of the cookie in Chase's mouth.

"I am charming," Chase said still mumbling while trying to chew the rest of the cookie.

"Oh, you sad delusional man," Dixie said patting him on the shoulder and going over to grab a new cookie.

Tyler laughed and said, "Give it up Chase. These women are not impressed with you."

"It's alright. I have a list of women who want all this," Chase said gesturing his hands down the front of his chest.

Ariel laughed, looked at Dixie and said, "Quick, shove another cookie in his mouth." Chase walked over to Dixie and opened his mouth wide.

"Hey, food is food," he said.

The five friends continued to finish off the cookies and said their goodbyes leaving Tyler and Zoey alone.

"You almost done?" Tyler asked.

"Yeah, I just need to finish this batch and make some icing to prep for tomorrow," Zoey said.

"Okay, I am going to get a quick shower and I'll be right back down."

"Okay."

Tyler kissed her on her forehead and went out the back door up to his apartment.

Zoey continued to make the icing and clean up from the day's work. She heard the water start running from upstairs for his shower. She suddenly had an urge to run up the stairs and join him. She envisioned seeing the water run down his chest and lathering him with her hands while massaging him into ecstasy. As she heard the sound of the water shut off, she shook her head to try and clear the images of Tyler's naked body against hers. Her heart started racing. Was she ready for this? Was he? Could she trust him not to hurt her? She felt like she could. He had shown how much he cared for her and she felt his protectiveness.

She turned back to the prep counter where her bowl of icing was sitting and turned to see Tyler leaning in the doorway.

"Hello Sweetness," he said with a smile.

Zoey beamed. "Hi. All cleaned up?"

"Yup," he said as he made purposeful strides to her.

"Hmmm. Shame. I like you kind of messed up," she said softly as her hand went behind her back and slid into the bowl. She scraped the bowl and then quickly wiped some icing down his face.

Half shocked, Tyler caged her in against the counter with his arms and looked intently into her eyes with desire, not even caring to wipe anything off. "You know, I like you kind of a mess too."

"You wouldn't..." Zoey said with a laugh.

"Oh, you better believe I would," he said with an evil smile. His hand rushed behind her as he placed it in the bowl. He held it up for her inspection and slowly ran it down her face. Her mouth was open in mock offense, but it gradually changed into a half-lidded gaze as he dragged his fingers to follow her neck and down to the cleavage resting just above her shirt.

Zoey tried to ease back and arm herself with more icing from the bowl as she used her other hand to lift his shirt.

He smiled with a small laugh. "What do you think you are doing Sweetness?"

"Getting what I want."

Tyler leaned and whispered in her ear, "When it comes to me, you can have anything."

Zoey let out a small breath and replied, "Good." Then suddenly her posture changed, and she smeared the icing all along his abs and up his chest. Tyler grabbed for more icing and went for his revenge on her stomach and chest. It became a chaotic mess of hands and icing. Only after the bowl was nearly empty did they stop smearing the confection, looking at each other and laughing, trying to wipe themselves off with clean spots from their clothes.

Tyler shook his head, "All your hard work."

"It's okay. I will just make more tomorrow. It wasn't perfect, anyway."

Tyler came closer to her and licked by her ear where a glob of icing was clinging to her neck. "It tastes perfect to me, or maybe that is just you."

Zoey gave a slight moan in delight. He continued to kiss her up her neck while licking off the icing to meet her mouth. Their kiss started out light at first. A sensual tenderness of desire and need. Then her lips parted, and he traced his tongue around her lips and entered her mouth. Her hands clinched at his chest and wrapped around his shirt as she pulled him closer. He lifted her up on the counter so that her face was level with his as they continued to deepen the kiss.

Tyler glided his hands from her hips to the undersides of her breasts where his thumbs began stroking her nipples between him and her clothing. Zoey felt her nipples tighten under her bra and felt an overwhelming need for his touch, for his hands to touch her skin. Tyler gave a deep sigh as Zoey spread her legs apart as he stepped between her thighs. She continued her kisses tracing the line of his jaw where she licked and sucked the icing from his face stopping at his earlobe to suck it completely in. The taste of the sweetness of sugar and Tyler's clean woodsy soap combined for an intoxicating scent.

Tyler grabbed at her shirt, pulled it over her head and discarded it on the counter. She returned the favor by pulling his shirt off and tossing it to the floor. Her black lace bra was spattered with white icing and her tight nipples were responding under the lace.

"Zoey, you take my breath away," he said while tracing his fingers on the edges of her bra.

Zoey blushed at his compliment and grazed her hands down his chest while she closed her eyes to memorize this moment. This exquisite moment where this gorgeous man told her that she left him breathless. It was intoxicating and empowering. She smiled up at him and brought him back to her lips to kiss him in appreciation. He glided his hands under her bra and caressed her nipples in a teasing circle.

"Tyler, oh my god..." she said as she ran her hands down his back and across to his front where she felt his erection hard and ready for her.

He sucked in a breath, looked into her eyes and said, "Zoey, I want you and if you need me to stop, please tell me now. I want to take you up to my bed right now and make love until you can't feel anything but me."

Zoey looked deep into his eyes and breathlessly said, "It seems like I already only feel you and I am not going to stop you." Zoey leaned over to his ear, tightened her fingers in his hair and whispered, "I want you...I want all of you...now."

With a growl of delight Tyler picked up their shirts and proceeded to pull her down from the counter and said, "We are leaving. Now."

Hopping off the counter, Zoey hurriedly pulled her shirt over her head, grabbed her keys and purse, and followed Tyler. As they were leaving through the back, Zoey set the new alarm and locked the door. It took longer than necessary since Tyler was kissing the back of her neck causing her to mess up a few times. She was finally able to turn to him and said, "Okay, ready."

"Thank God," he said as he bent down and threw her over his shoulder in a fireman's hold and proceeded to carry her up to his apartment.

She gasped in delight and said, "I can walk."

"Nope this is quicker," he said while climbing the stairs to his front door.

"Put me down, Tyler. I am too big; you will get hurt."

He stopped dead in his tracks and set her down by the top of the stairs in the hall. "Look at me Zoey," he said as she started to look away from him. "Zoey. Look at me." He lifted her chin so they could look into each other's eyes. "You are not too big. You are perfect."

"I'm not perfect."

"To me you are perfect. Every inch of you, from head to toe, you are perfect for me."

Her eyes began to tear up and she couldn't remember the last time a man made her feel this way. She was still looking up at him and said, "And you are perfect for me."

Tyler's breath deepened and determination lit his eyes. He again picked her up to finish carrying her into the apartment. Once the door closed, they frantically kissed and pulled off clothes making a pathway to his bedroom. Tyler was down to his boxer briefs and Zoey had only her bra and matching lace panties. When they made it next to the bed, she crawled backwards on her elbows, careful to keep eye contact with Tyler. He matched her every movement creeping further onto the bed. He was hovering over her, careful not to put his weight on her. Tyler kissed his way down her neck back to her breasts where her nipples were again hard waiting for his touch. She arched her back up to him offering better access, yearning for his touch.

He drew his hands behind her back where he unclasped her bra. His hands found the straps and slowly slid them down her arms to expose her bare breasts. Zoey's breath quickened as she felt the waves of desire and readiness for him.

His mouth made its way to her nipples where he wrapped his lips around them and gently sucked. The warm intense sensation cause Zoey to grab his hair and hold on tight. He looked up at her and asked, "Are you okay?"

"God yes."

Smiling he returned to the other nipple that she knew was still covered in icing. He smacked his lips and she could tell that, for him, the taste of her and the sugar was exquisite. She was his very own sweetness. His mouth glided down from her breasts and started to kiss lower. Zoey started to cover her stomach. Tyler shook his head. He gently took her arms and moved them to the side, looked her in the eyes and said in a low tone. "Remember? Perfect."

Zoey nodded and returned her hands to his head. He slid his fingers under her panties and pulled them down to toss them to the side of the bed. His lips and tongue teased their way back up her thighs to the warm place they met in the middle. He traced his fingers along her folds several times as she started to arch again. "Zoey, you are so wet and ready for me. I love how your body is responding to me."

"It has been responding to you from the day you found me on your couch," she said breathlessly.

He smiled and glided his finger into her folds. His tongue grazed upward to tease her clit in a circular motion. She began writhing beneath him feeling an orgasm start its first wave from the pit of her stomach. Groaning in approval, he began sucking on her clit and speeding the thrusts of his fingers until she came and quivered beneath him.

"Tyler, I need you now. I need to feel you inside of me."

He groaned and reached for a condom from the nightstand drawer. She took the condom from his hand and said, "Let me do this."

He nodded and discarded his boxer briefs. She opened the condom and rolled it down his length. He was hard and ready for her. She could feel the pulsing veins under her touch. He once again rolled her underneath him and began kissing her gently. She could still taste remnants of the icing and her body on his lips. It was intoxicating. She held her breath as she felt the head of his penis gently grazing her clit. "Tyler, please. Now."

He then gently moved his pelvis to align with hers and she felt the first soft push of him entering her. Her thighs widened to allow him to deepen their connection. He responded with another push. "God Zoey, you are so tight."

She started to close her eyes in pleasure, and he said, "Look at me Zoey. I want to see you. I want to see you coming apart for me."

She opened her eyes as he continued to push in and out of her. His thrust began to speed up bringing her yet again close to orgasm, only to slow down and kiss her beyond her senses. Finally, after speeding his thrusts again she said, "Come with me Tyler, be there with me."

That was it. That seemed to completely undo him. All reason and rhythm left as he sped up his thrusts and brought his hand down to rub his thumb in a circular motion on her clit. She made a soft cry as her whole body shook and her walls pulsated around his hard length. She felt the pulsing release of his orgasm with hers as he stopped and buried his head in her neck. He brought his lips to her ears and said, "That was amazing Sweetness."

Panting Zoey replied, "Yes it was. I didn't know it could be..." Just then Tyler covered her mouth in a kiss and ran his hand through her hair.

"It would always be like that with you. You completely unravel me."

Zoey felt her heart leap. She had never shared such an intimate moment like this. Sure, she had good sex before, but this was beyond good sex. It was beyond words. In this moment she had forgotten everything. The whole world, all her troubles were gone, and this man made her feel as if everything centered around her. It was amazing. She wrapped her arms around Tyler's neck and kissed him. Then like a blinding light from the darkness she knew that she was falling in love with him. There was no doubt he made her feel things she hadn't felt in years. She loved him but wasn't ready to say the words to him. Not yet. She didn't want to scare him away with how fast she had fallen for him. She found her way to his ear and then whispered, "And you make me feel whole."

TYLER SMILED AS HE withdrew from her, gave her a small kiss and left to discard of the condom. He gazed at himself in the mirror and found he had on a dopey grin. Yup. He was going to be one of those guys who would be at the mercy of a woman. Tyler searched himself for some fear or anxiety about letting a woman in again, but there was nothing.

He came back to the bedroom and saw Zoey wrapped in his sheet with a bare leg draped to the side. She was so alluring, and sweet. She had no idea just how amazing she was or how she made him feel. He couldn't believe that in such a short time his feelings had grown so much for her. When he was younger, he always thought that he would find love like his father did, who always told him that the moment he saw his mom he knew that was it. There would be no other woman who could affect him the way she could. He knew it was love at first sight. Tyler used to think it would be the same for him, but as he grew up that belief faded away. But now, as he looked at Zoey in his bed, he knew this was it. She was it, and he would tell her, but only when he thought she was ready. He was never going to let her go.

Then her voice broke his train of thought. "Hey you. Are you coming back to me?"

God yes. He walked over to the bed and wrapped his arms around her. She moaned in a sweet tone of comfort and content as she looked at him and said, "I am sticky from all the icing." With a smile she continued, "And the bed is all sticky too."

"Guess I will have to take a shower again." Providing a heated gaze, he looked at her and asked, "Care to join me?"

Zoey smiled and said, "Why Mr. Ashford you are ready for more so soon?"

He rolled on top of her where she could feel his erection brushing up against her hips and he said, "What do you think Ms. Carrington?"

She ran her hands though his hair and said, "Well, I think we should go take care of that then."

With a gruff laugh of delight, he stood from the bed, picked her up and carried her into the bathroom. He turned on the shower where they proceeded to make love again under the hot pulsating water.

After their second round of making love, they gathered their things and made their way to Zoey's apartment where they again got lost in each other's bodies. Completely sated and exhausted Zoey slept wrapped in Tyler's arms where they both fit perfectly into each other.

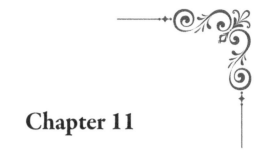

Chapter 11

The bright morning light glowed on Tyler's face as he awoke. He rolled over and found the other side of the bed empty. *Damn, she is a morning person.* He found his jeans and walked down the hall to the kitchen. He discovered Zoey in the kitchen wearing pajamas with her hair in a loose ponytail and singing while cooking breakfast. Without the earbuds again. She was swinging her hips and continued to sing "Fever."

He couldn't resist any more. He stalked up behind her, wrapped his arms around her waist and kissed her bare neck.

She jumped slightly in surprise, turned to look at him and said, "Well good morning, Ty."

"So, is this how it's going to be? I wake up alone every morning?"

Zoey laughed and said, "Well, I do own a bakery so once it opens, it will be even worse. I will need to get there around five each morning to prep for the day."

Tyler groaned and said, "Guess I will have to learn to adjust my schedule to optimize our time together."

"You don't have to do that."

"I know, but that is why I love being the boss. I can start and stop my day whenever I want."

"Well you are always welcome to get up with me each day, but good luck keeping up with me," she said with a little hip bump as she returned to the breakfast before it burned.

After they finished breakfast, Zoey had gone into the bedroom to get ready for the day. Tyler joined her and couldn't resist kissing her neck and rubbing her arms as she tried to dress. "You have a big day today. I think we should start it out right," Tyler said with a growl.

Zoey gave out a slight moan and said, "You are going to be a bad influence."

Tyler felt a rushing heat chase up his spine and rushing to his length as she melted into his arms. Zoey turned to face him and ran her hands up his chest.

Tyler brought his lips to hers, and she gasped as they explored each other's mouths in a fierce sense of urgency. He scooped her up and tossed her back onto the bed. "I am going to make sure that I am on your mind all day. You are going to think about how you couldn't stop saying my name this morning."

Tyler felt as if he was losing his mind. All he could do was explore every inch of her. He savored the taste of her skin. He was licking and swirling his tongue in torturous little circles down her body to where her center was ready and waiting for him. His tongue traced her from the bottom of her folded lips up to her swollen clit. Her body writhed underneath him with each stroke of his tongue. Finally, he took two fingers, entered her body and proceeded to suck on her clit in a strong steady rhythm.

Zoey suddenly gasped and said, "God, you are going to kill me."

"Don't worry. I'll die with you and it will be a beautiful death for us both."

The more her body responded to him the faster he stroked and harder he sucked. Finally, her body crested into the waves of orgasm and her walls quivered around his fingers.

She was breathless and just whispered his name, "Tyler..."

He smiled and moved his way back up to her and gave her a deep impassioned kiss. She wrapped her arms around his neck and gave a light bite to his earlobe.

"I need you...now."

He quickly reached in the drawer for another condom and ripped open the packaging. Zoey reached and coupled his balls while he rolled the condom down. She widened her legs to welcome him in and his eyes sparked with desire. As he entered her, he felt the world disappear around him and felt a falling sensation. It seemed as if his heart would pound out of his chest for love for this woman. With each stroke inside of her he knew she was the only one for him. He wasn't sure how long he was lost in his thoughts while he made love to her, but she brought him back to her when she grabbed his face with her hands and made him look her directly in her eyes and said, "You amaze me."

"Believe me Zoey, it is you who amazes me." He quickened his pace and Zoey raised her hips to allow even more of his length to enter her. He couldn't stop his body anymore and he lifted her to change the angle. She moaned in pleasure as her body spasmed under him and he joined her in his release.

He wanted to stay as close as possible to her for as long as he could. He rolled them over so he wouldn't have his weight on her and stayed inside her. As they laid together in tangled limbs, Tyler could hear his inner voice telling him something he could feel in the depth of his soul. *Mine.*

AFTER ABOUT AN HOUR of resting wrapped up in each other's arms, they finally got ready for their day. Tyler was leaning on the counter in the kitchen and asked, "Ready for your opening?"

"I am, but I am a bit of a mess. I still have so much prep work to do and I want to make sure everything is perfect."

"Do you want me to help?"

"No. I have Phil and Dana working tonight for the open house. They will be there a few hours before opening to assist with baking and any last-minute set ups. What are you going to do with yourself today?"

"Work. I have a couple of projects that I have to get done before flying out to Chicago to help with the rollout of the new program."

Zoey felt a pang of disappointment. "You have to go to Chicago?"

"Yeah."

"When?"

"In about two and a half weeks."

"How long will you be there?"

"Two weeks."

The corners of Zoey's mouth turned down, and she already felt a twinge of heartache knowing he would be gone for so long. She couldn't believe that she already felt such a connection to him, and that she knew she would feel a loss already. She needed to get it together. She sighed and looked at him and said, "Well, I will miss you."

He walked over to her and bent his head down and whispered in her ear, "I hope so, because I know I am going to miss you. But you better believe that I am going to make sure you have enough to remember me by before I leave."

Shivers rocked Zoey from her core. "I am going to hold you to that promise."

THE REMAINDER OF THE day ran in a blur of activity. Tyler could hear Zoey preparing for the open house. She was even singing louder today. At one point he heard her singing Walking on Sunshine. She still didn't sing in front of others, but he felt lucky that she seemed to feel comfortable enough to sing in front of him now. Later in the day, he occasionally heard the voices of Phil and Dana drift through his window in between the clang of dishes and pans being tossed around.

Tyler had run some coding for his new project and had a few conference calls to clarify details of the launch of his new software for the company in Chicago. He also worked with arranging training for the testers to provide feedback for any potential issues before he left for final implementation.

Tyler could smell the sweet flavors of the bakery drifting up into his apartment from downstairs. He couldn't wait to gorge himself on the various goodies. Chase was going to meet him at the apartment before going downstairs for the big event. Chuckling to himself he realized that he would finally be using the front door of the bakery instead of slipping his way through the back door like he normally did.

Then he heard a knock at his door and opened it to find Chase, Kyle and Derek standing in his hallway. Slightly surprised at the two extra guests he opened the door and allowed them all to come in. "Come on in guys," Tyler said as he looked at his extra two guests. "Wasn't expecting you two."

Derek looked at him in surprise and said, "You think I would miss Zoey's big day?"

"No. Just thought Chase was the only one coming to get me."

Kyle grinned and said, "Don't worry it isn't your pretty face that brought us up here. We needed an in."

Looking confused Tyler studied his brother and said, "What do you mean?"

Chase chuckled and said, "Dude there is a line around the block. Zoey might run out if we have to wait in the back of the line."

"Are you kidding me?"

"Nope, I never joke about missing out on food," Chase said while rubbing his belly. "Look at me, I am wasting away. I need food."

Derek looked at Chase and said, "I don't know how your mom ever had enough money to keep you fed."

A sadness came into Chase's eyes, but Tyler saw him quickly shake it away. "I am so charming, people just kept feeding me when she wasn't looking."

Tyler smiled and said, "They still do."

"You should have seen the breakfast Maria made me this morning."

"Maria?"

"Yeah, you know that girl from Wilmington."

Tyler was caught a little by surprise. "So, is it going to be serious?"

"Nah. She is still hung up on her ex. We had fun, but she cried saying that she was sorry, and she thinks she is going to get back with him."

Kyle winced, "Ouch. After sex with you she goes running back to her ex? That doesn't say much about your talent."

Chase shrugged. "I knew that she wasn't really going to stick. We had fun and believe me she didn't have complaints. I didn't want anything serious, anyway. She wasn't challenging enough. We had fun, and it ran its course."

Tyler shook his head. He could think of one person who could challenge him enough, but he was going to leave that one alone, at least for now. They needed to figure that out for themselves.

Derek looked at the men and broke the silence. "Okay, are we ready to go die from a sugar rush?"

"Absolutely," said Tyler and they all left down the stairs.

They went to the front of the building and Tyler couldn't believe it. The line was now down almost two blocks. He saw the girls close to the front of the line. Dixie was at the head of the line with her camera around her neck and was joined by Ariel and Josie. Tyler motioned the girls to follow him around the back of the building. They all followed him and found yet again the back door of the bakery wide open. Tyler peered in and saw Phil practically sprinting with trays of

food going up front, and Dana frantically icing some cookies. He didn't see Zoey right away, and he knew it was only
a few minutes until opening. Then his gaze caught hers coming from around the corner and she looked at them with
wide eyes.

"Oh my god guys, thank goodness you are here. We are
going to need help. I did not expect this kind of a turn out.
There is a line down the block."

Derek gave a slight grin and said, "Actually two blocks
Zoe."

"What?!?!"

"Yeah two blocks and growing."

"Oh...I...uh...geez. Can you guys help with plating for
customer orders and Phil and Dana can handle the registers
while I take care of everything else?"

Kyle looked at her and said, "Zoey, do you mind if Dixie
and I hang back to cover the story of the open house for
the paper? We can help after we do some interviews and get
some pictures."

"Sure, that would be great." Then an alarm from Zoey's
phone came ringing through. "Okay it is time to open the
doors. Guys, grab what you want now and stash it aside
for later. Whatever you want is on the house all night." She
looked around at them with a grateful smile and had to laugh
as Chase had already eaten half a cookie that Dana had just
decorated.

Zoey opened the doors and the people flooded in. It was
a crazy night. Everyone was patient and kind about the wait.
They were entranced by the selection and flavors that Zoey
offered in the shop. Kyle did interviews with the locals as

they enjoyed their night. Dixie flurried around the shop taking pictures of everyone and even the line outside the shop. Tyler found himself having fun helping out handing the food to everyone.

Derek looked at home since he always served people at the bar. He planted himself at the drink station serving coffee, juices and sodas. Josie took over as the designated person to keep crowd control. Her strong personality was perfect to handle allowing only a certain number of people inside at a time and granting permission for new ones to enter as others left. Ariel continually walked the small dining room to keep it clean and turn over the tables to allow for new customers. Chase mostly kept to the back to help Zoey with the rotation of stock. Zoey continued to bake additional treats and tried to keep up with the demand. Not only were people eating something for that night, but they were ordering packages to take back home with them.

THE NIGHT WAS PERFECT. Zoey beamed with pride at how well everything went. She knew that it could have been a disaster if it wasn't for the help of her friends. At the close of the evening the group rested in the dining room and started eating their well-deserved treats.

Phil came from the back and stated that everything was put away and ready for tomorrow. Zoey told him to go home and take the care package from the back with the blue bow home to his family. He thanked Zoey and left with Dana who offered to drive him home.

Chase sat back on his chair and grinned. "I am full."

The remainder of the group suddenly got quiet and looked at Chase in shock.

"What? I can be full. It happens," he said, slightly offended.

Dixie giggled and said, "The world must be ending."

"Hush woman," Chase growled.

Derek then stood and went to give Zoey a hug. "I gotta go. I want to check on the bar before heading home."

Zoey nodded and said goodbye. The others started to leave with Derek. Zoey thanked the group for the help and said goodbye to the others. Tyler helped her lock up the shop and again they went to his place for a change of clothes and then walked over to Zoey's apartment.

After making love Tyler and Zoey laid in each other's arms enjoying their quiet moment. Tyler finally was the first to speak. "Are you happy with how tonight went?"

"Incredibly happy. It couldn't have gone better. I can't believe how many people showed up. I made three times more in sales than I had anticipated. I think the whole town showed up tonight."

Tyler gave a slight laugh. "Not much happens around here so when it does, it kind of brings everyone out. Plus, all the coverage you got with Kyle's paper just amplified it."

"Well, I know it wouldn't have been as much of a success without everyone coming to help tonight. I am so thankful to them all."

"They know that Zoey. And they all love you, even Josie."

Zoey laughed. "She does seem like a tough girl, but I think she has a big heart she just doesn't show much."

Tyler nodded. "Yeah, she doesn't open up much to us. She talks about work but that is really about it." He paused for a minute and then said, "My mom said to tell you that your cookies were amazing."

Zoey popped her head up and looked at Tyler. "Your mom was there tonight?"

Tyler looked confused with her surprised reaction. "Yeah. She knows that we are dating, and she wanted to check out your bakery."

"Oh, I wish I could have known, I would have tried to make a better first impression. I was a frantic mess all night. And I don't even know which person she was. Why didn't you tell me that she was there?" She buried her head under the blanket trying to hide her embarrassment.

Tyler pulled down the blanket and smiled at her. He started rubbing her back in small soothing motions. "Calm down, Sweetness. You looked gorgeous, and you made an incredible impression. You opened this amazing bakery with the most delicious desserts this town has ever seen. You are sweet, warm and caring. Anyone can see that. Mom and Dad weren't there to judge you. They wanted to support the opening of your bakery."

"God, your Dad was there too?" Zoey buried her head in his chest.

"Yes. Zoey it is fine. Trust me."

Zoey sighed. "Okay, I just wish you would have told me. I could have at least made an introduction of myself, other than just running around my shop like a crazy person."

"I'm sorry, Sweetness. I didn't think it was a big deal. I will give you a proper introduction to them soon, okay?"

She nodded and then leaned in for a lingering kiss. She glanced at the clock and whimpered. "We need to get some sleep. I have to get up in five hours."

"Okay. Sleep it Is," he replied as he covered the two of them in her blanket.

Zoey laid her head back on Tyler's chest and drifted off to a peaceful sleep.

THE NEXT MORNING CAME quickly. Zoey was up in the shower and Tyler was packing his things to take back to his place to do some laundry. He thought about taking a power nap once he got home, but decided he wanted to try to adjust his schedule to hers. If he was going to try and match her crazy hours, he may as well start now. He was going to have to learn to be a morning person.

Zoey came out in a cute skater dress with skulls with pink bows on their heads and a crisscross cleavage cut. Tyler instantly felt a bulge grow in his pants. God, he needed to get a grip. Seeing that fabric crossing over her breasts was giving him all kinds of lusty thoughts. Trying to shake those thoughts from his head, he walked over to her and kissed her neck that was just exposed from her hair being swept up in a ponytail.

"Good luck with your first day."

"Thank you. Are you going to come down for breakfast before you start your day with work?"

"Of course."

"Good. Ready to go?"

Tyler nodded, and they left to cross the street to the bakery. He watched her walk into the shop and went upstairs to his apartment. He took a shower and found that he missed a call from his mom. He looked at his calendar and was grateful when he saw that he didn't have any appointments until 1:30 and called his mom back.

"Good morning dear."

"Morning Mom. Everything okay? It is kind of early for you to be calling."

"Everything is fine, well mostly fine. The car won't start this morning and I need to pick up your dad's medication from the pharmacy. I think it is just the battery, but I was wondering if you could help me out."

"Of course. Can you give me about forty-five minutes? I can also bring breakfast from the bakery for you and dad if you would like."

"That would be perfect. See you then."

Tyler finished getting ready and headed down to the bakery. By now it had been open for about fifteen minutes and Zoey already had a small line by the counter. Dana was handling the register while Zoey served the customer's orders. He watched how she interacted with grace and ease with her customers. She had a warm smile and was patient with each person while they made their selections.

Gazing in the case he saw the daily special, Red Hot Love Muffins, which were red with swirls of cinnamon and drizzled with white icing. He couldn't help but think about their escapades with icing just a couple days before and wondered if that had any bearing to the muffin name. Finally, it was his turn to place his order.

"Hi Sweetness."

Zoey blushed. "Good morning...again," she said as she smiled. "What can I get you?"

He leaned on the counter and looked over at the Red Hot Love Muffins. "I think I will have one of those."

Slightly embarrassed, she grabbed a muffin and put it into a bag.

Tyler was smiling wide now and said in a low tone, "Is that the same batch of icing from before?"

Zoey gasped and said, "Not the same batch, but yes the same recipe." Trying to recover she asked, "Anything else?"

"Yeah. A half dozen of mixed donuts."

Zoey laughed and shook her head. "Is that Chase's morning order?"

Amused Tyler said, "No, but that wouldn't be out of his possibilities. These are for my parents. Mom called and is having car troubles this morning, so I am bringing breakfast and going over to help."

"That's nice of you. Breakfast is on me. Will I see you later?"

He nodded his head over to the side opening of the counter. She followed him there, and he gave her a quick light kiss and whispered, "Definitely."

Breaking their little private moment, they heard a quiet cough behind them. "Nerd boy. Stop distracting the nice baker so we can all have breakfast." They turned to see Josie standing behind them and a small line of customers all with silly grins on their faces. When Tyler wasn't moving fast enough, she continued, "Out Romeo. I need my caffeine."

"Fine. Geez, you know you are a bit scary Josie."

"Yup. Now off with you."

Tyler smiled apologetically to Zoey and walked out the door with Josie making shooing motions with her hands.

ZOEY FINISHED WAITING on Josie and her other customers and finally had a couple of minutes to take a break. She told Dana she was going to take five minutes and to let her know if she needed help. Zoey walked over to Josie's table where she was pounding the keys on her laptop.

"Wow, you are an angry typer."

Josie looked up with a smile that would make children hide behind their parents. "Only when the other person is being a moron."

"How was your breakfast?"

"Amazing as always." She then shut down her laptop and looked at Zoey while picking up her coffee. "So, are you going to tell me that you still haven't had sex with Tyler?"

Zoey looked down. She wasn't going to lie to Josie, but she definitely wasn't used to the bluntness coming from another woman. Finally, she said in a hushed tone so that no one else would hear, "No, can't say that anymore."

Josie slammed down her cup and said a little loudly, "Fabulous! So how was it?"

"Shhh...geez Josie." Zoey started to look around her shop to see who could hear.

"Oh, don't worry about them. Erma over there is deaf as a doorknob. She can't hear a thing without her hearing aids, and she refuses to wear them. Mr. Three Piece Suit over there is too busy talking on his cell phone, and Ms. Too Much

Hair over there is listening to her iPhone. So how is the hot nerd?"

Zoey sighed and finally said, "He isn't a nerd, but he is incredible."

Josie shook her head with a smile and said, "Honey, he is a nerd. Did you see his t-shirt? I don't even know what it was referencing."

Zoey blushed. She knew the shirt. It had the spaceship Serenity trapped in a mason jar. "Firefly."

"What?"

"The shirt was about the show Firefly. The spaceship that was trapped in a jar like a firefly would be. The ship is from the show Firefly." She loved that show and had the whole season on DVD including the movie that followed years later.

Josie laughed and said, "I have never even heard of that show."

"It was a western space drama on for one season back in 2002."

"See he is a nerd, and apparently you are his perfect little nerd match."

Zoey was now laughing a little too and finally said, "Actually the term is geek. Geeks are cool, we are trending."

The two girls talked a few more minutes before Zoey had to get back to work. She was bonding with her new friend and was surprised that even as different as they were that she felt comfortable around her. A wave of comfort washed over her as she realized how much she loved her new life.

Chapter 12

Tyler pulled up to his parents' house, grabbed the pastries from the car and walked up to the front door. He used his key to get in and called out for his parents. His mom came from the back kitchen with a wide smile for her son. She looked good with her blonde shoulder length soft hair. Her green eyes sparkled with love as she saw her son approach. She was wearing a wrap dress and sandals that gave her even more height than her tall 5'9" build.

Tyler gave her a warm hug and handed over the donuts. "Hey Mom. Where is Dad?"

"Oh, he is upstairs getting ready. He wants to go with you to get the new battery and medication. I told him to stay here and get some rest, but he won't listen to me."

"He isn't an invalid Mom. You can't keep hovering over him."

"Oh, I know that, but if I hover over him too much, it gives me some leeway to give in on the little stuff, so I win the bigger stuff. I have to let him think he wins now and then." She gave a wink and smile to her son.

"Have you always been this evil?"

"Yes. How do you think I got my way with you boys all the time? Give in on the little stuff and hard line the big. Worked like a charm every time."

"You would think he knows your tricks by now."

"Honey, I never told him my tricks, and he was so busy at work he didn't notice how I managed to run a smooth home. Now, come sit with me in the kitchen while I get plates out for breakfast."

Tyler sat and watched his mom move about the kitchen and noticed that it was with a lot of the same effectiveness that Zoey had when she worked in the kitchen with deliberate and graceful moves. Then he heard his dad come in and joined him at the table.

"Good morning son."

"Hey Dad. How are you feeling?"

"Good. Your mom keeps me healthy."

"Well, I was bad and brought some donuts."

"Oh, thank god. I love you Hannah, but I really don't want fiber cereal for breakfast."

"Our son came to visit, so it is a special occasion, you can have the sugar this morning."

"Hey Ty, how about you come visit every morning?" Mark asked with a laugh. That earned a quick snap of the towel to the back of the head from Hannah.

"Don't push your luck sweetheart," Hannah said with a sweet smile.

Mark looked lovingly at his wife. Tyler knew that even when his mom was giving him a hard time his dad never wavered in his love for his mom. Mark grabbed a donut and took a bite. "Ty, this is amazing. Much better than the last owner. Does she know how good she is?"

Tyler sat back and got a starry-eyed gaze and said, "I think so. At least everyone has been telling her this. I have been lucky enough to have a lot of her food. She is amazing."

Hannah looked at her son with a wide smile. "So, the two of you are dating now?"

Tyler felt his heart pick up a few beats and replied, "Yes."

Hannah nodded. "Good. She seemed like a lovely girl from what we could see last night. You going to be serious about her?"

"I already am," Tyler confessed.

Mark took a studying look at his son and seemed to come to a conclusion and gave one small nod. He thankfully redirected the conversation away from Zoey for now. The remainder of breakfast, they chatted about how the opening night went, Tyler's upcoming trip to Chicago and other projects for his work. Finally, Mark stood and said, "Okay Ty, let's get going." Leaning over he kissed Hannah, told her he loved her and would see her in a couple of hours.

They got into Tyler's car with the dead battery and made their way into town. Mark was the first to speak. "So, it happened, huh?"

Tyler not understanding the question said, "Huh? What happened?" God he was hoping his Dad wasn't asking about sex.

Mark smiled and said, "You fell in love. Ty, it is all over your face. I saw it at the bakery too when you looked at her. I know that look. Trust me."

Tyler sighed. There was no denying it to his dad. "Yeah. And it was just like you said. I knew right away; I know she is it. I can't explain it."

"Okay so let's start at the beginning. Tell me about how you met her and go from there."

Tyler told his dad the whole story. He explained how he found her on his couch, the nights at the bar with friends, poker night, the break in at the bakery and all the time he had spent with her alone in between. Of course, Tyler left out the intimate details.

"Do you think she loves you too?"

"Yes, I do. I know she is just a bit skittish because of her past bad relationships. And it hasn't been just the men she dated. Her dad left when she was young and doesn't have contact with her anymore. Then the one guy she was with that seemed to be good for her died while they were in college from a brain aneurism. But she does seem to be letting me in and trusting me more. I just have to be careful until she can understand that I love her and am not going anywhere."

Mark was beaming. Tyler knew that his dad wanted the best for him, and anyone could see that Zoey made him happy. "Well we would love to meet her outside of her work. Could you bring her over for a barbeque on Friday? We could invite Kyle too so maybe she might feel a little more comfortable since she already knows him. Is Kyle dating anyone?"

Tyler frowned, "You don't know?"

Mark sighed and looked out the passenger window. "He doesn't talk to us as openly as he does to you or Derek. He is stingy with personal information."

"Oh. Well, he isn't dating anyone. At least not from what he has told me."

"His time will come. Anyway, have they caught the guy from the break in yet?"

"No, but we think we know who did it. There just isn't enough evidence to do anything about it right now."

"That is tough. Are you making sure she is safe?"

Slightly embarrassed he looked away from his Dad and said, "There is an alarm on the bakery and apartments now. And I am with her every night."

With a smile Mark said, "Good. I am glad you are there."

Tyler took a small breath of relief. "Thanks."

Then with a chuckle Mark continued, "Ah, Ty. I didn't think you were still a virgin."

"Ugh. Dad, stop. Please." Mark continued to laugh audibly as the two continued to finish their errands for the day.

TYLER WENT HOME AND finished up things for work and decided to start cooking dinner. He knew the bakery was closing and Zoey would need a good dinner after her busy first day. He sent her a text.

Tyler: Hey Sweetness, I am cooking dinner so when you close up come up to my apartment.

Zoey: You're cooking? Should I be scared? I have seen your pantry. Pathetic.

Tyler: I do have some hidden talents.

Zoey: I have seen your hidden talents, and I have been impressed.

Tyler: Sweetness we have barely scratched the surface.

Zoey: Ooooo. Promise?
Tyler: Yes. Now hurry up and get your sweet ass up here.

ABOUT AN HOUR LATER she came knocking on his door. He opened the door with a wide grin and obvious stains on his shirt from cooking. Zoey could smell garlic coming from the kitchen.

"What are we having for dinner?" Zoey asked as she took in a deep breath.

"Chicken carbonara pasta and garlic bread."

"Wow, carbonara. They don't sell that in a jar. I am impressed."

She walked in and saw the dining room table set with food and candles. Her heart was skipping. This man was making her heart give every piece away to him bit by bit. She couldn't believe how lucky she was. She turned to him and leaped up to him for a long passionate kiss.

Zoey could feel Tyler getting aroused and after they pulled away he said, "Sweetness if you don't sit down right now to have dinner it is going to get cold and we may not eat food tonight."

Regretfully, she let go of his neck and went to sit down at the table. Tyler served the pasta and listened as Zoey told him about her day. She was excited. The people from the town were warm and friendly. They loved her food and told her they would be back on a regular basis. She also told him about the two consultations she set up for wedding cakes. Tyler seemed impressed, then he grew wide eyed when he found out how much people pay for wedding cakes.

"Wow Zoey. That is more than some people make in a week."

"Yeah, I know. People get crazy about these cakes. I think I am going to need to hire an additional person on top of Dana and Phil. Dana has a natural talent for pastries, and I would like to train her on the more detailed works for decorating cakes so she could help me. She has been a food network junkie and knows a lot already from watching *Cake Wars* and *Ace of Cake* reruns."

Tyler shook his head. "There are shows about just cake?"

Zoey perked up. "There are several. I love them too. Someday I would love to even compete on *Cake Wars*, but I am still a long way from that level of artistry. Speed is not my friend. I am clumsy and that is not a good combination with cake."

"I should say not. Oh, I was at my parents today and they invited us to a barbeque on Friday at their house. My dad is great on the grill."

"Okay sounds great. Should I bring anything?"

"You don't have to, but I know my Dad would love anything you make. Mom only lets him have sweets on special occasions and meeting you would definitely qualify as a special occasion."

"Awe thanks. Is Kyle going to be there too?"

"Dad is inviting him so I would think so."

"Okay. I will figure out something to bring."

"Good. I also got you a present." He pulled out a small gift bag taped together at the top.

"You didn't have to buy me anything."

"It isn't a big deal," he said sheepishly.

She opened the bag and pulled out a key and key chain with R2-D2 on the end.

"It's my apartment key. Now you won't have to knock when you come up."

Zoey grinned. "I was going to make you a copy of mine but haven't gotten a minute to breathe yet."

"That is because I have been busy taking your breath away."

She laughed and said, "That is for sure."

She stood and started to clean from dinner and Tyler came back from behind and whispered in her ear. "Leave it. You have done enough work today."

"I can clean up dinner. You cooked."

"No way. Absolutely not." He then picked her up in the fireman's hold and walked them back to the bedroom and made sure she didn't have any energy to get back up again.

THE REST OF THE WEEK for Zoey and Tyler went much the same. They spent the night either at Tyler's or Zoey's and he ate breakfast at the bakery before working. At night, he would cook dinner for both of them. Some meals definitely turned out better than others. One particular night after burned grilled cheese they had to order from the diner. Tyler was getting used to going to bed earlier and getting up with Zoey each morning. Things had calmed down and they were even starting to think that the break in was just an isolated incident.

Once Friday arrived, Zoey found herself growing even more nervous as the time grew closer for the barbeque. She never seemed to do well with her boyfriends' families. Even with Trevor his family kept her at an arm's length. He had a brother and sister, who while they were polite, never made any true attempt at connecting with Zoey. She always felt isolated at the family events and sometimes felt guilty that Trevor had to stay by her side to keep her from feeling out of place. Trevor's parents never bonded with her. She tried several times to win them over with cakes, cookies and pies and while they would say a polite thank you or acknowledge her talent, they still never gave her affection during any of their interactions. Trevor had always tried to assure her that this was just how his parents were and they did not display their emotions. They were so different from Trevor who always told Zoey how he felt and what he was thinking, she had a hard time reconciling how he became the person he was.

Zoey was trying to put finishing touches on her hair and her hands began to shake. She was going to lose it. She desperately wanted to make a good impression on Tyler's family, and she knew just how important Hannah and Mark were to him. She put her hair clip back down and took in a deep breath. *Breathe Zoey*, she thought to herself. She straightened her spine and reached down deep for courage and put on her best smile.

In the mirror she saw Tyler leaning on the bathroom door frame. "Hey Sweetness. Is your hair giving you problems tonight?" he asked while looking at her clip on the counter.

She eased at the sight of him. "Just a little."

"Want some help?"

"If I need my boyfriend's help to fix my hair, I am sure I would be breaking some kind of girl rule. Josie would be so disappointed in me. Give me just a couple more minutes, please."

"Ok, but if you don't hurry Mom will show up on our doorstep to drag us to the house."

Zoey laughed. "Well we can't have that. I will be right out."

Tyler looked hungrily at Zoey and gave a slow nod. Zoey quickly shook her head and said, "Oh no...you can't give me that look and tell me we have to leave soon. You need to get out before I jump you right here, right now."

Tyler gave a slight groan and covered his eyes. "Alright I am leaving. We can play later." Then he walked backwards out the door.

A FEW MINUTES LATER Zoey managed to win the fight with her hair and left the apartment with Tyler. He opened the car door for her and she got in while he handed the cake to her and then shut the door. They began the drive to Tyler's parents' house and Zoey started to fidget with her hands around the edge of the box of the cake. She was visibly shaking, and Tyler was beginning to grow concerned.

"Zoey, are you okay?"

She took a shaky breath and replied, "I am just nervous."

"Why? Everything will be fine. They are going to love you." *Just like I do*, he thought.

Zoey began to shake a little more and Tyler pulled over growing more concerned. He didn't want her to walk in the door looking like she was going to cry. Zoey looked confused as he pulled into the grocery's parking lot.

"What are you doing?" Zoey asked.

"You are upset, and we are going give you a minute before we get there. Now talk to me. What is going on in that pretty little head of yours?"

Zoey looked as if she was going to deny it, but instead took a deep breath. "I don't do well with the parents. I have a terrible track record."

Tyler was shocked. How could anyone not be charmed by her? She had a natural sense of caring and irresistibility. "What do you mean?"

"Out of all the boyfriends I have had, none of their families have liked me, or at least didn't make an effort to be overly friendly."

"What about Trevor's family? He seemed like he was a good guy and must have come from a good family."

Zoey explained that his family never accepted her during their whole relationship and how they were always distant. She continued to explain, "I don't think they took me seriously since we were so young."

"You were together for years though, and they didn't get close to you?"

"No, and when he died, it wasn't them who called to tell me what happened. I was told by Trevor's roommate. Actually, his roommate called Derek's phone because he couldn't get ahold of me. Then Derek told me."

"Aw, Sweetness I am sorry." Derek never mentioned that he had to be the one to tell Zoey.

Zoey shrugged. "I am okay with that. It was probably best that Derek was there to tell me. Derek went with me to the funeral. I tried to approach Trevor's brother and sister at the church, and they turned their backs on me and refused to acknowledge my presence. I didn't matter to them."

There was a minute of silence while Tyler rubbed Zoey on her cheeks. Finally, she continued. "Anyway the rest of the men I dated that introduced me to their family had such dysfunctional relationships that I just got used to not getting close to them. But you are so close to your family and you are so important to me, I just don't want to mess this up."

Tyler's heart was breaking. He hated to see her like this. He silently cursed all the people in her life who shook her confidence. He bent his head down to kiss her and then held her head in his hands. "Listen to me. I know that they are going to love you. This whole town loves you already. Please don't let the idiots from your past shake you like this. And remember you already know Kyle and he adores you."

Zoey smiled and nodded. "Yeah, he is great."

"And I promise everything is going to be fine. Five minutes after we are there, I know you are going to feel so much better. My parents are amazing, and they are close to Derek's mom who has been raving about you for years."

Zoey seemed to be calming down. Tyler believed what he was saying to his core.

Zoey leaned in and kissed him again and said, "I do feel better. Let's go."

They finished the drive and still arrived five minutes early. Tyler opened the door and took the cake from Zoey, using his other hand to help her out of the car. They walked up to the door and were instantly greeted by Hannah and Mark.

Tyler gave his parents a hug and handed the cake over to his dad. They walked into the front living room and Tyler made the introductions. "Mom, Dad this is Zoey. Zoey these are my parents, Hannah and Mark."

Zoey started to extend her hand for a greeting and Hannah just rushed in and gave her a big hug. Zoey froze for a brief second and looked a bit in shock. Hannah exclaimed as she was hugging Zoey, "It is so nice to meet you. We have heard so much about you. Both from my sons and Amanda."

"Thank you, Mrs. Ashford. It is very nice to meet you."

"Oh, please call me Hannah." She was beaming at Zoey. Looking at her, her smile brightened even more and she gave Tyler a sly wink.

Mark stepped forward to greet Zoey and also gave her a warm hug. "Zoey, I have to say I have gotten spoiled from your baking, and it is very nice to meet you too."

Zoey looked as if she may start to cry. Tyler could see how the warm reception was affecting her. "It is nice to meet you as well sir, and don't worry, I will make sure to send Tyler with treats over as often as I can."

Mark laughed and announced, "Tyler, I like this one. Hurry up and marry her."

Tyler's face flushed, and he gave a crooked smile at his dad. Hannah stepped in before the men could scare Zoey any more. "Boys quit overwhelming the poor girl. Come on into the kitchen. I have appetizers all set out." Turning to Mark she continued, "And sweetie you need to start grilling soon."

THEY ALL WENT INTO the kitchen and started eating from the veggie tray. Hannah and Mark asked Zoey how the bakery was going and how she was settling into town. Zoey was grateful for the easy conversation. She found herself at ease with his parents. She felt infinitely better and thought this is how it is supposed to be. Then she heard steps coming from the next room and Kyle came into the kitchen. He greeted his family and Zoey with a hug.

"What have I missed?"

"Not much yet. We just started. Everything okay?" Hannah asked.

"Yeah, I was just finishing up with a story about a house fire that happened this afternoon."

"Oh, is everyone okay?"

"Yeah. Minnie Kaplan's daughter got mad with her ex-boyfriend and decided to burn all of his pictures and stuff and used a little too much accelerant. The damage wasn't too bad, but she was mostly just embarrassed."

Zoey thought back to some of her past relationships and remembered when she thought about doing much of the very same thing and had to smile.

"Hey Zoey, did you see the article about your open house?" asked Kyle.

"Yes, I did. It was a great article. Thank you again so much."

"You don't have to thank me. Your opening was big news for our town, and everyone raved about your food. Speaking of which, are we allowed to eat the cake before dinner?"

Hannah snuck up on her son and gave him a light tap on the head. "Absolutely not. Just because you're an adult now doesn't mean you can break the rules in my house."

Tyler laughed at his brother. "Dude, have you lost your mind?"

Kyle groaned. "Thought I could get away with it since we had company."

"Mom still scares me. Don't push it."

Zoey had to laugh at the family. They had such a comfort level with each other. Even with her family it was always a lot more formal.

Mark finally looked at his two sons and said, "Boys, how about you come with me outside to the grill and leave the girls here to relax." They nodded and Tyler grabbed the platter full of meat while Kyle grabbed the beers and followed their dad out the back door to the deck.

Hannah turned to Zoey and asked, "Would you like a glass of wine?"

"Yes, that would be great thank you."

Hannah poured her a glass and handed it to her and the two sat on stools at the island and watched the men out the window. "Tyler hasn't told me much about the two of you so forgive my mother's curiosity, but how did you meet?"

"I am surprised he didn't tell you."

"No. He probably told Mark, but I have been out of the loop."

Zoey blushed. "Well just a fair warning, it is a little embarrassing."

Hannah laughed. "Honey, those are the best stories."

Zoey nodded and proceeded to tell her about the Diet Coke disaster, sleeping on Tyler's couch, the apartment mix-up and how they had been hanging out with mutual friends.

Hannah looked happy as she took Zoey by the hand and said, "That has to be the sweetest story I have ever heard. I know Tyler is crazy about you and I am happy for the both of you."

"Your son is incredible, and I adore him. Actually, you have raised two good men. Kyle is great too."

"Kyle worries me more than Tyler. Tyler has always been an open and accepting person. Kyle is open with friendship, but he doesn't allow anyone into his heart. He is his own worst critic and after he came back from Philadelphia, he withdrew even more."

"I hope this puts you a little more at ease, but I have seen him with all of us. He is very open and kind. As for loving someone just give him time, I have a feeling that will resolve itself soon enough." Zoey remembered how she had watched the interactions with Kyle and Ariel grow closer each time they were together. She believed that something would happen soon, but he needed to realize it on his own time.

"I hope you are right."

The two continued talking while the boys finished preparing the meal. Hannah told Zoey stories about the boys when they were younger, how she met her husband and her upcoming surprise to Mark for a cruise to the Caribbean. The men then came back with dinner ready on the platter. Zoey stepped up to help Hannah plate the food.

They all sat down to dinner and fell into easy conversations. Towards the end of dinner Tyler leaned over to whisper into Zoey's ear, "See, I told you that they would love you."

She shivered at the heat of his breath to her ear and then leaned back to whisper into his ear, "The feeling is mutual." Tyler put his arm behind Zoey's back and starting rubbing up and down her spine. She wanted to just jump into his lap and melt into him. She looked at him as he was driving her crazy by tracing little circles on the small of her back.

Tyler leaned over again and whispered, "I can't wait to get you home, and have you all to myself."

Zoey gave a slight gasp. They still had to make it through dessert before they could leave, and she was already craving to feel his body over hers. She took her hand into his and gave a slight squeeze under the table. Tyler then started to shift uncomfortably in his chair. Zoey looked at him and smiled in understanding.

Tyler finally cleared his throat and said, "Dad, you ready for some cake?"

Mark sat up straighter and said, "I was ready when we brought it into the kitchen."

Zoey jumped up and said, "Let me take care of that for everyone." She grabbed the plates from the counter and proceeded to slice and serve the cake.

After finishing the dessert, Hannah got up to clear the plates. Zoey started to rise to help again, but Hannah would not hear of it. She told Zoey that she was their guest and to relax.

"Don't argue with her. You will never win," said Kyle.

Mark started nodding his head in agreement. "I have only won two arguments with her since I have known her.

The first one was convincing her to date me. The second was when I knew our second child was going to be a boy. She was convinced that Kyle was going to be a girl."

"Thanks Dad," Kyle said rolling his eyes.

"She was so convinced that she bought a special dress to bring him home in. She still has it stuffed in a drawer upstairs. It even had a matching little hat with the name embroidered on it."

Zoey's eyes brightened. "Oh, you have to tell me the name."

"Not cool Dad. Aren't we supposed to be telling embarrassing stories about Tyler and not me?"

"Nah," Mark said. "This is much more fun. KAYLA."

Zoey burst with a loud laugh. "His name was going to be Kayla?"

"Yeah. Since he turned out to be a boy Kyle seemed like an easy switch."

Tyler was laughing at his brother whose face was reddened. Kyle turned to Tyler and said, "Keep laughing nerd boy."

Tyler immediately stopped laughing and looked over at Kyle with wide eyes. "You wouldn't."

With an evil "I'm going to torture my brother" look he said, "I would."

Zoey was laughing at the brothers and then couldn't resist and said, "Oh, please do."

Tyler turned to Zoey and said, "Hey, you are supposed to be on my side."

"I am, but if he has childhood dirt on you, I totally want to know about it."

With almost a bounce in his step Kyle got up from the table and disappeared for less than a minute and returned with Tyler's freshman yearbook from high school. He had it opened to a page with Tyler's picture and there he was in all his nerd glory. He was way too thin with braces and black-rimmed glasses. His hair was a disheveled mess of bushy waves that draped over his forehead and looked like he was drowning in his t-shirt. Kyle puffed up his chest in victory.

Zoey looked at the picture and then back to Tyler. He definitely shed the nerd look and was quite handsome now. She let a giant smile grow and tried to hold back her laughter. Finally, she said, "Well those braces paid off nicely. I love your smile. What happened to your glasses? I know you don't wear contacts."

"I had LASIK surgery after college. Best money I ever spent."

Zoey nodded. "Well you still looked adorable." She leaned over and gave Tyler a kiss. Tyler started to try to give the kiss a little more passion when Kyle gave a loud cough. They pulled away remembering that they weren't alone.

Kyle shook his head and they could hear him muttering something about being bulletproof.

Zoey finally said, "Where is your picture from school? Fair is fair."

Tyler groaned and said, "No it isn't. He looked perfect in school. All the girls fell all over themselves to get his attention."

"He is just jealous."

Tyler looked at Zoey and said, "Not anymore."

SHORTLY AFTER, ZOEY, Tyler and Kyle said their good-byes to Hannah and Mark. Hugs were being given from everyone and Hannah welcomed Zoey to come back any-time.

When Tyler was the last to hug his mom, she whispered in his ear, "I love her. Don't let her go."

Tyler whispered back, "That is the plan Mom."

Once Tyler and Zoey got back to her apartment, she put away the leftovers that Hannah sent with them into the fridge and he began kissing the back of her neck. Between his kisses he said, "They loved you."

Zoey sighed in pleasure and said, "I loved them too. You and Kyle are really lucky."

"I know I am." Then he spun her around to face him and lifted her up off her feet so he could kiss her. Their tongues danced with passion and need. Zoey tangled her fingers in his hair.

Once their kiss broke, he was still holding her in the air with his arms wrapped around her thighs. She looked into his eyes and said, "So you have me all to yourself now. What are you going to do with me?"

That was all the encouragement he needed. He picked up Zoey and carried her into the bedroom where he showed her what he was going to do with her...twice.

Chapter 13

Saturday morning Zoey opened the bakery and was still amazed that she consistently had a line of people waiting for her to open each day. She put out her daily special sign for her Devil May Care Puffs and found Chase to be the first in line.

He was in his full sheriff's uniform and gave Zoey a bright grin. "Thank god. I'm starving."

"Well, we can't have a cranky hungry armed sheriff going around town, now can we?"

"I don't recommend it." Chase's normal easy posture was much stiffer than Zoey was accustomed to. She wasn't sure if it was from all the gear he had to wear or if he just easily slipped into this persona when he was on duty.

"Well come on in Sheriff, I have just the thing for you."

She got his normal black coffee and bagged up a bear claw and a couple of puffs from the daily special. He went over to the table to enjoy his breakfast before he started his shift and watched Zoey as she worked.

Zoey was able to clear out her line just as Phil walked in to start his shift. Chase walked over to her and asked, "So, how did dinner go with Hannah and Mark?

"Great," Zoey said honestly. "Actually, it went so much better than I could have even hoped for. They are so open and warm. I've never felt so welcomed."

Chase nodded. "Yup. That is just how they are. Tyler and Kyle included. Is your family going to come to visit soon?"

The thought of her mom and stepdad coming up filled her with anxiety. She loved them, but things could be strained at times, but the thought of Xander coming down gave her a warm comforting feeling. "I don't expect my parents anytime soon, but my brother Xander has been trying to clear up four or five days to come out here and see the shop."

"No sisters that cook like you?" Chase asked hopefully.

Zoey laughed. "No, sorry it's just me."

"Ah well, can't blame a guy for trying."

Phil started calling out to Zoey for help with the pastries in the back. She quickly said goodbye to Chase and went back to work.

SHORTLY AFTERWARDS, Tyler, Dixie and Josie came for breakfast. The trio sat at a table by the front windows and talked about their week. Tyler occasionally got distracted by watching Zoey work and charm the residents of the town.

Finally, Josie shook her head and said, "So you do love her."

Dixie stared at her friend. "Josie!"

Tyler shook his head and said, "What?"

Josie narrowed her gaze and said, "You do love her, don't you?"

Tyler just paused and didn't know what to say to Josie.

Dixie put her hand on his arm and said, "You don't have to answer her."

Josie shot Dixie a look who squirmed in her seat and continued to say, "We adore this girl. I want to make sure that you are not going to break our friend's heart, that you really care about her and if you love her."

Tyler really didn't want to admit to Josie that he loved Zoey. At least not until he had a chance to tell Zoey first. "I am not going to break her heart Josie. Don't either of you worry about her breaking my heart?" he asked hoping to redirect the questions.

Quickly both Dixie and Josie said, "No."

Then the three heard a male voice from the counter area talking to Zoey and Tyler turned his gaze just in time to hear the guy say, "You sure are a pretty little thing." Tyler narrowed his gaze and realized it was Austin Sutton. Austin was a fireman, and to be honest, a nice enough guy. Tyler went to school with him and played against him in the softball league during the summer. Austin was similar in height and build as Tyler. He constantly charmed with women with his light brown hair, blue eyes and a southern drawl. Being originally from Texas, his slow sweet accent was naturally charming. Many women fell at his feet, but he seemed to be very picky about the women he found interest in. To his credit he didn't like the pretty girls with no brains. He liked intelligent women who challenged him.

Tyler saw Zoey blush and say a polite thank you to Austin. Tyler felt his heart sink a little and let a slight growl escape watching the exchange with Austin and Zoey. Then he felt a hand on his arm and heard Dixie's voice, "Down boy. Let her handle it."

He quickly turned his head to Dixie and gave her a pointed stare. She wasn't impressed.

"Please, Chase gives me scarier looks when I keep food away from him."

Tyler turned back around to hear Austin ask Zoey out to dinner. Zoey appeared a little confused and asked, "Are you asking me out on a date?"

Austin smiled and said, "Yes, I guess I am."

"Oh, that is really sweet of you to ask, but I have to tell you, I already have a boyfriend."

Surprised Austin asked, "Really? Well he is a lucky guy."

Zoey shook her head and said, "No, actually I am the lucky one, but thanks." Zoey looked over at Tyler who was now looking at her with clear affection on his face. Austin picked up the clues as she finished waiting on him, and then walked over to Tyler's table.

Austin nodded to the group, "Good morning ladies," then looked at Tyler and nodded. "Tyler."

Dixie got a little dreamy eyed. "Hey Austin. Good to see you."

Austin looked at Tyler and said, "Hey Tyler, listen I had no idea she was with you. I didn't mean any disrespect. You are a lucky guy. She seems great."

Tyler relaxed a little and said, "Thanks. We haven't been together long, and yes she is great."

"Well good for you. So, that look you gave me earlier where you wanted to kill me...we are all good now?"

Tyler gave a slight laugh and said, "Yeah we're good."

After Austin said his goodbyes to the group, Josie turned to Tyler and said, "I am so proud of you. You didn't let your inner caveman take over and make an ass of yourself."

Tyler gave a sideways glace to Josie and said, "Thanks, I think."

"Did Zoey tell you that we are going to have a girls' night tonight?"

"Yeah. I am going to hang out with Chase after our run today."

Dixie looked at him and asked, "What time are you going to be home? We still don't think Zoey should be alone, so we are going to drop her off to you after we're done."

"I should be home around eleven or eleven-thirty. Chase has the morning shift again tomorrow, so he turns into a pumpkin early."

Dixie laughed. "I had to take pictures for the police department one day when he only got four hours of sleep and he was a big giant grump. It took me shoveling three donuts down his throat to make him tolerable."

"He has always been that way."

"Has Chase heard anything about Zoey's break in?"

Tyler shook his head. "We are waiting to hear from Lexington PD next week. They said that there should be more information then. He won't give me anything more than that."

The day passed with relative ease. Zoey found that she had a comfortable rhythm with her days at the bakery. While it could be chaotic at times with the different rushes throughout the day, she had worked out some of the kinks from opening week.

She heard a light knock from her back door and opened to find Ariel holding a bottle of wine with a look of satisfaction.

Zoey looked at her friend and said, "You look happy."

"I am," Ariel beamed. "I hired a new girl to help so that Myrna and I can have some days off."

"Really? Do I know her?"

"Probably not, but she has been to the bakery. She was holding a muffin when she came into my shop to fill out an application."

"So, what do you know about her?"

"Her name is Lana, and she is twenty-eight years old. She moved here about a year ago with her now ex-fiancé. She is going to college at night for a nursing degree and worked in a greeting card store when she lived in Raleigh."

"That sounds promising."

"Yes, it is."

Looking at the clock on the wall Zoey said, "Well, I guess we better go. Josie and Dixie are waiting on us. If we are too late Josie will kill us."

They walked over to Josie's and found that dinner was ready, and Josie and Dixie had already started with the wine. Zoey dropped the French silk pie on the counter and went to the couch to join Dixie.

Dixie looked over at Zoey with a giggle in her voice. "I still can't believe you got Austin to ask you out."

Zoey shook her head. "You mean that fireman this morning?"

Ariel dropped her fork loudly on her plate. "Austin Sutton? Austin Sutton asked you out?"

Zoey looked at Ariel in surprise. "If that is the fireman, yeah I guess so."

Josie came walking in with her plate and sat in the oversized chair and said, "You should have seen Tyler nearly lose his shit."

Zoey groaned. "He heard all of it?"

"Darling the whole bakery heard it. And they also heard you tell Austin that you had a boyfriend. Perked ole nerd boy right up."

Ariel looked at Zoey and said, "Zoey first let me say, I love you like you are my sister, but quit stealing all the hot guys."

"I only want one of the hot guys. You can have the rest."

Ariel looked at Dixie and said in a quiet whisper, "Austin Sutton, holy crap."

Dixie nodded and put her hand on her friend's shoulder and said, "I know one guy who is up higher on your holy crap meter."

Ariel sagged further into her chair and said, "Yeah, but that isn't going anywhere." Redirecting the spotlight Ariel looked at Josie. "What is going on with you? I heard from Derek you got the attention of some guy at the bar this week."

Josie waived a dismissive hand in the air. "Oh, he was nothing. Fun to play with but I sent him on his way."

Dixie shook her head. "You are worse than any of the guys. You don't let any of them stick around."

"God no. You let them stick around too long then you find out just how awful they truly are. This way I still like them when they leave."

Ariel looked at Zoey and said, "Josie is tough on them. She made poor David Willis cry."

Josie took a long sip of her wine and smiled. "During and after sex."

"Oh my god Josie," Ariel said with a wide-eyed expression.

Dixie sat back and said, "Don't worry girls. Just wait, it will come for her too. We will all have our fun when we see how the mighty have fallen."

Then from the coffee table the tone of R2D2 came from Zoey's cell phone. Zoey reached down to read her incoming message.

Dixie shook her head and said, "Wow, you are Tyler's dream girl."

Zoey sighed and said, "I hope so." She swiped her phone to read her message.

Tyler: What are you girls up to?

Zoey: Eating pasta, drinking wine and picking on Josie.

Tyler: Wow, you guys are brave, and stupid.

Zoey: She loves us. No worries.

Tyler: I miss you.

Zoey: I miss you too.

Tyler: I can't wait to see you tonight.

Then she heard Dixie's phone go off. Then Dixie announced, "Chase said to stop distracting his boy."

The girls all laughed, and Zoey sent a final message to Tyler.

Zoey: Chase just scolded us. Go have fun with your friend.

Tyler: Ok Sweetness, see you soon.

TYLER TOOK A SLOW DRAW from his beer while Chase returned from the kitchen with a plate of wings. Tyler took a wing and said, "I can't believe you texted the girls on me."

"I am trying to save a little of your manhood."

"Believe me my manhood is getting plenty of exercise."

"Yeah, Josie told Dixie you guys have been very vocal every night and just how happy you really are."

"Ugh. Really? She can hear us?"

Chase shrugged. "You guys share a wall, and the insulation is thin."

"Someone could have told us before now."

"You really think Josie is going to tell you? She loves eavesdropping to have blackmail material."

"Well thanks for the heads up, but you could have warned me earlier."

"Nah. I like getting the dirt too." Chase took a drink and looked thoughtfully before continuing. "You still going to Chicago next week?"

"Yeah. I have to. I am my own boss, but I also don't have anyone to pawn the work off onto."

Chase nodded. "I don't think Zoey should be alone yet. Do you have a plan?"

"Yup. I have this kick ass bodyguard staying with her for the first four or five days."

"Yeah, who is that?"

"Josie."

"Holy crap, the big guns. What about the rest of the time?"

"Derek said she could stay with him." Tyler's voice dropped and had a disappointed tone.

"You okay with that?"

"Yes," Tyler said with a pause. "No."

"She isn't Jane you know."

"I know, and I know Derek wouldn't do that to me. Plus, they have made their relationship very clear to all of us."

Chase set down his plate of food and looked earnestly at his friend. "If you really want this relationship to work with Zoey, you need to have full faith in her. Guys are going to be around her. Derek told us how she usually had all guy friends. She likes sports, poker and Star Wars for God's sake, so guys are going to want to talk to her."

"Yeah, and I love all that about her, but I do find myself a bit jealous of the bond she has with Derek."

"She has known Derek since she was eighteen. Of course she is close to him, but she is *with* you." Chase picked up his plate again and continued. "And I will deny this if you ever repeat it, but I am jealous of how she looks at you. Out of all the women I have been with, none of them look at me the way she looks at you."

"You are turning into a softie."

"Nah. Just a moment of weakness. You stopped me from eating. It's the hunger talking."

AT THE END OF THE NIGHT Zoey left Josie's apartment and walked down the hall to hers. She found Tyler sitting on the couch with the TV on, his head tilted on the back of the couch and his mouth agape. Shaking her head, Zoey walked over to him and wondered how he fell asleep sitting up. It was the cutest thing she had ever seen. She carefully knelt on the couch next to him and went to kiss him on the cheek.

Tyler snapped his head up with the touch of her lips and she got startled and jumped back. He took a second to shake his head, woke up and turned to see Zoey smiling next to him.

"Hello gorgeous," Zoey said while stroking his hair.

"Hi Sweetness. Did you have a good time with the girls?"

"Yes. We had pasta and wine. Dixie and Ariel started singing Katy Perry towards the end of the night. It all went down the rabbit hole after that."

"Did Josie sing too?"

Zoey laughed. "No. She wasn't that drunk. And did you know that she made David Willis cry?"

"Yeah. It was the saddest thing. The poor guy was lovesick, and she kept turning him away. He even sent roses, chocolates and stuffed animals. Ariel made a fortune off him trying to buy his way into her heart."

"I don't think the way to her heart is with those kinds of gifts. He obviously didn't know her very well."

"Do any of us, really?"

"No, I guess not. So how was your night with Chase?"

"Good. You know how it is, wings, beer, sports."

Zoey sighed. "Yeah, I know. The girls wouldn't let me turn the game on."

"They still hope to convert you to their feminine ways."

Zoey shook her head. "Never gonna happen. Too stubborn. I DVR'ed the game, so don't tell me what happened."

Tyler wrapped his arms around her and turned her over so that she was under him on the couch. He put his forehead to hers and said, "God you are so sexy, and believe me I love your feminine ways."

"You just love my feminine parts."

"Well those too." He started kissing her neck, and she was overwhelmed by his masculine scent. Zoey arched into him and released a slight moan with his touch. She felt his arousal pressing against her thighs and then ran her hands up and down his back.

"I thought you were tired."

"When it comes to you, I am never that tired."

"Well then I guess I will just have to wear you out." They got up from the couch and managed to make their way to the bedroom where they both ended their night in total exhaustion.

Chapter 14

Tuesday morning, Detectives Buxton and Morris went to Main St Café to meet Shane's boss, Alex Winbush, to question him about the suspension that Shane had at work. When they arrived, Alex had already been seated and was enjoying his dark roasted coffee. Alex prided himself on being a fair and kind man. He ran his company with efficiency and was well respected in the community. At the age of thirty-seven he had accomplished a lot with his company and knew that his employees were a large part of that success. Being a happily married man with two young children he also expected a lot from his employees to show ethical behavior in and out of the office. He wouldn't tolerate endangering his company's reputation. When the detectives reached out to question him about Shane's suspension, Alex requested to meet them out of the office, and would provide full disclosure and cooperation.

The two detectives sat across from Alex at the table towards the back of the café. Detective Buxton was the first person to speak. "Hello Mr. Winbush, we appreciate you taking the time to meet with us today. We want to ask you some questions about Shane and his suspension."

Alex set down his coffee, "Yes of course. What would you like to know?"

"First, how long has Shane been in your employment?"

"I hired him about five and a half years ago."

"And before the most recent suspension did you have any problems with him?"

"Nothing more than occasional crankiness. He is good at his job, but he is not the most popular person in the office."

"Was there ever anything with his interactions that gave you cause for concern?"

"Nothing in the office. The only thing that gave me concern was when we saw him at the restaurant with his ex-girlfriend."

Morris straightened in his seat and asked, "Do you remember which ex-girlfriend?"

"Her name was Zoey, but I am sorry gentlemen I don't remember her last name. She was a sweet little thing. My wife and I had met her a few times during corporate and holiday events when she would come with Shane. She even would drop off her desserts to the office on occasion."

"What exactly was the cause for suspension?"

"Ethics violation."

"Could you provide details of that violation?"

"My wife and I were at Sidebar Grill when we saw Shane burst in. We were sitting up by the front door and he was in such a hurry that he didn't see us sitting there. I watched him approach Zoey and a man that she was having lunch with. At the time I couldn't hear what was being said, but it didn't look like it was going in a good direction. The two men exchanged angry looks with each other, and Zoey looked a little scared and uncomfortable. She gave the man she was with a hug goodbye and she and Shane left the restaurant. I had a bad feeling about what might happen as they left so I told my wife to call the police if I signaled her from outside."

"You thought that there might be a need to call the police?" asked Buxton.

"I was hoping not, but I grew up with an abusive alcoholic father and I know the look a man can get when things are going to get out of control. I approached them in the parking lot so Shane couldn't directly see me, but I could hear what was being said, and I could step in if necessary."

"That was noble but could have ended badly for you."

"I couldn't just sit there. I am not made that way."

"Okay, what happened once you were within earshot?" asked Morris.

"I heard Shane call her names and was screaming at her just inches away from her face. She was crying and flinching with each word he was saying."

"This didn't seem like enough cause to call the police?"

Alex narrowed his eyes and said, "It has been my experience that if you call the police when someone is just yelling nothing happens and sometimes it makes it worse after they leave." Alex's tone made it obvious that he was speaking from past experience.

Morris nodded his head seeming to understand the man's frustration. "Do you remember what he said to her exactly?"

"He called her a 'fat cheating whore' a 'bitch' and said that she was never allowed to see her friend again."

"Do you know who she was with?"

"No. I've never seen him before. But when Shane talked about him, he said 'friend' in a sarcastic tone. I thought about stepping in, but he had Zoey get in the car and slammed the door shut before I moved forward."

"So, you suspended him for this?"

"Yes. To be honest, I called my attorney because I wanted to fire him, but I also didn't want a lawsuit. My attorney advised me that it would be in my best interest to suspend him for the ethics violation that we have in all of my employees' contracts. When they sign with us, they agree to present professionalism inside and outside of the office. Inappropriate behavior is grounds for disciplinary action up to and including termination. I was advised that just observing an argument between a couple is not grounds for termination, but I could suspend him for the unprofessional verbal altercation."

"When did you deliver the suspension?"

"The following Tuesday."

"How did he take it?"

"I thought he was going to throw something. He became extremely angry, but then I saw a switch go off in his head. He calmly took the disciplinary papers and said that he would be back to work after the suspension was over, and that he was sorry that I had to witness his fight with Zoey."

"Did you hear about anything else between him and Zoey after that?"

"Nothing beyond the fact that they broke up." He paused and took another sip of his coffee. "What happened to bring you to my door, gentlemen? I have been very open with you about my employee, and I need to know if I should be concerned for my other employees' safety."

Morris looked thoughtful for a moment and then responded, "Zoey moved to North Carolina and opened a bakery there. Someone broke in and vandalized the bakery. Windows were smashed, display cases broken, holes in the walls, and derogatory names were written in the shop."

Alex exhaled, sat back in his chair and his concern for the woman shone in his eyes. "Is Zoey okay?"

"Yes, she wasn't there at the time."

"And you think that Shane went from Lexington to North Carolina and did this to her?"

"It is a possibility."

"You should talk to Shane's new girlfriend. I don't know her name and have only seen her once but his secretary should know who she is."

"We have that information but thank you."

"Is there anything else I can answer for you gentlemen?"

Buxton rose to leave and said, "No thank you, but we would appreciate it if you did not advise Shane of our conversation. This is a continuing investigation and we need it to remain confidential for now."

"Of course." Alex knew all too well what could happen when a cornered man gets spooked, and he had no doubt that Shane did this to Zoey. He recognized the behaviors and could not have this in his office. If Shane was capable of doing this, there may be other dishonest things he was doing in the office.

After the detectives left, Alex called his secretary. "Jessica, pull all of Shane's account files for the past three years and send them to me. Please be discreet about what you are doing. In fact, if you would do this before or after hours, I will pay you double time to get this accomplished."

Jessica advised him that some files were already at the off-site facility for storage and may take a week or two to receive them. Alex said that it was no hurry and that he wanted to make sure this was done right. He thanked his secretary and advised her that he would be back in the office in late afternoon. Alex knew deep down that this extra effort would pay off.

Alex thought about the lifestyle that Shane led. He always had tailored suits, an extravagant car and a home that seemed beyond the means of his salary. The first time he had been to his employee's home he did think it was odd that he could afford such a place, but he knew that he lived with his girlfriend and thought perhaps it was affordable with their combined salaries, but now he wondered if he had been naïve. Maybe Shane had been maintaining his extravagant lifestyle through unlawful means. If he was taking advantage of Alex and his company, he would make sure he would pay for his crimes.

Alex called his attorney and advised him that he would be dropping off files to his office to have sent to forensic accounting to research a suspected employee of illegal activities.

DETECTIVES BUXTON AND Morris were in the car on the way to the station and Morris turned to his partner and said, "I think we have a motive for the break in at Ms. Carrington's shop."

Detective Buxton nodded. "Yeah, but what I don't understand is why the slow burn? I would have thought he would have taken out revenge more at the time of the suspension."

"Didn't they say this was her first shop and that she worked in an office here in Lexington before her move to North Carolina?"

"Yeah."

"Maybe seeing her happy pushed him over the edge."

"We need proof that he was in North Carolina. Let's get a warrant for his bank records and see what happens."

"Agreed. Give that sheriff a call and give him an update."

CHASE SAT AT THE STATION and ran a hand over his face and gave a big sigh. He just got off the phone with Detective Buxton, who gave him an update about their discussion with Alex and that they would be pursuing a warrant for Shane's banking and credit card information for evidence of his travels to North Carolina.

Chase felt a knot in the pit of his stomach and just knew that this wasn't over yet. He wondered if Zoey knew about Shane's suspension at work. He turned to his computer and pulled up the file for Zoey's case and went to update with the latest information from Lexington. The more he typed the more frustrated he was getting, and he pounded harder on the keyboard. Then he felt a hand on his shoulder. He turned around to see Dixie's concerned face looking down at him.

Dixie gave a slight squeeze and said, "Hey, you okay?"

Chase sighed and replied, "Yeah, just getting frustrated with work stuff." He couldn't go over the details of Zoey's case with Dixie even though he wanted to talk to her. She always seemed to have a way of calming him down.

Dixie leaned on the edge of his desk and studied him. "Is there anything that I can do to help?"

"No but thank you. Did you finish with the pictures from the accident scene?" Chase had contacted Dixie to take pictures of an auto accident that included one fatality just on the outskirts of town. They needed pictures for evidence and the department often contracted Dixie for the more important cases.

Dixie's mouth dropped at the corners and Chase watched her eyes well up with the beginning of tears. "Yes. I will be sending you the pictures later today for your file."

Chase could see the emotion on Dixie's face, and he stood up to lean on the desk next to her. "You know that if these scenes that we send you to get to be too much you can just tell me. I can train one of these bozos to take better pictures."

Dixie shook her head. "No, I am okay. I know how important they can be, and I want to help when I can."

"I appreciate that. Are you going to McKenna's tonight with all of us since Tyler is leaving for his trip to Chicago in the morning?"

"No, I have a date."

"Anyone I know?"

"Well since you know the entire town, I would have to say yes. It's Jay Rosen."

"The mechanic?"

"Yes."

Of course, Chase knew that guy. He had a reputation of being fair to his customers and didn't rip them off with unnecessary repairs. He didn't own the shop but was the assistant manager and had been there since he was in high school when he started as just a tech. He was an average looking guy with average intelligence. He was nice enough, but he didn't think that he was good enough for Dixie.

Dixie frowned at him and said, "What is with that face?"

"What face?" Chase asked, but he knew what face he had given and didn't mean to let it show.

"That slightly shocked and confused face. You think I can't get a date?" Dixie looked like she was getting mad now.

"God no Dix. I just..." *Crap* he thought *there is no good way to finish this sentence.* "I didn't know you were interested in the guy." *There, that was better.*

"Oh. Well, I wasn't, or at least I wasn't chasing after him or anything. I just went to get my oil changed and he asked me out to dinner, so I said yes." Chase knew that Jay wasn't the type of guy she would normally go out with. Her usual type was a bit more handsome and confident, but her recent track record had been so horrible maybe she was trying to go for a different type.

Chase stood away from the desk and looked at Dixie for a second before speaking. "Good. I hope you have a good time. Maybe you and your *date* can stop by McKenna's after dinner. I think everyone will be there."

"Maybe we will."

"I have to stop at Zoey's bakery. I can walk you back to your studio."

"Okay. Let's go."

As Dixie and Chase walked through the square Chase was grinding his teeth and his jaw ticked a few times.

Dixie looked up at him and said, "Are you going to tell me what's bothering you?"

"Can't, at least not now." His thoughts were circling around his conversation with the Lexington detectives. He also thought there had to be something he was missing to help provide solid evidence to link Shane to the break in. The best way to protect Zoey would be to nail this guy to the wall.

"When you can talk, will you let me know? I haven't seen you like this in a long time."

Chase stopped and looked at Dixie and fought to bring back his ease and charm. "I will."

They arrived at Zoey's shop and Dixie continued to walk to her studio as Chase turned into the bakery. As Chase approached, he saw that Zoey had a full dining room. Josie was in her usual corner table typing away on her laptop and writing furiously on some files that she brought. She lifted her head and nodded a hello to Chase and then went back to work. Tyler's mom and dad were sitting at another table enjoying pastries and obviously caught up in their own little world. Other town residents were also enjoying their afternoon. He looked behind the counter and found Dana and Zoey reorganizing the cases with the last of the pastries for the day.

Zoey was a little more disheveled today than he normally saw her. Her hair was up but several strands had fallen from hard work through the day. She had what looked like icing on her apron and pink food coloring staining the fingers of her left hand.

Chase greeted her with a smile and said, "Hi Zoey, busy today?"

"It was crazy today. We got a tour bus that came in and then the shuttle from the senior center came over about thirty minutes later. At least things have calmed down now. Is there something I can get you?"

With a slight frown Chase said, "I am not here for the food."

Zoey shifted her weight from one foot to another. "Oh, okay. Tyler okay?"

Chase nodded his head, "Yeah, this isn't about him, it is about the break in. Is there somewhere we can go to talk privately?"

Zoey nodded. "Yeah, we can go into the back," she continued and turned to Dana. "When my interview gets here can you give them a drink and let them know I may be a few minutes?"

"Sure, no problem," Dana replied.

Zoey then followed Chase back to her office and closed the door.

Chase smiled at Zoey and asked, "You are hiring another person?"

"Yes. I am so busy I can justify the extra person and maybe even be able to schedule two days off a week instead of just the one."

"I am happy to see it is going so well for you."

"Thanks. Now what did you want to talk to me about Chase?"

Chase stood straight and took a deep breath. "Did you know that Shane had gotten suspended because of a fight that you and he had at a restaurant?"

Zoey gave him a wide-eyed blink. "No. Why would he have gotten suspended over a fight that we had outside of his work?"

"Apparently his boss was there and observed how he had spoken to you in the parking lot. He said that you were having lunch with another man when Shane came in, took you away and proceeded to argue with you outside. His boss suspended him on an ethics violation that is part of his contract for his employment. Do you know what fight he is talking about?" There was a part of the story that bothered Chase. Zoey was having lunch with another man. He didn't think that she was the type of girl who cheated on her boyfriend, but now she was with his best friend who he knew was head over heels for this girl.

Zoey appeared to think about it for a minute and finally said, "That had to be the lunch I had with Derek."

Relieved that it was Derek she was with, and not some other guy she was seeing, he asked her to provide him with details of the lunch.

Zoey recounted the specifics of the conversation with Derek and then what happened after Shane showed up. "When Shane put me in the car and slammed the door shut on me, I knew I had to leave and soon. I was embarrassed of the person that I had become with him. I was embarrassed that Derek saw me that way. I had lost all my friends that I had in Lexington because of this man, the man I kept defending, the man who I felt didn't love me anymore, or maybe he never really did."

"And nothing strange happened after you left him while you were still in Lexington?"

"No, I was living in a small apartment in a gated complex, but when I moved in, the security of the complex wasn't really a consideration about where I lived. He was verbally abusive but had never physically threatened me. I thought that by leaving I was safe. Why would he wait so long to do something like this to me? Why not while I was still close to his hometown?"

"Usually something triggers revenge. It has been my experience that if someone moves on in a new relationship and shows that they are happy without the other person it can cause reactions like what you went through. My theory was that his trigger may not have been you in a new relationship but opening the bakery and moving on happily without him."

"I heard that he had a new girlfriend."

"Often times that doesn't matter. I know that he may still feel the need to cause problems for you, so I want you to continue to be vigilant. Tyler is leaving for Chicago tomorrow. Are you still going to have someone stay with you?" He already knew what Tyler had told him the other day but wanted to make sure Zoey understood how important this was.

"Yes. I tried to tell Tyler it wasn't necessary, but I will be staying with Josie and Derek until he gets back."

Normally Chase wouldn't agree that another woman would count as protection, but he had seen Josie at the gym boxing with her trainer and he also had seen her at the gun range. He had no doubt that Josie could handle almost anything his deputies could. "Don't tell Derek I said this, but I think Josie is scarier than Derek."

"Yeah seriously, what did she do before she moved here?"

Chase shrugged. "You have no idea how much I want to break the rules and do an extensive background check on her. She is great, but none of us really know much about her, but she has been great to Ariel and Dixie and that is all that matters."

Zoey looked at her phone to check the time. "Do you need to ask me any additional questions?"

Chase shook his head. "No, but I will see you tonight at McKenna's?"

Zoey opened the door, and they started to leave towards the front. "Yes, of course. I am going to miss Ty while he is in Chicago."

"I know he will miss you too. You guys are good for each other. I am happy for both of you."

Zoey turned and smiled at him. "Thanks, now we just need to get you all fixed up."

"Hey, what about your best friend first?"

"Nah. He isn't ready yet."

"And you think I am?"

Zoey patted him on his chest and sweetly said, "Yes you are, you just haven't figured that out yet."

Chase gave out a loud short laugh. "Not likely."

Zoey stopped at the case and grabbed a cupcake. "Here take this and get back to work now."

Grudgingly he took the cupcake and took a big bite. With his mouth slightly full he said, "I am not next."

Zoey shrugged and said, "Okay big guy, whatever you say."

Chase was going to argue but then a call came through from dispatch and he said a hasty goodbye and turned to leave.

Chapter 15

At McKenna's, Tyler, Zoey, Kyle, Ariel and Chase were having drinks and playing group trivia. Their secret weapon, Josie, was running late and Dixie was still on her date with Jay. Derek stopped by with refills for the group and said, "Man, you guys suck tonight. I can't believe you are losing to the old ladies."

Kyle grunted. "Maybe if the questions weren't so concentrated on 1950s references, we would be doing better. Who made these questions?"

"I let Tiny make them tonight." The group sat a little lower in their seats. They were not going to criticize Tiny. Tiny was actually Tim Cooper. He was a bear of a man at 6'5" with tattoos visible on his neck and forearms. He had served some time in prison for beating a guy within an inch of his life for hitting his sister. The judge had decided to still teach him a lesson about vigilante justice and sent him to prison. While he was there, he served as the cook and as his skills improved remarkably, he became the warden's personal chef. He was actually a very talented cook. The aroma from McKenna's could grab your attention from a block away.

Tiny found that once he was released from prison, he had a hard time finding a job. Derek had been friends with the warden who was a regular customer at the bar. The warden recommended Tiny when Derek said he was looking for a new cook. He advised Derek how he served a punishment that seemed a little too harsh for trying to protect his sister and deserved a fresh start. Tiny did not disappoint. He worked hard and treated the staff with respect. Derek never hesitated to tell people what a great asset to the bar Tiny was. Often Derek was looking for more ways to include him in the day-to-day operations of the bar.

"I can bring Tiny out here so you can complain to him directly if you like."

Kyle looked down and glanced at the others and said, "Nope. We're good. Thanks."

Derek chuckled and walked away from the group.

Kyle looked around the bar and said, "I know Josie was late for a meeting but where is Dixie?"

Chase took a long pull off his beer and said, "She is on a date."

"Really? Anyone we know?"

"Jay Rosen."

"The mechanic?"

Chase ground his back teeth together and replied, "Yup."

Ariel looked a little confused at Chase and said, "Jay is a nice guy. I hope she is having fun."

Zoey and Tyler saw how agitated Chase was getting and they gave a knowing look to each other.

Josie finally appeared and slid into the booth next to Chase. "Hey big guy. Did you leave us any food?" She paused and looked at him and continued, "Or from the look on your face you haven't eaten yet?"

Kyle smirked and said, "He ate already, but that isn't his problem." Chase glowered at his friend and Kyle said, "Save that look for someone else." Saved by a new trivia question, the topic of conversation was diverted.

As the night continued Tyler was putting Zoey on edge. He kept touching her in places that were driving her wild. He was trying to be discreet but wanted to rev her engines to almost a breaking point. He started with slow rubbing circles on the small of her back. Later he moved his arm around her and started grazing his thumb on the side of her breast so that no one could see him. When Dixie showed up later with Jay, he moved his hand under the table and put his hand up her skirt to rub her inner thigh. Once his hand started to move up a little higher, she had to pull his hand down and laced her fingers into his. She leaned over and whispered in his ear, "If you don't stop soon it is going to get really embarrassing really quickly."

Tyler whispered back into her ear, "Soon I am going to be tasting a little more than this beer, and you are going to quiver under my tongue."

Zoey looked down and said quietly, "Oh God."

Josie slid out of the booth and came to the other side to sit next to Zoey. Confused Zoey looked at Josie. "Had enough over there?"

"I can't believe I am going to say this, but I would rather sit with you love birds than deal with grumpy papa bear over there."

Zoey looked at Chase who was now sitting next to Dixie with Jay on the other side of her. "And you thought leaving Dixie in between the two of them was a better idea?"

"Well more fun to watch at least. When did the good sheriff start going down this windy road," Josie asked Tyler.

Tyler just shrugged. "This was news to me. I am not even sure he knows what he is doing, or maybe he is just having a bad day."

Josie sat back and gave a slight evil smile. "Well this going to be fun to watch. I give it two months before something blows up."

Zoey giggled and said, "I say less than two months."

Josie looked at Ariel and Kyle who were quietly talking to each other not even noticing the rest of the group. "And how long do you think before that works itself out?"

Tyler was the first to speak up. "A lot longer. I have tried to talk to him before about it. My parents have even tried to talk to him and he gives us the silent treatment if we try to push too much. He stopped talking to me for three days last time."

Zoey was surprised and said, "You didn't tell me any of this."

"Not really my place to say anything. They have danced around this since we were kids. Kyle says he isn't good for her and won't budge."

Josie shook her head and said, "Ty I can't believe I am going to say this, but you are the only guy in our group who isn't a complete idiot."

Tyler straightened in his seat and kissed Zoey's hand. "Thank you. I knew I couldn't risk losing this girl to someone else."

By the end of the night Tyler, Zoey and Ariel were the last ones left at the bar. Derek was talking to his wait staff and bartender to start closing out the night. He grabbed his phone from the bar and joined his friends at the booth. He sat next to Ariel and asked, "Did I miss anything?"

Tyler cleared his throat and attempted to not laugh. "Well, Chase was a grump all night."

"Why, because your ugly mug is going away for a couple weeks?"

Zoey laughed. "No, because of Dixie and Jay."

Derek looked really confused. "Why would that bother Chase? Jay is a good enough guy."

"Seemed like a jealous temper tantrum."

"Why, Dixie goes out on dates all the time?"

"That is the million-dollar question tonight," Tyler said.

"Ok. Did I miss anything else?"

Zoey looked at Ariel and said, "Nope. Not really."

"I leave tomorrow for Chicago. Zoey said she will stay at your place after Josie leaves, right?" Tyler asked.

"Yeah. I have that guest room all set up for her."

Zoey hated that she was going to abandon her apartment and stay further away from the bakery, but after the discussion with Chase she felt like it would still be a good idea to not be alone.

Tyler squeezed Zoey's hand. "Okay. If anything happens, call me right away."

Zoey was starting to get a little annoyed with the two men. "Hey! You both realize I am sitting right here, and I am not a child that you pass off to a babysitter, right?"

"Ok Zoe. Sorry. We are stupid men. Forgive us," Derek said as he tilted his head and started batting his eyelashes. Tyler then joined with the same gesture and cuddled on Zoey's shoulder.

"Ugh. You guys are impossible."

Derek finally sat back up straight and said, "Yes, but you love us."

"You do have a certain charm about you that I can't help but to adore," Zoey said as Derek gave a cheesy wide grin that belonged on a toothpaste commercial.

Ariel finally tired of the boys' antics and took her hand on Derek's face and squished his lips together to make a fish mouth. "Okay brother of mine. Take me home so they can enjoy the rest of their night."

With Ariel still holding his face Derek said, "I am supposed to just leave so that cad can take advantage of my friend?"

"Yes, you are. Now get your butt moving," Ariel said as she shoved Derek out of the booth.

ZOEY AND TYLER MADE it home to a frenzied round of lovemaking and Zoey drifted off to sleep as soon as she cuddled into Tyler's arms. He laid motionless without a sound to listen to her breathing at a slow and steady pace. His arms tightened his embrace and whispered to her, "I love you, and I am going to try my best to get back here as quick as I can."

Tyler held his breath waiting to see if she heard him or woke up to his words, but she just continued her rhythmic breathing and small movements that burrowed deeper into his embrace.

ZOEY WOKE THE NEXT morning to see Tyler picking up his suitcase to leave. She rubbed her eyes and said, "Hey you. Time to go already?"

"Yeah. Kyle will be here in a couple minutes to take me to the airport."

"You chose Kyle to wake up early?" Zoey asked in astonishment.

"I know, but I trust him to get up on time and you have the bakery to take care of."

Zoey sat up in bed and gazed at Tyler all dressed in his khakis and polo shirt. He looked devastatingly adorable. Her heart was doing little flips and her fingers yearned to lift his shirt to feel his toned chest. As her thoughts began to wander, they both heard a knock at the door.

"Damn. I need to get the laptop packed and grab a couple more things," Tyler said while making spinning motions around the room.

"I'll get the door. Take care of whatever you need to." Zoey walked to the front door and opened to see a very disheveled Kyle holding his travel coffee mug. His hair was standing on end and he looked like a complete mess.

"Geez Kyle. Did you just roll out of bed and come straight here?"

"No. I rolled out of bed and made coffee. *Then* came over." He looked down at his jeans and fitted t-shirt and gave a slight shrug. "I don't remember getting dressed though."

"Maybe you had some help."

"If I had some help, I would be in a better mood." Kyle looked at what Zoey was wearing and gave a grin. "So pink bunny pajama bottoms do it for my brother?"

Zoey looked down and said, "Just about anything does it for your brother." Seeing Kyle grimace a little she gave a slight grin and said, "Would you like a detailed list?"

"God no." Then he shouted to the back room, "Ty! Get your ass in gear before your girl scars me for life."

"I'm coming. Quit growling." Tyler emerged from the bedroom with his laptop bag slung over his shoulder and wheeling his suitcase behind him. He made quick strides to Zoey and wrapped his arms around her thighs and picked her up to give her a passionate kiss.

Kyle stood there looking at the two of them and rolled his eyes. When they continued, he glanced at his watch and cleared his throat. "Ty, let the girl breathe."

They broke their kiss and Tyler glared at his brother. "God, you need to get a woman. Why don't you go fix that?"

"I do just fine thanks."

Tyler shook his head and looked at Zoey. "I will call you when I land, and just about a million times a day. It will be like I am still here."

Zoey nodded, still a little breathless from his kiss, and said her goodbyes to the two men.

When Zoey arrived at the bakery, she saw Dana waiting at the front door. Zoey had asked her to come in early to work on daily prep so she could work on a wedding cake that had been an emergency order from a bride whose other bakery had backed out of her order.

After a few hours, Zoey had an interview for another part-time employee. When she walked out front, she found a little old lady sitting at the table dressed in what looked like her Sunday best including her feather adorned hat. She smiled at Zoey and her dentures popped out of place. Zoey wondered if she hired her just how many times those dentures would fall into the cake batter. Zoey thought she may also be a little more than confused. The application said that she graduated with her high school diploma six years ago under her education section.

"Hello, I am Penny Nolan," the woman said as she reached out her hand to Zoey. Zoey held Penny's frail hand and returned the introduction.

Zoey took an assessing look at Penny and saw quite a bit of mischief in her eyes. "So, Mrs. Nolan you are here for the part time position with the bakery?"

"Yes. I am a very experienced baker and need something to do with my extra time."

Just then another man seated at a nearby table decided to join in the conversation. "She doesn't need the job; she just wants to get closer to the gossip."

Zoey gave a sideways glace at Penny. "The gossip?"

Penny sighed. "Oh fine. Yes, I want the job and I have an ear for local gossip now and then. But I can't help it if people like to tell me things."

Zoey heard a hard loud "HA!" coming from the next table.

"Well, I would need someone who can help with prep and deliveries. It is a physically demanding job. The trays and pastries can be very heavy and sometimes wedding cakes can be up to two hundred pounds fully constructed. You would be on your feet for the entire shift and it is a fast-paced environment. Is this something you feel comfortable with?" Zoey was hoping she was getting her point across. While Penny looked like she could handle herself well, she didn't think the job would be the best fit for her. Zoey had even noticed how she had lost ten pounds since she began working in the bakery.

Penny took a minute to consider the demands of the job. "Well dear, I didn't realize a bakery would be that intense. Maybe I will just continue to come in and enjoy your fine baking." She reached her hands out, clasped Zoey's hands into hers and looked around her surroundings and whispered, "So how about you tell me all about your little romance with our resident hot computer nerd?"

"What?" Zoey gasped.

"Oh, come now. The whole town knows that you and Tyler are going all hot and heavy."

Laughter came from the man at the next table and Zoey could hear him say something about good luck as he got up and left the shop. Zoey shook her head to clear her mind. She could remember her grandmother, and how she was always nosing into her personal life, but this woman didn't even know her. *Small town life* she thought.

Zoey finally said, "Mrs. Nolan I appreciate your time today and I will let Tyler know that you said hello." There. Hopefully, that would be enough for the curious older woman.

As she was trying to excuse herself from Mrs. Nolan, her phone that had been sitting on the table buzzed. She had muted the phone for the interview and the screen lit up from a text message from Tyler.

Tyler: Hello Sweetness. Just landed. I miss those sweet lips on mine. Talk soon.

Penny was quick and sharp. She read the text before Zoey was able to put her phone away. With a smile Penny said, "Well looks like things are progressing nicely with the two of you. If he misbehaves just let me know. I will get him straightened out real quick."

Penny hurriedly said goodbye and walked out the front door. Zoey was dumbstruck. What just happened? Zoey was beginning to think that the old lady wasn't even interested in the job, and just wanted to scope her out for the gossip. Good lord.

Josie came over from her usual table and looked at Zoey shaking her head. "You do know that text will be all over social media, right?"

"What? I am sure she doesn't mess with all that stuff."

Josie belly laughed—a whole uncontrollable silly belly laugh. "You are in for a rude awakening. That old bat has Facebook, Instagram, Snap Chat...you name it. She gets bored and loves to interfere in peoples' lives. And honey you have been a topic of hers a few times."

Zoey's face grew pale. "Oh my God, Josie. Why didn't you guys tell me about this earlier?"

"I thought you knew. Or at least Tyler or Derek would have told you about it. You were kind of big news with the break in and opening of the bakery."

"Well, I expected that from the paper, but not some old lady."

"Eh. She's harmless, but if she feels like your life needs fixing, she has a nasty tendency to meddle on social media until you get your life back together."

"Really? Who else has she terrorized?"

"Kyle was a focus for a little while after he came back from Philly. There have been many others, but our little group has escaped most of the focus, so far."

Zoey sagged down in her chair and shook her head. "And the sad part is, I still need another part-time employee. She was my last applicant."

Josie placed her hand on Zoey's arm and said calmly, "You will find someone. People always need jobs."

The remainder of Zoey's day ran by in a blur of activity. She had a consultation for a child's birthday cake that rivaled in size of any wedding cake. The mother wanted a carousel cake that actually spun like a real carousel. Zoey said that it shouldn't be a problem, but it would cost extra for the motor and structural adjustments that would be needed to get the desired effects. The woman said that money was no object and then decided to complicate it a bit further by requesting to add colorful lights on the canopy top. Zoey wasn't the best with lighting and mechanical aspects of large cake demands, but knew that if needed, she could ask for assistance from Tyler or Facetime Xander if she got desperate.

Zoey was getting ready to close for the day when Josie came and knocked on her office door. "Hey, hope you don't mind. Dana let me in as she was leaving."

"No problem. We headed to your place now?"

"I thought we would go to McKenna's for dinner and then home."

"That sounds perfect. I would love to see Derek. Anyone else coming?"

"Not tonight that I know of. Chase is covering an extra shift and Dixie has had a busy day and said she needed to rest. I called Kyle and Ariel but all I got from Kyle was a text saying he was too tired, and Ariel didn't respond."

"That is weird. Is she okay?"

Josie shrugged. "I think so. I peeked in her storefront window and she was dealing with an angry customer. The guy was yelling at her and I was going to stop in to help but she stood up on her tiptoes and was poking the guy on his chest. She was giving it back to him as good as he gave it. So maybe we will hear from her later."

"The poor thing. It is a gift shop. What on earth could someone get so upset about when buying gifts?"

Josie laughed. "You need to have her tell you about just how upset people got with her during Christmas time. If she didn't have what they were looking for they got a bit crazy."

The girls made their way to McKenna's. It was a slow night, and they found Derek sitting at the bar going over paperwork. Zoey bounced over to her friend and wrapped him in a hug from behind.

Derek turned around and smiled. "Hey Zoe. Missed you too." Then he saw Josie and gave her a nod. "Hi Josie."

"Derek. You joining us for dinner?"

"Yes, we are slow, and I am going home after we eat."

After they sat down at their booth for a few minutes they were joined by Ariel. She let out a long-suffering sigh as she sat down and said, "I had the worst day at work today. What is with people? This guy was looking for a certain collectable piece that I didn't have. I told him I would be more than happy to order it for him, and I would have it ready for him in about a week. And then he just freaked out. He called me a useless bitch and said that Amazon could do better."

Josie turned and said in a tight voice, "Please tell me that is the asshole that you were poking in the chest earlier."

"Oh...you saw that?"

"Yes. I was going to step in, but you were holding your own."

"Yeah, that was him. By the time I was done telling him how it was and how he needed to correct his manners he did apologize. He bought a different figurine, but I still wanted to smash it on his head."

Zoey laughed. "I had no idea you had such a temper."

Derek said, "Are you kidding me? She never took any of my shit growing up. I made her into a tough cookie."

Ariel slid him a look. "You think that all my greatness is due to you?"

"Of course," he said, beaming.

"Brother dear you better sleep with one eye open tonight. I may have a soft voice and dress like a walking debutant, but I am definitely not a push over."

Derek laughed and then looked at Zoey. "Hey, you want to play a game of pool? I know the owner, and he will let us play for free," he said with a wink.

"Stop wasting your charm on me sir, but I would love a chance to kick your ass."

"I have a bar. I have been practicing."

Zoey smiled. "Okay, let's see how this goes." Zoey was not out of practice either. Shane had a game room with a pool table and dart board. She had a lot of alone time in that house and practiced when she got bored.

Derek allowed Zoey to break, and then she sunk two striped balls. She looked up with an impish smile and a glint in her eyes. "Wow. Imagine that. I got lucky."

"Lucky, huh? Are you telling me that you got better since college?"

"Only a little. I am not going to try to hustle people. That can get a girl in trouble." Zoey missed her next shot and went to stand by the wall while Derek took his shot.

"So how are things going with Ty?" he asked as he sunk his first ball.

"Really good."

"So just how good? I need more details than that."

"I didn't realize you wanted all the orgasmic details."

Derek hit the cue ball wrong and it went flying off the table. "God, Zoe please don't give me those details."

Zoey bent over and picked up the ball and said with a giggle, "I know, I just wanted you to screw up the shot." Zoey lined up her shot and asked, "What exactly do you want to know?"

"Is he treating you right? Is it going too fast for you? Do you need some space?"

"Okay, stop right there." She straightened up and looked him in the eyes from across the table. "I am a big girl, and I am going to make damn sure I don't make the same mistakes that I did before. So yes, he is treating me right. You know him and have for years. Do you really think he wouldn't treat me right?"

"No, not really. But he does seem to be diving in with both feet quickly. Do you feel ready for all of this?"

Zoey missed her shot and went to the barstool. "It has been months since Shane. And I didn't think that I was ready at first, but when he touches me my heart just stops. I get butterflies when he smiles at me, like I am some dumb teenager. And when I am not with him, I miss him even if it has only been a few hours. The whole thing is crazy, but a good crazy."

Derek nodded and then went next to her after missing his shot. "Is it like it was with Trevor?"

Zoey felt a pang hit her in the chest. That pain never seemed to go away. Each time she heard his name her mind would drift away for a few minutes and she could feel her eyes glaze over in sadness. It had lessened over the years, but never seemed to leave completely. "In some ways yes, but in so many ways no. With Tyler, it is a more grown-up version of the feelings that I had for Trevor. Trevor was my first love. It was always wonderful with him, but with all the experiences I have had since him, good and bad, I am a different person. And feel love differently." Zoey wiggled her hips as she sunk her next two balls.

"So, you are in love with him?"

Zoey sighed and gave a pointed look at Derek.

"Right. Have you told him yet?"

Zoey missed her shot and Derek slid by her to take his. "I haven't said I love you directly, but I am sure he knows."

"Has he said it yet?"

Zoey took a breath before replying. "No. Sometimes I think he wants to tell me, but he still hasn't said those words."

"You may have to say it first."

"Uh-uh. No way. That is the death card. Having a girl say it first rings of desperation. What has happened when one of your girls said it first, or for that matter when anyone ever said it to you?"

Derek gave a slight laugh. "I let one girl stick around who said they loved me," he said with a wink at Zoey.

Zoey rolled her eyes. "I don't count, and you knew it wasn't romantic love."

"It counts."

Zoey let out an exhausted grunt. Then her phone lit up and started ringing. She saw that it was Tyler and answered the phone. Derek made a motion to ask if she wanted another drink. Zoey nodded and Derek headed to the bar.

"Hey Tyler. How was your flight?"

"Good. We landed a little early and I was able to check in and get some work done. How are things for you?"

"Good. I am at McKenna's with Derek, Ariel and Josie. Ariel had a bad day at work and Derek and I have been playing some pool."

"You kicking his ass?"

"Of course."

"I miss you already."

"I miss you too. This is going to be an awful couple of weeks."

"Maybe we will get lucky and I can get done early to come home."

"That would be awesome, *and* I would make sure your greeting home would be worth your extra effort."

Tyler gave a throaty groan. "I will do my best." Then a knock in the background came through. "Zoey, I have to go. Room service just came with my dinner. I miss you and will call you tomorrow."

"Okay miss you too. Night Tyler." She desperately wanted to tell him that she loved him but did not want the first time she said it to be over the phone. She turned to place the phone on the table where their drinks were, but when she turned the cue stick hit a man dressed in a pricey designer button-down shirt and dress pants. The man's drink tilted and spilled all over his shirt and onto the floor. She gasped and began to apologize to the man who was now soaked in beer. "Oh my gosh I am so sorry. Let me..."

"Jesus, are you a fucking idiot?" the man shouted.

Stunned Zoey just blinked. People were turning to look at her and she wanted to crawl under the table. "I... I'm sorry. I didn't mean to... let me get you another drink."

"You really are a stupid fat bitch. You ruined my shirt." He was screaming now, and Zoey backed up as far as she could until the back of her thighs were hitting the edge of the pool table. The man matched each step forward as she stepped back. Then Zoey saw a hand grab the man by his

shoulder and spun him around. Derek had turned him to
face him with a red flushed face.

"You need to apologize to the lady," Derek said with a
scowl.

"That fucking bitch ruined my shirt. It probably costs
more than she makes in a week."

"You need to leave. Now."

"You can't make me leave."

"Yes, I can. I own the place." By now others joined behind Derek including Josie and Tiny from the back kitchen.
The man's friend who came in with him also stood behind
him in a show of solidarity.

Zoey was shaking uncontrollably. She was still only
about two feet from the man who was now clenching his
fists. Zoey didn't want Derek to get hurt over this. She took
a deep breath and tried to gently step in between the men.

"Sir. I am happy to pay." The man glowered at her and
looked down at her with disgust and closed the gap between
them. Then Shane's voice came slamming in her mind. *You
are such a fucking idiot. Can't you do anything right?* Those
words were playing on repeat in her mind.

One night she had tried to cook dinner when Shane
came storming into the kitchen and slammed his briefcase
on the counter. Zoey had just pulled dinner out of the oven
and his temper startled her, which caused her to drop the
glass pan with the chicken she had just made. The pan
crashed to the ground and shattered while the chicken and
grease spread all over the kitchen floor. Shane closed the gap
between them and yelled those and other hateful words at

her while he threw the shattered pieces around the kitchen causing a bigger mess.

Another night Shane brought a file home from work, and she had moved it off the counter so she could cook dinner and put it on his desk. Later, he was looking for the file and she asked him what he was looking for. After he told her it was the file he put on the counter, she explained that she moved it from the kitchen and into the office. He yelled at her about how he had put it in the kitchen for a reason and again called her a fucking idiot. Every time he wanted to remind her just how worthless she was, he would move closer into her space and raise his voice so she would know just who was in control in their relationship. The volume of his voice vibrated in her ears each time and the fear always made her motionless, just waiting for what would happen next.

Derek's voice brought her back to the present. "Zoey, get out of here." Derek then looked back at the man and continued, "Consider your bill paid in full and get out."

Zoey felt a hand pull her from in between the two men and found herself getting dragged back to the other side by Josie. She could hear the indistinguishable arguments coming from Derek and the man. Looking to the other side she saw Ariel on her cell phone. A loud crash came from the direction of the men. She couldn't tell what happened or how it started but the two of them were tangled in each other's limbs and Tiny was taking the man's friend by the arm and escorting him out of the bar. Zoey reached her hands up to her mouth and feared for her friend's safety.

Suddenly she saw Austin pulling the man away from Derek along with a few other firemen who were splitting up the fight. Once they were separated, Derek swiped his arm across his mouth to wipe blood that was coming from the corner. The man was now sitting in a chair where Austin and two other firemen were standing over him to make sure he didn't cause trouble, but she could see him studying her. He had blood from his nose and mouth and wiped it off all while keeping a steady stare on her. Zoey's breath quickened and she could feel her head lighten and heart race. Shane's voice was still echoing in her head. *Fat lazy bitch... worthless... boring...fucking idiot...cold fish...stupid.* Her legs began to wobble and before she could fight the haze back to the present day, she felt two hands cupping her face.

"Zoey, look at me. Jesus, slow your breathing down sweetie." It was Derek. She knew his voice, but her memories were blinding her now and she couldn't shake it off. "Josie get her a chair quick!"

Zoey felt Derek ease her into the chair and finally was able to slow her breathing down and escape the flashbacks. She shook her head and looked Derek in the eyes.

"There you are. Are you okay?" Derek asked.

Zoey took a shaky breath and said, "Yes, but oh my god Derek you're bleeding."

Derek gave a shrug. "I'm okay."

Then from behind him, Chase and a deputy came walking up to Zoey and Derek.

Chase looked at Zoey with a frown. "You okay Zoey?"

Zoey nodded. "I am not the one who got hit." Then she gave a slight nod to Derek who was again bleeding by the corner of his mouth.

Derek stood up and looked at Chase. The deputy went over to the man who was still surrounded by the firemen. "Someone called you?"

Chase looked over at Ariel and said, "She did."

Ariel looked at Derek and said, "Did you really think I was just going to watch the two of you beat the shit out of each other without calling Chase?"

Derek shook his head. "Mr. Sunshine over there got a little out of hand and I had asked him to leave. He got pissed and then started to hit me. Tiny escorted his friend out while he decided to try to destroy my bar and my face."

Zoey stood up, "Chase this is my fault. I spilled beer on him, and he got mad."

Derek growled. "This isn't your fault. He didn't accept your nice apology and acted like an asshole."

Chase pinched the bridge of his nose with his hand and said, "Okay Derek, come with me and let's talk about what happened." The two men disappeared into the kitchen.

Josie wrapped her arm around Zoey's waist as they watched the other man get placed into handcuffs. The man was now sitting in the booth while the deputy was talking to the fireman and getting details of the incident. The man glared at Zoey and continued to smirk at her, like he knew he was better than her, and she was worthless. His stare continued to grow into an almost soulless gaze. Zoey started to panic. What if Chase had to arrest Derek too? She started to feel nauseous and increased her breathing and heart rate again. Shane's voice again intruded inside her head. *You destroy everything you touch. You can't do anything right. Nobody will ever love you. I can't blame your dad for leaving you.*

The room started to spin. Sounds began to muffle as her blood rushed through her head and into her ears. She was going to pass out.

Josie saw her starting to sway and made her sit back down again and yelled, "Austin, get your ass over here!"

Zoey could feel Austin grabbing her by her wrist to take her pulse. "Zoey, can you hear me? I need you to slow your breathing down. You are hyperventilating and you will pass out if you don't calm down." He turned to Josie, "How long has she been like this?"

"I don't know—a few minutes, maybe."

Zoey's head started to clear, and she looked at Josie who had a worried expression on her face. She cleared her throat and said in a whisper, "I'm okay." She concentrated on slowing her breathing and felt her face start to warm back up.

"Good Zoey. That is better." Austin started looking around and finally looked at Josie. "Where's Tyler? Someone should go get him."

Josie shook her head. "He is out of town for work. She came here with me."

"Get her some water."

Josie nodded and went to the bar to get the water.

Austin looked back to Zoey, who was looking much calmer now and had color returning to her face. "Girls' night out gone all wrong, huh?"

Zoey shook her head. "Derek will love to know you think of him as one of the girls."

Austin laughed. "Well he certainly fought like a girl." Austin glanced down at his watch and still had his hand on

Zoey's wrist taking her pulse. He nodded and let go as Josie came back with the water.

Zoey accepted the glass and took a drink.

The three sat in silence for a few minutes and Chase and Derek came back up front. As Derek walked over to them Austin was still squatting in front of Zoey assessing her in an EMT pose. Derek looked at Josie who shook her head.

"Zoe, you okay," he asked.

"I'll be fine," Zoey said. She looked at Chase and asked, "Are you arresting Derek too?"

Chase shook his head. "No. We are taking the other guy in though. He started the fight and destroyed bar property. Everything will be okay."

Austin stood beside Zoey and looked at Derek. "She was hyperventilating. She almost passed out. She should go home and get some rest."

Josie looked at Chase and asked, "Do you need her for anything, or can I take her home?"

Chase shook his head. "No, I am good. Take her home."

Josie stood beside Zoey and said, "Let's go sweetie."

Zoey was too overwhelmed to argue and was frustrated with herself. She wasn't hurt and yet she panicked to the point where Josie thought she needed medical attention. She didn't want attention drawn to her like this. She should have been able to handle what happened without nearly passing out.

They got to Josie's apartment and Zoey sat on her couch. Josie brought Zoey a glass of water and a blanket. Zoey looked up and thanked Josie. For a while they just sat in silence. Josie seemed to know the value of keeping secrets and being willing to talk when she was ready. Zoey's eyes were glazing over and reliving memories in her head. Finally, Josie stood and said, "I am going to take a shower and get ready for bed. Is there anything else I can bring you?"

"No, thank you."

Zoey heard the rushing water come from the bathroom when she heard a knock coming from Josie's front door. She opened it to find Derek standing before her with a couple bruises and cuts on his face and holding her phone up in the air.

He quirked a smile and said, "Your phone was ringing off the hook. Tyler is going crazy. You better call him back."

"Thanks for bringing it to me. Do you want to come inside for a few minutes? Josie is in the shower."

"Yeah, thanks. I left Tiny in charge for the rest of the night. I wasn't feeling like being a people person anymore."

Derek came inside and sat down on the couch with Zoey. Zoey found several texts and missed calls from Tyler. She winced and said, "I think I need to call him really quick. Do you mind if I call him first?"

"No, please do. He freaked when I picked up your phone."

Zoey dialed and Tyler picked up before it seemed to go through just half a ring tone. Tyler's frantic voice came booming through the line, "God Zoey, Chase sent me a text that you got involved with a bar fight and Austin was treating you at the scene. What the hell happened? Are you okay?"

Zoey started to cry. She desperately wanted Tyler's reassuring arms around her to chase the memories and Shane's voice away. She could only manage a whisper at first, "I'm okay. I am sorry."

"Awe, Zoey you don't have to apologize to me. It's okay. Please, just tell me what happened."

She felt Derek place his hand on her arm in an attempt to calm her down, then she continued. "Derek and I were playing pool. Then after I spoke to you on the phone, I turned with the cue stick and bumped into a man and spilled beer on his shirt. I tried to apologize, but he was so mad and started yelling at me and calling me an idiot. I still tried to say that I was sorry, and he called me a fat bitch."

"Are you kidding me?" Zoey heard Tyler's clear frustration and could almost see him rubbing the back of his neck the way he always does when he gets upset.

"No. Then Derek stepped in and told him that he needed to apologize. It looked like the man was going to hit Derek, so I stepped in the middle of them both and tried to offer to pay for his shirt, but he advanced in on me like..." Zoey couldn't finish. She lost her voice and started to cry again. After a long pause she heard Tyler's soft kind voice break through.

"Like what Zoey?"

After a sigh Zoey said, "Like Shane used to do when he would yell at me, and I was afraid he was going to do something more. Anyway, someone pulled me out from between them, and I don't really know much of how it happened from there but this guy and Derek were fighting and glass was breaking. At some point Austin and some of the other firemen broke up the fight. Chase and one of his deputies showed up. The deputy arrested that guy while Chase was talking to Derek in the back."

"When did Austin have to take care of you?"

"It was while Derek and Chase were in the back room. The man was sitting in the bar and kept looking at me. He was glaring at me as if I were nothing and he knew he could get away with anything." Zoey sighed. "I know that look. I lived with that look for too long. Then all the things that Shane used to say to me came flooding back and I couldn't stop it. Some of them were the same things this man said to me earlier. I felt like I was back in Lexington and just stuck there, waiting for the silent punishments I had to suffer through every day. All of a sudden, I couldn't breathe, I couldn't get enough breath into my lungs and the harder I tried to stop suffocating the worse it got. I felt like I was drowning, and my head became so light. Josie got Austin to come over and was able to calm me down enough before I passed out."

Zoey could hear Tyler struggling to get his breathing under control. She knew this was the most that she had told him about her relationship with Shane. After a few moments Tyler asked, "What happened with the guy?"

"They arrested him and then I left to get back to Josie's." Zoey looked over at Derek who was running his free hand through his hair.

"I am coming home. I will get the first flight I can get out of here."

"No. You have a job to do. You can't risk your company's reputation because some guy put me in a tailspin."

"I don't want to leave you alone when you are dealing with all this, and I am not just talking about this asshole."

"I am not alone. I am at Josie's, like each of you insisted. And Derek is here right now too. I will be okay until you can come back. This was a fluke. We have been to McKenna's before and nothing like this has ever happened. It just threw me. I wasn't expecting to run into another version of Shane."

Tyler sighed. "I know you are right, but I would just feel better knowing you are in my arms, safe. Please promise me that you will call me right away when or if something like that happens. Chase is a great guy, but sucks at telling a story. I had all kinds of things running through my mind when he said Austin had to treat you at the scene."

"I promise. Now get some rest so I can call you early to wish you a good morning."

"Ok. Good night Sweetness."

"Good night." Zoey hung up the phone and put it on the table in front of her and Derek.

Derek was frowning and then Josie came from the hallway in shorts and a tank top. Josie took the chair and arched an eyebrow at Derek. He shrugged at her and said, "I brought Zoey her phone. She left it at the bar, and Tyler was blowing it up after Chase ratted us all out."

Josie shook her head. "Great, now nerd boy will never trust us with her again."

Zoey gave out a huff. "Hey! I am sitting right here."

Derek leaned over and gave her a hug. "We know. Just trying to make you smile."

Zoey sniffed. "You guys suck."

Josie looked at Derek and gave a wink. "We know, but we are the two resident bad asses, and we have a rep to uphold."

Zoey thought for a second and said, "I think Chase would take offense to not being included in the bad ass list."

Josie just smiled and said, "I just think of him as a hungry bear who can arrest people. He is all cuddly when he is fed."

Zoey looked out the window behind Josie's couch and sighed. "Maybe I shouldn't have come here. I am causing too much trouble. I didn't mean to..."

Derek put his hand on her face and moved it to look at him. "Stop it right there Zoey. You are not trouble. There are people out in the world who will always cause problems. They will take it out on you or someone else they find. I wanted you here. Ariel wanted you here, and I can safely say that there are so many more people here now who want you here too."

Josie nodded in agreement. "He's right you know. Who gives a crap if other people cause problems? Screw them. We love having you here. And don't let nerd boy hear you talk like that or he would be on a plane back here so fast your head would spin. Besides, if you leave, he would go back to sulky depressed nerd boy which was just annoying."

"He was sulky?" Zoey asked. She found that so hard to believe. He had always been so light and easy since she had met him.

Derek nodded. "Josie's right. He mostly kept to himself up in the apartment and worked on his computer. I mean he would come to the bar or poker night, but he didn't talk much, at least not until you broke into his apartment."

With a slight smile Zoey said, "I didn't break in. I had the key."

"There's my girl."

The three of them sat and talked for a few minutes about the nights events and as it started to grow silent Josie spoke up. "I have to confess I heard most of your call with Tyler. What did you mean by silent punishments with Shane?"

"It took a long time to leave Shane. I didn't see our relationship as abusive. He never hit me. For some reason that seemed to provide enough reason to stay and suffer through how he would treat me. If I did something that he disapproved of he would find ways to punish me. He would place wedges between me and my friends and family, or he would withhold the kind of affection I wanted."

"What do you mean by affection?" Derek asked.

Slightly mortified, she wasn't sure she wanted to clarify but knew that she needed to talk to someone. "One night we had a fight because I was late getting home because of work. He didn't believe me. He thought that I was cheating on him. I tried to cuddle up to him to show him that I cared about him, but he wouldn't move or let me in." She looked away from them both because she couldn't look either of them in the eye while she confessed the next part. "He said that he wouldn't give me what I wanted until I gave him what he wanted."

Josie immediately understood what Zoey was saying and said, "Bastard."

Derek was still confused. "What did he want?"

Zoey continued. "He wouldn't kiss or hold me until I would go down on my knees and..."

Derek immediately put his hand in Zoey's and said, "Stop. You don't need to finish that. God Zoey, I wish you would have reached out to me sooner."

"I know. I wish that I would have too. There were so many little things like that, that just happened over and over again. The whole thing is just mortifying. Each time I look back at all the things I did or the things he said to me it rips at my soul. The more time I spend here with people who care about me the more I know and understand how awful it was. Tonight just brought back some flashbacks, and I didn't handle it right."

"Have you told Tyler about all of this?"

Zoey shook her head. "Some of it but not all the details. I know I should open up more to him about it, but sometimes I am afraid that if I tell him everything, he might be disgusted with me."

Josie set her water down, cleared her throat and said, "Sweetie, with Tyler, that is something you do not have to be worried about. That boy is crazy about you, and I am talking about the crazy that I have never seen before. I am pretty sure he is in love with you."

Zoey looked at her two friends and said, "He hasn't said it yet. I don't know."

Derek said, "We do. Trust us. He is completely in love with you, and I am happy for you. He had just better realize that I am not going anywhere either. I will always be your best friend."

Zoey smiled and said, "Always."

Chapter 16

It had been a quiet week since the incident at McKenna's when Chase's cell phone buzzed on his desk. He quickly recognized the number as Detective Buxton's. *Finally,* he thought. He picked up the phone and greeted the detective.

"Thanks for calling. Please tell me you were able to get something from his financial records," Chase said.

"Nothing. We checked his credit cards and his bank accounts. Then we got a subpoena for the girlfriend's records to see if he charged it to her account, and we got nothing. He must have used cash the whole trip."

Chase scrubbed his hand down his face. "Have you guys had any interactions with him lately?"

"No. We were able to do this quietly behind the scenes."

"Do you think he would still be a threat to Zoey, or has he refocused his attention?"

"We don't think he would be ballsy enough to go back for more over there, but you know as well as I do that we can't give any guarantees."

"Right. I really appreciate all the extra effort you guys put into this."

"Of course. We hate this as much as you do. My partner and I know that he did this, but we have no proof to help you out. If anything changes or comes to light, we will call you right away."

"Okay, thanks."

Chase pulled Zoey's file and looked again at all the evidence pictures and reports from that night. He really wanted an arrest on this. His best friend's girlfriend and he couldn't fix it or at least provide some justice. Frustrated, he made some notations on the file and placed it back in the cabinet, slamming the drawer shut. He needed to update Zoey on her case. He briefly thought about stopping by the bakery but decided that delivering bad news would best be done after working hours to give her some time to process. He knew that Josie was out of town again and Zoey was going to be at Derek's tonight. He would stop by Derek's after his shift was over to talk to her.

Ariel was slicing up the lasagna she made and went to sit with Zoey for dinner. Derek was still at the bar and wouldn't be home until after twelve so the girls had some quality time. "Have you talked to Tyler?"

Zoey nodded her head. "Yes, but our conversations have been so short. He is exhausted. I know that he didn't get back to the hotel last night until after eight-thirty his time. I was so tired from my day too, so we spent a lot of time just kind of breathing and then we fell asleep with our phones in our hands. My phone was dead when I woke up."

"That is so sweet and romantic though."

"It is just sweet and romantic from the outside. I miss him, and it scares the hell out of me that he affects me so much and this quickly. I am so afraid I am going to be left in pieces at the end of this."

"I don't think it is going to end like that. He is not that guy."

"I know that, but Trevor wasn't that guy either and through no fault of his own he left, and I was just shattered in pieces. There are still small things that hit me all these years later that seem to find one of those broken pieces of my heart—and then uses that piece to rip it back open again. They say that time heals all wounds, but what they don't tell you is how much it hurts to break them open again. And this goes for all memories...good and bad." Zoey flashed back to the scene at the bar when the man reminded her of how Shane made her feel worthless and alone.

Ariel watched with her soulful eyes at her friend who seemed to rip open more wounds and said, "I understand that too, but the new memories are what helps all the old memories hurt a little less each time. When you are with Tyler do those painful memories come back?"

Zoey thought for a few seconds and replied, "No. When we are together, it is just me and him. Everything else just seems to disappear."

"That is incredible and rare. Embrace it."

Breaking the silence the girls had just settled into came three loud knocks on the front door. Zoey looked at Ariel and asked, "Were you expecting someone?"

Ariel shook her head and went to peer out the window to the porch. "It's just Chase."

"Seriously, did he just smell the food and drift over here?" Zoey asked with a giggle.

Ariel looked back at the pan, frowned and said, "I didn't make enough for him."

Ariel opened the door and let Chase in. She looked up at him and asked, "You came for dinner?"

Chase grimly shook his head. "I need to talk to Zoey. Can you give us a couple minutes?"

Zoey stood up with a slight panic and said, "Is Tyler okay?"

Chase nodded and blew out a breath. "Yes, he is fine. I was here about the break in."

"Oh. Okay, well Ariel can stay. Anything you tell me I will just tell her later, anyway."

Chase rubbed his hand across his jaw and inhaled deeply. "Lexington PD called today, and they were not able to get the evidence we were hoping for to arrest Shane. I still hope that something will come up, but I have to you tell you that it isn't looking good. He may get away with it."

Zoey sat back down and looked at the floor. "It's okay Chase. I knew it would be hard to prove anything. And who knows, it may not have been him."

"Oh, it was him. I have no doubt in my mind."

"Okay, but nothing has happened since that night. Do you think I am still in danger?"

"I think the risk is lower, but I can't give any guarantees Zoey."

"Well how about the babysitters? Can I ditch the babysitters?"

"Hey," exclaimed Ariel.

Zoey looked over at her friend with an apologetic look. "Sorry Ariel but I haven't had any time to myself, and I just feel silly now sleeping at everyone else's house. I need my independence back."

Chase looked at the two women and sighed. "I don't feel comfortable with you alone yet, but I understand why you are getting frustrated. How about you put up with your 'babysitters' at least until Tyler gets back? If he found out that I knew ahead of time that you were trying to stay on your own and didn't stop you, he would kill me. He should be back in about a week, right?"

Zoey groaned in frustration. "Yes."

Chase tilted his head and looked at Zoey with a stern gaze.

"Fine," Zoey said, "but only until Tyler gets back."

"And you think when he gets back you are going to be alone? That is funny," said Ariel.

Zoey rolled her eyes and said, "That is different."

Chase then longingly looked at the lasagna and back to Ariel. She recognized that plea for food and said, "Okay fine. Come on I will serve you a piece."

Chase sat next to Zoey at the table while Ariel got him some dinner. Chase looked at Zoey and said, "Where's Dixie? I didn't think she would miss a chance for girl bonding night."

"She is out with Jay again," replied Zoey.

Chase's jaw clenched. "isn't that like the third time this week? She is just ditching her friends now?"

Ariel set the plate in front of Chase. "Here grumpy bear. Eat this, and she isn't ditching us. We are all going to Zoey's for girl's night when Josie gets back."

Ariel looked at Zoey who just gave her a shrug. Zoey thought that if Chase and Dixie didn't figure their stuff out soon, it was going to get really ugly. But this was something that should be addressed by the best friend and not her. She made a mental note to talk to Tyler about it when he got back.

CHASE FINISHED HIS meal and thanked the girls for dinner. After he got into his car, he called Tyler.

Tyler answered a little breathlessly. "Hey, what's up?"

"I have an update about the break in."

"Great. Please tell me that asshole got arrested."

Chase groaned. "No, afraid not. We weren't able to get any financial evidence to tie him to coming out here, and you know we weren't able to pull anything from the scene."

Tyler's frustration rose. "So, this asshole is going to get away with terrorizing her?"

"It isn't looking good. Something may come up but for now yes, he is getting away with it." Chase then heard a loud thud coming from the background of Tyler's end. "I just told Zoey about it. She is at Derek and Ariel's."

"How did she take it?"

"She was disappointed, but she is okay. She is getting tired of all the babysitters, and honestly I don't blame her."

"She needs to stay with them at least until I can get back."

"She is. I talked to her, and she promised to stay until you get back. And when is that exactly?"

"I am coming back in day after tomorrow. I have been working fourteen-hour days to get this project and training done so I could surprise her and come home early."

"She will love that."

"Yeah, I know. Listen I have to go. I need to get back to work so I can come home."

"Okay. See you soon."

THE NEXT MORNING ZOEY and Dana were working when it finally slowed down enough for Zoey to take a small break. She went back to her office and looked at her phone and saw that she'd missed a call and a text from Tyler. God, she missed him. She opened her text to see his message.

Tyler: Good morning Sweetness. Sorry we couldn't catch each other last night. Miss you and can't wait to see you soon.

Zoey sighed and sent a reply.

Zoey: I miss you too. We have a lot of catching up to do.

For the past few nights, she had tried to talk to Tyler, and he was working late to finish the project. Another night he had gone out to dinner with the CEO of the company and she didn't want to interrupt. He had called her when he got back, but she was so tired she had fallen asleep. She was frustrated with how little they were able to talk since he had been gone but she understood how important this was for his business and tried to keep a positive attitude. Zoey sighed and returned a few emails and then went back up front to help Dana.

At the front of the line she saw Kyle and Derek. They looked like they just came back from the gym. Kyle ordered the daily special of I've Got the Blues Muffin, which was a blueberry streusel muffin.

Derek looked at the daily special and frowned. "How is it going Zoe?"

Zoey gave a shrug and said, "Okay."

Derek arched an eyebrow at her. "Really going to give me that line of crap?"

"Have you talked to Chase?"

"No, but Ariel told me what he said. I am so sorry Zoey."

"It's okay. Frustrating but okay."

"Anything else?"

"Not really."

Dana gave a short laugh. "She misses Tyler."

Zoey turned to frown at Dana. "Yeah that too."

Then the front door of the bakery chimed and in strolled a man in his late twenties who was well built and dressed in a navy-blue polo shirt and khakis. Nearly filling the doorway, he was tall, with short brown hair and sunglasses pushed to the top of his head. He approached the counter, and as Zoey was able to focus her gaze, she gave a little shriek of excitement and ran up to him. She wrapped her arms around his neck as he picked her up in a giant hug.

Kyle looked stunned. He looked at the pair as they were hugging. He then looked at Derek who had a big grin on his face. In a protective growly voice he said, "Who is this guy?"

Derek grinned and placed his hand on Kyle's shoulder. "Calm down, it is just Xander." Derek walked over to the pair and greeted Xander.

Kyle stood there dumbfounded. "And that was supposed to help me how?"

Zoey finally let go of Xander and said, "I can't believe you are here. You didn't tell me you were coming."

"I wanted it to be a surprise. I missed you and wanted to check this place out. I have a lot of time off at work, so I decided to take a week and come for a visit. I hope you don't mind."

"Are you kidding me?!?! This is fantastic. I have missed you so much."

Derek greeted Xander with a handshake. He had known Xander since he was a teenager when he would come to visit Zoey at school. Xander had always liked Derek, and the two had always gotten along very well. Xander never went through the bratty phase that most teenagers did. He was always respectful of everyone and had a lot of love for his sister.

Zoey saw Kyle's face looking a little confused, and she brought Xander over to meet him. "Kyle, this is my little brother, Xander."

Kyle's face suddenly looked like a light bulb went off in his head and Zoey had to give a small laugh. He extended his hand to Xander and said, "It is very nice to meet you."

"Nice to meet you as well," Xander said accepting Kyle's greeting.

Zoey looked between the two men and then said, "Kyle is Tyler's brother, and Derek's best friend."

Xander nodded. "So where is Tyler? I really want to meet this guy."

Zoey's face fell a little. "He is in Chicago for business, but if you are staying for a week, you should get to see him before you leave. You are going to stay with me, right?"

Xander shrugged. "I thought I might stay at one of the B&Bs."

"Absolutely not. You are staying with me." Zoey was supposed to stay with Derek again that night, but she knew he would feel okay with Xander staying with her. She gave a pointed look at Derek who just nodded with understanding. "Is your stuff in the car?"

"Yeah, but can you feed me first? I drove straight through and have been looking forward to your food."

Zoey smiled and led him over to the counter when he ordered coffee and a chocolate croissant.

ARIEL CAME INTO THE bakery and joined Derek and Kyle who were sitting at the table to enjoy their breakfast. She looked over at the counter where Zoey and Xander were talking. She gazed over at Xander and got a starry-eyed smile. "Who is the hot guy with Zoey?"

Kyle shot her a look and said, "The hot guy?"

Ariel rolled her eyes and said, "Yeah the tall muscular brown-haired cutie over there."

Kyle's jaw clenched and Derek laughed.

Derek finally said, "That is Zoey's brother, Xander."

Ariel's eyes widened. "That is Xander? Wow."

Kyle gave a slight huff. "He isn't that wow."

Ariel looked at Kyle and smiled brighter. "Don't worry, you are still a giant stack of hotness too."

"And I am not wow worthy?"

"Don't push it Ashford," Ariel said with a shaking of her head. She got up to go and introduce herself to Xander.

Kyle watched Ariel walk over to them and laugh as she started talking to Zoey and Xander.

Derek watched his friend and said, "This is a mess of your own making. You could fix it whenever you wanted. You know that, right?"

"It can't be fixed. You know that."

"Anything can be fixed. You just have to want to fix it." He placed a hand on Kyle's shoulder and got up to join Zoey, Xander and Ariel. Kyle finished his coffee shortly afterward and gave a small wave to everyone as he left.

THAT NIGHT ARIEL, DIXIE, Jay, Xander and Zoey went to McKenna's for dinner. They had just ordered their drinks when Dixie asked, "Where is Kyle? He never misses McKenna's when we all go out."

Ariel frowned. "I called him and invited him out, but he said he had to work tonight."

Zoey asked Xander, "How are things going with that one girl?"

Xander took a long pull from his beer and said, "She has a name Zoey."

"Of course, she does, but I have never met her so it is hard to keep a name in mind when she refuses to meet your family."

"Don't start. And her name is Laura. She is busy with work; she can't just take off whenever she wants. She has responsibilities."

Zoey's frustration was starting to bubble again. Laura and Xander had been dating for over a year and a half. When she did live in Lexington, she was less than two hours away from Xander. When Zoey made the trip up to Cincinnati,

Laura suddenly had meetings or other commitments. If she hadn't heard the woman in the background whenever she called Xander, she would have sworn he made her up. Once, Zoey made Thanksgiving dinner and Laura was expected to make the trip with Xander, but he showed up alone saying that she had to stay home to work on some reports.

"I just think that you should be with someone who takes your priorities into consideration too. This includes your family."

Xander tapped his fingers on the table the way he always did when he was holding something back. "Zoey, she does support me and my decisions. I am sorry that you haven't met her yet, but you will I promise."

Zoey nodded. She knew her brother could take care of himself, but she still had this gut feeling that this woman was nowhere near good enough for him.

Zoey's phone buzzed along the table with a text message.

Tyler: Hello Sweetness. How are you?

Zoey: Good, I am at McKenna's having dinner with everyone.

Tyler: That is great. I just wanted to say that I miss you and can't call tonight. I have to work late again but I promise you will have plenty of my attention tomorrow.

Zoey: It's okay. Everyone is keeping me busy. We will talk tomorrow. Miss you like crazy.

Zoey was disappointed, but she knew that he was trying to get the project done so he could come home on time. She wanted to tell him about the good news that Xander was in town but figured it could wait until tomorrow when they could talk on the phone.

Xander noticed the disappointed look on her face after the texting stopped. "You okay?"

"Yes...no. Tyler is working a lot and said he couldn't talk tonight."

"Are you worried that he is lying to you?"

Zoey sighed. "No. I trust him. He explained everything he has to do to complete the project before he left town, and to be quite honest I can't believe he could finish all this in two weeks instead of three or four. Really if he explained it to you, you would have a better idea that he would be crazy busy. He talked about imaging new computers, installation of his new software and training the staff for the new program."

Xander winced. "Well, imaging new computers can be time consuming. You are basically starting from scratch and have to install everything from email, software to even printers. Then it can take longer if you have employees standing over you asking a ton of questions about computers that have nothing to do with the reason why you are there."

"Remind me again why you work in computer science when you don't even like working with computers."

Xander gave a short laugh. "Money. Actually, it is good money and I don't have to deal with the public, most of the time anyway."

Zoey saw Chase stride into the bar and waved him over. She saw a brief look of confusion when his eyes found Xander sitting next to Zoey. Then his face dropped looking at Dixie with Jay who had his arm draped around her shoulders looking familiar and at ease with each other. Once he reached the table he said, "Hey guys, how is it going?" His eyes fell back to Xander.

Zoey smiled and said, "Really good. Chase this is my brother, Xander. He came to visit me for the week."

Chase's posture relaxed and a wide smile came across his face. "Good to meet you. Hope you have fun with your sister."

"Nice to meet you too. How do you know my sister?"

"She is dating my best friend, and well I have been friends with all these knuckleheads for years. Not to mention I am addicted to her food."

Xander laughed. "Who isn't? I got to live with her food for years and then she took it away from me."

Zoey glared at her brother. "I went to college. Then you went to college and you moved away from me, so hush."

Xander finished his beer and replied, "Yeah. I should have stayed so I could have protected you from that asshole."

Chase laughed. "I like this guy."

Xander stood up and offered to get refills. The girls all nodded. Chase and Jay stood and followed him to help with the next round.

Zoey suddenly felt a quick crumple of napkin hit her cheek. Ariel sat with her arms crossed not looking remotely sorry. "You never said your brother was so hot."

"Contrary to popular belief, just because I am from Kentucky doesn't mean we ogle our relatives. But I am aware that he is cute. He never has had problems with dates. Girlfriends, yes. Dates, no. Besides, what am I supposed to say? Hey, I have a hot brother, but he lives in Cincinnati—you want to meet him?"

Dixie laughed. "She has a point. It is a shame you couldn't get him to move down here. I can tell you guys are close."

Zoey smiled. "Yes, we are, but with his career there isn't much for him here. He makes good money over there and he seems happy. He does the same thing that Tyler does but works for a large company with great benefits and pay."

Ariel sighed. "I get it." Ariel then turned her focus to Dixie. "We don't see you as much. How are things going with Jay?"

Dixie looked over at the guys at the bar waiting for their drinks. "It is good. He is a sweet man. He is very attentive and devoted."

Ariel shook her head. "Geez Dix. You sound like you are talking about your dog and not a lover."

Dixie nearly spit out the last of her drink. "God Ariel! I didn't compare him to my dog."

"No, just his traits. Look when Zoey talks about Tyler, she gets all starry eyed and blushes. You just rattled off a list of nice qualities and had the emotional tone of reading your grocery list."

Zoey wanted to protest about the starry-eyed comment, but she could feel her face blushing. Stupid bodily reactions. She thought about what Ariel said about Dixie and Jay and couldn't agree more. She looked at Dixie and realized that she wasn't ready to face the truth yet and just waited for Dixie to react.

Jay returned with Dixie's drink and kissed her on her cheek while Zoey and Ariel watched for a reaction. Ariel shook her head and said, "Grocery list."

Zoey leaned over to her friend and whispered, "Since when did you lose that cute romantic side."

Ariel shook her head and whispered back, "I haven't, but that," she said as she nodded to Dixie and Jay, "isn't romantic. He likes her a lot more than she does him." She looked down at a silver bracelet with a single charm in the shape of a tree. "I know how much it hurts to be in that situation. I feel sorry for Jay, and for Dixie. This isn't going to end well."

LATER THAT NIGHT ZOEY found herself alone with Xander in the apartment getting ready for bed. They talked for a couple hours about Zoey's new life and more details about Tyler.

"You light up when you talk about him you know," Xander said taking the last cookie from the coffee table.

Zoey felt her face blush. "I know. I can't help it. He is so different from the others. I just get a little afraid sometimes."

"Afraid of what?"

"I dunno. Maybe that I don't deserve him, or that I am disrespecting Trevor by being happy with someone new."

Xander turned and looked at his sister. "Zoey listen to me. First, I hope he is as great as you and everyone else has been telling me, and if he is, I can't think of another person who deserves this more than you. Second, Trevor would want you to be happy, whatever that would mean for you. He wouldn't want you to waste your life waiting for him when he is never coming back."

Zoey looked up as her eyes welled with tears. "I know that he isn't coming back."

Xander sighed. "I know that you know that, but dating guys who were disasters didn't give you this guilt. It didn't show up until a good man came into your life." Xander took Zoey by the hand and continued. "You deserve the best of everything. This includes being happy with Tyler if he is the right one."

"I think he is."

"Good, and you know I am not leaving until I meet this guy, right?"

"Yes Xan, I know. He should be home in a few days, and you are going to love him."

"I will love him as long as he treats you right and takes care of you."

The next morning Xander got up with Zoey and went to the bakery to help her with the shop. She loved having him around and the playful banter they had in the kitchen. After they were done with prep, they worked the front counter during morning rush.

Thanks to Penny Nolan's Facebook page and small-town gossip, word had spread that Zoey's hot brother was in town and helping out at the bakery. Zoey had never seen so many women in her bakery. Then when it came to the regular customers, she noticed how many of the women were not in their normal yoga pants, but instead low-cut blouses and full makeup.

After the parade of young single women slowed down Dana looked exhaustedly at Zoey. "Either your brother can't work here, or we are going to need to hire another person."

Zoey nodded. "I can't believe how crazy it got. I even told several of them he has a girlfriend back home hoping it would slow us down. And I don't even like the girlfriend. Normally I would love to parade a bunch of women in front of him to wake him up."

The two women looked over at Xander who was talking to Ariel and Dixie at a front table. Several women around them were eyeing him in his tight-fitting polo shirt and tried desperately to get his attention away from the girls.

Zoey shook her head. "I am going to have Xander take the day off tomorrow and maybe have Derek take him hiking to give us a break. Watching all these women drool on my little brother is getting a little icky."

Dana laughed. "Good idea."

Chapter 17

Tyler stretched as he got up from his seat on the plane. It was a bumpy flight, and he was ready to get back to Zoey. Looking down at his watch he calculated that he should be able to make it home no later than 6:30. He wasn't able to talk to Zoey as much as he wanted while he was gone and he was excited to see her soon. Working the longer hours so he could leave earlier than expected was going to all be worth it. He was proud that he was making it home three days early. Chase had reported back to him how frustrated Zoey was getting with the "babysitters." He figured that she would only allow it for another day or so before she brought out her stubborn streak and decided to go home alone.

Tyler retrieved his luggage and met Kyle at the designated pick up spot. Kyle grunted a small greeting and handed Tyler a bottle of water. Tyler was all too familiar with Kyle's mood swings and knew when not to poke the bear, but after ten minutes of silence he finally spoke up. "You okay?"

"Why wouldn't I be okay?" Kyle grunted.

"Oh, I don't know. You have that moody pissed off look on your face."

Kyle turned to look at Tyler and made a circling motion with his hands around his face. "This is not my pissed off face. This is my super happy face because I missed my brother."

Tyler laughed. "Is it work?"

"No."

"Mom and dad get on your nerves?"

"No," Kyle said in a long drawn out voice.

Only one other person could put a scowl on his face like this, but Tyler wondered whether to push it. Then he decided he only had ten miles left stuck in the car so why not risk it. "Ariel?"

"Why would I be mad at Ariel? She can do whatever she wants with whoever she wants."

Tyler laughed softly to himself. *Yup. It is Ariel.* "I was just asking. I ran out of people who piss you off."

"I am not mad at Ariel."

Tyler thought about pushing the topic but then thought better about it. "You want to join me and Chase for a run tomorrow?"

Kyle shook his head. "Nah. I am going to the gym, but thanks."

"Well, just let me know if you change your mind."

XANDER AND ZOEY GOT home from working a long day at the bakery. It was after six and Zoey was covered in sugar, icing and coloring. She told Xander to make himself at home and grab a snack while she got a shower. He looked down at his shirt and he was just as big of a mess as Zoey. Not wanting to sit on her furniture with his sugar laced clothes, he took off his shirt and jeans. After putting on some athletic shorts, he went to the kitchen to grab some paper towels and wipe down his arms and chest from the sugar that somehow made it under his shirt. As he was wiping down, he heard someone coming up the stairs. He knew that Josie was out of town and no one else lived on the floor with the girls. He grabbed a kitchen towel and slung it over his shoulder after drying his hands and made it to the door.

He opened the door just as Tyler stepped up to the door-frame. Tyler had flowers in his hands and took a step back as he found a shirtless Xander standing in front of him.

Xander knew that Tyler wasn't due back for a few days, and so he took a defensive stance in the doorway. "Can I help you?"

Tyler didn't respond for a minute. He stared at Xander who was half naked with Zoey's towel over his shoulder. "Is Zoey here?"

Xander felt his protective instincts heighten. "She can't come to the door right now. She is indisposed."

Tyler looked around the apartment behind Xander and finally said, "Right then. Um...Thanks." He turned around and left to go down the stairs.

As Xander shut the door, he shook his head. *Zoey's boyfriend is gone for a couple of weeks and some creep comes knocking on her door.* Just then Zoey came out from the hall-way dressed in pajamas and looked at Xander with an eye-brow raised.

"SOMEONE WAS AT THE door?"

"Yeah some guy came with flowers."

"Who was it?"

"I dunno. Some tall blonde guy wearing a Marvel t-shirt."

"What did you say?"

"I told him you were indisposed."

"What?!?" Zoey ran to the window and caught sight of Tyler walking across the quad just as he looked back at her apartment. "Tyler!" Zoey sprinted from the window and went out the door in just her pajamas and no shoes. She ran down the stairs and made it out the door to face the quad just as Tyler was making it to the other side getting ready to cross the street.

She screamed out his name and kept running. He didn't hear her at first. He was at the curb waiting for some cars to pass before crossing the street. Zoey picked up her pace. She screamed his name again.

Tyler turned around and saw Zoey running towards him. He stepped off the curb and was standing just below the sidewalk as Zoey caught up to him.

Zoey stopped breathlessly and saw anger and hurt in Tyler's eyes. She started to reach out to him, but he took a step back further into the street.

"You're here," she said breathlessly.

"Yeah. Obviously, I was trying to surprise you, but turns out you surprised me," he said with a sharp tone.

"What's wrong? I don't understand why you are mad." Zoey's heart was plummeting.

Tyler clenched his fists and jammed them into his pockets. "You can't be serious. I leave for a business trip, you have some half naked guy in your apartment, and you don't understand why I am mad?"

Zoey started smiling and then laughing.

Tyler was starting to look hurt. "You're laughing at me? You break my heart and you are laughing at me?

Zoey stopped laughing. "Tyler, that is my brother, Xander. He came to visit and wanted to stay so he could meet you."

Tyler's color started to return to his face. He took a step back towards the sidewalk where Zoey stood. He was still processing what she said. "Your brother?"

"Yes, you big dummy. My brother."

The relief showed clearly on Tyler's face along with a blush. Was that embarrassment? He took a step back up on the sidewalk and started towards Zoey. He stopped when she put her hand up to him.

Frowning Zoey said, "You thought I was cheating on you?"

Tyler hung his head down and replied, "Yeah. I mean he came to the door and wasn't wearing a shirt and said you were indisposed."

"And you couldn't just wait for me to come out and talk to me?"

"I know. It was stupid. I'm sorry."

Zoey stepped forward and started poking her finger into his chest. "You are right it was stupid. I have missed you like crazy. I can't believe you thought I could hurt you like that. You stupid idiot. I love you and you just—"

Tyler's eyes grew wide, and he grabbed her hand mid-poke and he smiled. "You love me?"

"What?"

"You said you love me?"

Zoey gasped. She didn't mean to say it, especially not like this, but she wasn't going to take it back. She took a deep breath. "Yes, I love you. You big idiot."

Tyler bent down, wrapped his arms around her thighs, picked her up and crashed his mouth on hers. Finally, after they broke their kiss he said, "God, Zoey I love you too, and I missed you." He kissed her again. "I came home early to be with you. I couldn't stand being away so long."

Zoey laughed into his neck and said, "I was going crazy. I missed you and wanted desperately to tell you that I love you."

"Aw, Sweetness. I have wanted to tell you that for so much longer." He started to set her down but saw her bare feet. "Where are your shoes?"

Zoey blushed. "I wanted to get to you so quickly that I ran outside without them." Then Zoey and Tyler heard a throat clear from behind. They both turned around to see Xander standing with a broad smile and holding Zoey's sneakers.

Tyler set her down as Xander gave her the shoes. The two men looked at each other for a second before Xander finally spoke.

"So, I hope that you are Tyler."

"Yeah," Tyler replied. "And you must be Xander."

Xander nodded.

Tyler rubbed the back of his neck and reddened his face. "I have been looking forward to meeting you and I am sorry about earlier. When I saw you...uh without your..."

Xander put up his hand. "No need to apologize. I know how it looked." He stopped with a shiver, "And I didn't do anything to stop you from believing that I was uh...well, ugh." He looked at Zoey and continued. "She said you weren't coming back for a few days and so I thought you were some random creep showing up on her doorstep, or worse one of her exes that I never met."

Tyler nodded in understanding and extended his hand in greeting. "Well, it is nice to meet you."

Xander accepted his hand and said, "Nice to meet you too."

Zoey had finished putting on her shoes and wrapped her arms around Tyler's torso. Tyler took his arm around her shoulders and they looked up getting lost in each other.

Xander shook his head. He had heard their declaration earlier to each other and couldn't resist embarrassing his sister. "So, you love my sister?"

Tyler didn't even blink. He looked down at Zoey, smiled and said, "Yes I do."

They looked longingly at each other and Xander began to feel a little out of place. "Zoey, I am going to head over to McKenna's for a bit. I have the spare key. I will just let myself in later... much later."

Zoey giggled. Tyler looked at Xander and said, "We are going back to my place and will be there all night. It is that one over the bakery right there. The apartment will be empty. I hope you don't mind me stealing your sister from your company for the rest of the night."

"Not at all. Have fun. I will catch up with you tomorrow and don't give me any details."

Tyler grabbed Zoey and carried her in a fireman's hold across to the street to his apartment.

Laughing she said, "Put me down Tyler."

"Nope. Not a chance. I am not letting you go for a long time." He growled and took a little love bite from her hip as they continued walking. "Mine," he growled.

Zoey shook her head. "Yes, Tyler... yours."

They made it into his bedroom where he laid her out on his bed. He crawled over the top of her and gazed into her eyes with his lips just a breath's apart from hers. His intense gaze and closeness had Zoey breathing heavily. He finally said, "Did I forget to mention that I love you?"

"I might have heard something like that, but a girl could never hear it enough."

"Sweetness, I love you. I love you from your crazy pajamas, your mad baking skills, your smile and laughter, and how you surprise me every day." He kissed her lips and then made his way down her jaw to her collar bone continuing light brushes with his lips.

"Tyler, I love you too. I love you from your silly t-shirts, your good but less than superior poker skills, your kindness and how you make my heart feel complete every day."

They continued to explore and kiss their way across each other's bodies and whisper declarations of their love for each other. Hours later they laid in each other arms completely sated as Zoey began to fall asleep. Tyler kissed her shoulder and asked, "You are completely mine?"

Zoey turned her head around and placed her hand on his cheek. "Forever and always...yours."

THE NEXT MORNING TYLER heard a knock on his door and found that Zoey had already left the bed to start work at the bakery. Groaning he put on jeans and padded his way to the door. He was surprised when he opened it to see Xander standing there.

"Hey, Zoey is already at the bakery."

Xander gave a crooked grin to Tyler and said, "Yeah I know. I have already been down to see her. Actually, I am here for you, and I brought breakfast." He extended a small white box that held donuts to Tyler.

"Oh, thanks. Come on in." Tyler moved out of the way to allow Xander inside and walked to the kitchen. He opened the refrigerator and asked, "Can I get you a drink?"

Xander shook his head. "No thanks. I had some downstairs."

Tyler took out some orange juice and sat on the stool next to Xander. He waited for Xander to speak since he looked like he had something on his mind.

Xander fidgeted and then finally spoke. "I came over here for a few reasons. First, I want to apologize for how our first meeting went. We weren't expecting you for a couple more days and I thought you were some asshole bothering her while you were gone."

Tyler shook his head. "There is nothing to apologize for. I appreciate that you were looking out for your sister. I know she adores you and I have been looking forward to meeting you. I hoped to make a better first impression too. We're all good."

Xander quirked the corner of his mouth in the beginning of a smile. "Good. I also came out here to check you out. Zoey's past relationships have been disasters and I feel like I failed as a brother to protect her."

"You didn't live in the same town, and from what she told me she hid a lot from everyone."

Xander shook his head. "Then why was Derek able to see something was wrong with one little lunch when I saw her all the time?"

Tyler sighed. "Derek and Zoey have this weird special friendship. I have to admit it is a little intimidating, but I am sure she tried much harder to protect you from what she was going through. You are her little brother and she feels very protective of you and cares very much what you think."

"What I think is that I always want the truth from her, the good and the bad."

"She knows that. She felt bad that you found out online about the break in and didn't get a chance to call you about it."

Xander nodded. "Yeah, that really scared me. Then she started telling me about dating a new guy and how happy she was, and no offense, but I had to come and see for myself that you were okay. Derek had assured me that you were a good guy, but I still had to come down here."

Tyler set down his glass and looked at Xander. "You called Derek."

Xander gave a slight laugh. "Of course, I did. If he told me he didn't like you, I would have been down here much sooner." Xander looked down and started to fidget with his watch. "However, after seeing the two of you together last night, I feel much better. I can see you care about my sister."

Tyler made sure to look Xander in the eyes and said, "Yes, I do. I love your sister. She is the best thing to have ever happened to me. I will always support and care for her."

Xander nodded. "I believe you."

"Good."

Clearing his throat Xander stood up and said, "Anyway I also thought we could get to know each other so I thought I would invite you to join me and Derek on a hike this morning. We are leaving in about thirty minutes."

"Sure. Sounds good. I just need to get a shower and get dressed."

"See you down at the bakery then?"

"Yeah, be right down."

LATER THAT EVENING Zoey was finishing some prep work and was singing and dancing along to "Zoot Suit Riot" when she turned around to see Xander, Tyler and Derek watching her from the back door. She jumped and gasped at seeing them. "Geez guys, you scared me to death."

Tyler was the first to speak. "Sorry Sweetness. We couldn't help it."

She shook her head and looked at the three men. "Well, how could I be mad at my three favorite men?"

Derek smirked and said, "I am her most favorite."

Xander gruffly said, "Ha! Dream on. I am her most favorite."

Tyler shoved the two men aside and strode over to Zoey. "Sorry to break it to you boys but that title belongs to me." Then he picked her up and kissed her deeply as the two others stood wide-eyed.

Xander gave a loud groan. "Seriously, come on man, that is my sister you are mauling."

Zoey broke the kiss and giggled against Tyler's lips while her legs were still dangling in the air. She looked over at Derek and Xander and said, "You are all my favorites. Just different kinds. My brother, my best friend," then looking at Tyler, "and my love."

Xander started to pout. "I am your only brother."

Zoey gave a small laugh. "But you are still my favorite."

Derek gave a small shove to Xander and said, "Winning by default. So sorry man."

Xander gave a small punch to Derek in the gut. "Hush old man."

Derek rubbed his stomach and said, "I am not old, and Tyler is older than me."

"Yeah, well you irritated me more."

Laughing Derek said, "Yeah, but I didn't molest your sister in front of you."

Tyler finally set Zoey down and she went to hug both Derek and Xander. "I love you both, now play nice."

The remaining days with Xander in town were perfect. Zoey enjoyed getting to spend time with Xander both alone and with Tyler. Before Xander left to go back to Cincinnati, he had a chance to talk to Zoey.

"I like Tyler, he seems like a good man."

Smiling she said, "He is. I am so glad that you were able to spend some time with him before you had to leave."

"Just do me a favor Zoey. Keep your independence too. Keep your friends close in your life. With your past relationships you got lost and disconnected from people you cared about. I don't ever want you to go through that again."

"I won't, and the friends I have made out here are all in the same circle. Both people I knew before Tyler and people I have gotten to know since him. I can't begin to tell you how full my life feels right now. Even the townspeople who just come into the bakery are such good people, this place truly feels like home."

Xander nodded. "I can see that. Your friends and this town are great."

"You could move out here too. I would love to have you here with me."

"My life is back in Cincinnati, you know that."

"I know that you have a good job that you couldn't care less about, and a girlfriend who doesn't seem to care enough about you."

"Don't start."

"Sorry, I just want you to be happy too."

"Tell you what...if there ever comes a time where I am truly unhappy, moving here will be at the top of my list."

"Promise?"

"Yes. I promise."

Chapter 18

A few weeks after Xander left to go back to Cincinnati, Tyler took a morning off to visit his parents. Thinking back about the time he had spent with Zoey since he came back from Chicago, it had been perfect. They had a natural ease and comfort with each other. He had never known just how love was supposed to be. The best part of his day was when Zoey would come home from the bakery smelling of sugar and fruit. Her warm smile and openness always amazed him. There was a contentment and sense of completeness each day with her. He pulled into the driveway of his parents' house, and his father came out from the garage with a wrench in his hand. Shaking his head, Tyler got out of the car to greet his dad.

"What is wrong with the car now Dad?"

Mark laughed and wiped his hand on a shop rag. "Nothing. I was just installing new spark plugs."

"That's good. Mom inside?"

"Yeah, she has breakfast waiting on the both of us."

"Well we can't keep her waiting." The two men walked in the house to find Hannah setting the table.

Tyler walked up to his mom and greeted her with a kiss on the cheek. "Everything looks great, Mom."

"Well thank you, sweetie."

"Wow we have bacon too?"

"Turkey bacon."

Mark gave a slight groan. "She won't let me have the good stuff. It is always turkey bacon, turkey sausage, oh and let's not forget turkey ground beef."

Tyler laughed. "She is looking out for your health Dad."

"I would rather have one of Zoey's pastries."

Tyler nodded. "Yeah, well this is better for you."

"So why do you get to eat her food all the time and I don't?"

"I get to kiss the cook, I run with Chase and I am not recovering from a heart attack."

Mark grabbed a piece of turkey bacon and put it on his plate and gave Tyler a sideways glance. "Traitor."

Hannah hit Mark on the top of his head with a kitchen towel. "You leave my sweet little boy alone."

Shoving a piece of toast in his mouth Tyler said, "Yeah Dad, leave her sweet little boy alone."

The playful banter continued between the three of them for the remainder of the breakfast. Tyler helped his mom clean up from breakfast while Mark read the paper at the table. Once they were done, Tyler and Hannah joined Mark sitting on each side of him.

Tyler cleared his throat. "I wanted to talk to both of you about something."

Concerned Mark put his paper down and looked Tyler directly in his eyes. "What's wrong?"

Tyler put a hand on his dad's shoulder and said, "Nothing Dad. Actually, everything has been perfect. That is why I am here."

Hannah's eyes twinkled, and she gave a knowing smile to her son.

Tyler looked at his parents and took a deep breath before continuing. "Zoey is amazing. I am completely in love with her, and I want to start a life with her. I am going to ask her to marry me."

Hannah jumped up from the table and went over to give her son a huge embrace. "Oh sweetie, I am so happy for you. We just love Zoey and can't wait to make her a part of our family."

"Thanks Mom. I know she loves you guys too. I know this is fast, but I know this is right."

Mark stood and put his hand on Tyler's back. "Son, you know I have always said that if you know it is right, don't waste time. I knew I wanted to marry your Mom from the moment I saw her."

"Yeah, I think I fell in love with her the day she crashed on my couch." Tyler turned to his Mom and continued. "Can I have Grandma's ring to propose to Zoey?"

With tears in her eyes Hannah said, "Of course. You know she set that aside for you. Let me just go get it."

After Hannah left the kitchen Mark sat back down and asked, "When are you planning to propose?"

"Saturday after work. This gives me time to get the ring sized for her. I already took one of her rings from her jewelry box and took it over to Eternity's to get her ring size. They are just waiting for me to bring the ring over and promised it could be ready in a couple days."

"I knew I raised a smart boy."

"Thanks Dad."

Hannah came back into the kitchen with a small black box in her hand. She handed it over to Tyler who opened the box for the first time since his grandmother died several years before. It was a beautiful ring. It was white gold with a single round diamond with spiral filigree from the diamond down to the sides of the ring. He closed the box and smiled at his parents. "Thanks Mom, she is going to love this."

"You're welcome, and we can't wait to officially welcome our new daughter to our family."

LATER THAT SAME DAY Shane's boss, Alex, had received the phone call that he had been waiting for from his attorney. The attorney had advised that the financial forensic accounting had been completed on Shane's records. They found that Shane had been embezzling funds from the company for nearly five years. He had been careful with his transactions, and it had taken some extra steps to verify that there were padded purchases on his accounts. Over the five years it amounted to nearly 150,000 dollars. The accountants had also found a charge at a gas station in North Carolina on the day of the break in at Zoey's bakery. Alex spoke with the attorney about bringing the files to his office and to prepare the paperwork so that he could fire Shane and present the documents to the police to press charges.

Alex was furious. He had given Shane every opportunity with his company and he took advantage of him. Not only had he been stealing from his company, but Shane had terrorized that poor girl. All of this was going to come to a stop. It was late in the day so he would not be able to confront Shane until the next business day, but he was relieved that he would no longer be a part of his staff. Since the visit from the police about the incident with Zoey, Shane had been increasingly agitated with the staff and decreased his productivity. Alex had given Shane's secretary special assignments that took her away from the office as much as possible after noticing how Shane had been treating her passive aggressively.

He considered calling the police department immediately about what he had discovered, but decided that he wanted to deal with Shane directly first and then he would deal with the legal consequences.

Alex arranged for security to be stationed in the office when he would have the meeting with Shane the next afternoon. He set the appointment for 3:30 with Shane's secretary and requested for Shane to come to Alex's office. Alex's secretary, Jessica, arranged for one of the security officers to box up Shane's personal items from his office so that he could be walked directly out the door once the meeting had ended.

THE NEXT DAY SHANE was sitting at his desk already in an agitated mood. He had fought with Roberta the night before and he'd lost a few clients at work. He looked at the reminder to attend a meeting with Alex, figuring it would be about the clients that he lost. He prepared some files about new potential clients so that he could defend his position. As the day progressed, he became more agitated about the upcoming meeting. Just before 3:30 he made his way over to Alex's office. He was greeted by Jessica, who advised him to have a seat by Alex's office door while he finished with his conference call.

Shane fidgeted in his seat while anxiously waiting for Alex. He had several things to do and Alex shouldn't keep him waiting. He scheduled this meeting not him, and if Alex was going to bring up productivity numbers Shane decided that he would address time wasted with meetings that didn't seem to accomplish anything. Suddenly, a large man in a dark suit and military style cut came into the waiting room and took a seat next to Shane.

Shane looked over at the man who was at least 6'4" and 250 pounds. He wondered if the man was a new client, because he surely wouldn't be a new employee. He would be very intimidating to customers. The man sat calmly and gave a stony look to Shane while they both waited.

Jessica looked up and said, "Shane, Alex is ready for you now."

"Thanks." He stood up to walk into Alex's office and saw from the corner of his eye that the large man stood up as he entered. He thought that was odd but shook it off as he entered the office.

Alex stood up and said, "Sit down Shane." He opened a file folder that held a significant stack of paperwork. "I am going to get straight to the point. The office has analyzed account files for team members, and we found several discrepancies on your reports and statements. We have a zero tolerance for falsification of records and padding expenses. So, I am releasing you from our employment effective immediately. There will be no severance package."

Shane clenched his fists around the arm of the chair. "Alex, you can't do this. I am sure I can go over these reports to explain the expenses to you. Whoever you have looking at these records just didn't understand what they were looking at."

"No, Shane. We understand perfectly. You took advantage of this company and I will not tolerate it."

"You know that isn't true. I have worked hard for this company."

"You may have worked hard, but you also decided on your own that you could compensate yourself directly from my company, and quite frankly I think you need professional help."

Shane abruptly stood up, and the chair flew back behind him. Enraged he exclaimed, "What?!?!"

Alex rose calmly to look Shane directly in his eyes. "You need help. You have anger and control issues."

"You don't know jack shit about me."

"Do you really think I don't know what kind of man you are? I know who you are—you are a risk to everyone who comes in contact with you."

Shane pounded his fists onto Alex's desk. "You don't know what you are talking about."

The door to Alex's office opened quickly with the large man from the waiting room looming in the doorway with his arms crossed. Shane looked back at the man and then back to Alex.

Alex looked at the man and asked, "Are we all set?"

The large man nodded in confirmation.

Alex looked back at Shane and said, "You are to leave the office with Gus here. Your personal items from your office have already been collected for you. Do not return to this office for any reason. We will express mail your last check."

Shane looked from Gus and back to Alex. He knew that he couldn't win any confrontation with Gus or even Alex. He took one last swipe on Alex's desk and knocked over items that were by the edge of the desk before walking out Alex's door.

ALEX SAT DOWN AT HIS desk and Jessica came in to help him with the items that Shane had thrown. "You don't have to help. I have this." Then Alex's phone rang on his desk. He looked at Jessica and asked her if she could answer it while he continued to clean up.

Jessica answered and looked concerned at Alex. "Alex, it is your wife. Your son got injured at school and is at St Joseph's hospital."

Alex quickly stood up and took the phone from Jessica. "Honey, is he okay? Alright. Hang in there I am on my way." He quickly grabbed his keys and phone and left the office. He had intended to call the Lexington PD about Shane after the meeting but that would have to wait.

LATE SATURDAY AFTERNOON Detective Morris received a phone call from a nurse at the local hospital who stated that she had an unconscious patient under their care who didn't have any identification when she was found on a sidewalk. She was badly beaten and had his business card in her pocket.

Detectives Buxton and Morris arrived at the hospital and greeted the nurse at the front desk of the emergency center.

She started walking the two men to the back room where the woman was still unconscious. "We would normally call the reporting line for this, but I figured since she had your card, we should start with you first."

Morris nodded, "I appreciate that. You did the right thing."

The nurse finally pulled the curtain back where they could see a woman who had been badly beaten. Her face had several bruises and contusions. There were finger bruises around her neck and her arm was already in a cast.

Morris addressed the nurse. "You said she didn't have any ID on her? What about a phone?"

"Her phone is with her personal effects in the bag over there, but it was smashed beyond repair. We couldn't use it to contact anyone on her behalf."

Buxton tightened his mouth in a thin line and said, "We know who this is. Is she going to wake up?"

The nurse said, "We expect her to. We hope it will be soon."

"Okay thanks. We will take care of it from here. Thank you."

The nurse nodded and left the room.

Buxton looked at Morris and said, "This is that girlfriend from the Blossom Hills case."

"I thought so too. I remember giving her my card. Dammit. What happened?"

"Pretty sure that this is the work of the boyfriend. Let's go pick him up."

The two detectives made it back to Shane's house and found the front door open and evidence of a struggle. The glass kitchen table was shattered, and pictures were knocked off the walls. There was a fist-sized hole by the wall of the kitchen. They also could see blood on the floor and some smeared on the walls where the pictures had fallen to the ground. They cautiously continued to search the house and did not find Shane anywhere inside.

Morris went into the bedroom and found all the drawers open with clothes dangling out the sides. The closet also was nearly empty where men's clothes should have been hanging. "He left in a hurry. I don't think he is planning on coming back."

"And it looks like he decided to arm himself too." Buxton pointed to a small gun safe that was thrown on the floor with a couple of bullets still in the case.

"Call it in. And we need to contact Blossom Hills too. Just in case he still wanted to cause trouble for the baker."

Chapter 19

Zoey had an incredible day. Tyler had been surprising Zoey continually with small gifts. He sent flowers to her at work with a card that said, "Sprinkled with Love" in honor of the pajamas she was wearing when they first met. He had Phil deliver a six pack of Diet Coke with a bow on it and another note that said, "I am so grateful for the great Diet Coke disaster." Later, he dropped off a small BB8 figure with a note saying that he would roll with her anywhere.

Zoey couldn't wait for the promised steak dinner. She had sent Phil and Dana home and was almost ready to close for the day. She walked up to the front of the bakery to lock the door and found a man in a jacket and baseball hat walk up to the door. She opened the door to allow in one last customer and suddenly found herself being shoved to the ground.

Shocked, Zoey tried to crawl back away from the man as he kept advancing on her. She was trembling so much that she couldn't get her limbs to cooperate and get on her feet. The man turned around and locked the deadbolt into place. He flipped the sign to closed and turned back to her. Finally, she managed to get up and started to scream.

"Shut the fuck up," the man shouted. He threw off the baseball hat and Zoey found herself looking directly into Shane's coal-black eyes. His face showed a determined hardness and shadows darkened under his features.

"Oh god," she gasped. She turned and tried to run to the kitchen so she could escape out the back door, but Shane was too fast. He caught up to her and shoved her from behind to the ground through the doorway and into the kitchen.

Zoey stood up and knew that she couldn't overpower him. "Shane, please. Don't do this."

Shane stepped forward, raised his arm, and let out a deep growl as his hand came swinging downward. Zoey felt a blinding pain across her temple. The force made her lean down and had the air knocked out of her as she felt a kick to her stomach. She was back on the ground bending over as he continued to kick her repeatedly. With each contact she felt her fear increasing and couldn't catch her breath. A loud crack could be heard coming from her chest and she knew that had to be a rib breaking. He grabbed Zoey by her hair and dragged her across the floor.

When he finally released her, they were by the prep counter. He seemed to be taking a small break to collect his thoughts. Zoey finally looked up and found his eyes. She whispered a plea for him to stop and it just angered him further. Shane pulled her up by her hair to stand in front of him again. She was able to stabilize herself on the prep counter with her hand and then found the panic button on the underside of the table. She pushed the button down as she silently thanked Mrs. Glover for the alarm system. *Someone please help me*, she thought. Suddenly she felt cold steel under her chin pushing her head to look at him. *Oh my God, it's a gun.*

"You are going to pay for everything that you have done to me. But first I am going to get what you still owe me you fat whore."

UPSTAIRS TYLER HAD been preparing dinner for the night when a flashing light suddenly blinded through the apartment. It was the strobe light for the silent alarm going off above the door. "Shit, Zoey!" Tyler threw open the window and stumbled his way down the stairs. He could hear a man's voice and Zoey's sobs. His heart sank. He made it to the bottom as he heard a thud and Zoey cried out in pain. He made it into the back door just in time to see the man had Zoey pinned against the wall with a gun pulling up her skirt. Tears were streaming down her face along with streaks of blood.

"Shane, please don't do this," Zoey cried in between sobs.

Tyler instinctively ran full speed towards Shane and tackled him to the ground. Without Shane pinning her, Zoey crumpled to the ground. She was having problems breathing and was spitting out blood. Tyler and Shane were still wrestling for control. Shane had managed to get an upper hand by grabbing a knife that had fallen to the ground and stabbing Tyler in the shoulder. While Tyler was trying to get the knife out Shane had managed to grab the gun and stood on his feet.

"Get up," he growled.

Tyler stood up with his hands in the air and attempted to look around for how he could gain an advantage. At last he heard sirens in the background. He knew Chase had to be on his way from the alarm getting tripped. He only had to distract Shane long enough.

"Listen, Shane, right?"

"Yeah."

"You could still walk away from this. Just leave out the back door and we will let you go, but if you shoot us, or hurt Zoey any more than you already have, I promise you I will find you. And if it isn't me, it will be someone else who cares about us."

"You really want me to spare this little whore? Did you know she cheated on me?"

Then Zoey's voice came out softly. "Shane, I didn't cheat on you. You didn't trust me. I never slept with anyone else."

"Spare me. I know all about you and your little college friend. I saw you two together."

"You saw us having lunch." Then Zoey started coughing and more blood started coming out from her mouth.

Tyler felt his heart hammering in his chest. He wasn't sure how injured she was but knew that if she was coughing up blood, it was bad. "Zoey calm down, okay?"

Shane pointed the gun directly at Zoey. Tyler ran over to be by her side. He looked calmly at Shane. "You made your point. She suffered. Now just leave."

He cocked the gun and pointed at Tyler's stomach. "No, I don't think she has suffered enough. She needs to lose you just like I have lost Roberta now. A shot to the gut would be a nice, slow painful way for her to watch you die. Don't you think?"

Tyler watched Zoey study Shane's face. His eyes flared and dilated as he raised his arm. Zoey let out a painful scream and dove in front of Tyler, as the loud crack of the gun went off.

Tyler felt Zoey slump down in front of him. He quickly realized that she had stepped in front of the bullet for him. "Oh God Zoey, no! Stay with me baby."

"I can't lose you too. I wouldn't –" Whatever she was going to say was cut off as her eyes closed and her face paled.

Shane gave a menacing laugh. "Perfect."

Then a second crack sounded, and Tyler expected to be shot but instead he saw Shane fall back and the gun slide across the tile floor.

Then he heard Chase's voice, "Tyler put pressure on her wound. Now!"

Tyler laid Zoey on the ground and applied pressure to the bullet wound. She had been shot in the chest. Tears fell furiously as Tyler tried to stop the bleeding. From the corner of his eyes he could see Chase restraining Shane as another officer came through the back door. Zoey was still unconscious as Tyler continued to talk softly to her. "Stay with me Sweetness. I can't do this without you. Zoey...I love you."

Chase told Tyler that the ambulance was on the way and the room started gathering more people. The deputies attended to Shane and Ariel had made her way to the back door. Chase told her that she couldn't be there, but to let everyone know they will be transporting Zoey to the hospital.

"I heard the shots," Ariel said through her tears.

Chase put his hands on her shoulders. "I figured you did. Now go call Derek and everyone. They are going to need them. Okay?"

Ariel nodded and disappeared around the corner.

Tyler was still holding Zoey's wound and Chase finally noticed that he was bleeding onto Zoey. "Did you get shot too?"

"No, I got stabbed."

"Let me put the pressure on the wound. You're injured."

Tyler shook his head. "I am not leaving her."

"I am not asking you to leave her. I am asking to let me help her since you are injured too." Chase took his hands and placed them over Tyler's and nodded for him to release her wound. He finally moved and cupped her head with his hands. He started to stroke her hair but just found that he was smearing her blood into her hair. He was getting nauseous. This was supposed to be their happy day. He was asking her to marry him tonight and now he might lose her.

Finally, the paramedics arrived and began to work on Zoey. Tyler got up and followed them into the ambulance. Once they arrived at the hospital, they immediately took Zoey into surgery. Tyler received some stitches for the knife wound and found himself in the waiting room with Derek, Ariel, Kyle, Dixie and Josie.

Kyle was the first to approach. He gave his brother a hug and Tyler winced in pain from the contact from his wound. "Sorry. Mom and Dad are on their way."

Tyler nodded. He saw Derek holding Ariel who was red nosed from crying and shaking in his arms. Derek looked up at Tyler not releasing his hold from Ariel. "Please tell me that bastard is dead."

Tyler sighed. "Honestly, I don't know if he is alive or not. Chase shot him and I saw him go down, but I really don't know. I didn't ask."

The group had already been at the hospital for an hour and were still waiting for more news on Zoey. Everyone was on edge. Dixie looked up from her phone after receiving a message and said, "Chase said he should be here in a couple of hours."

About fifteen minutes later Tyler's parents arrived with Derek's mom, Amanda. Hannah and Mark embraced Tyler and attempted to comfort him. Amanda joined Ariel and Derek and held her daughter. Derek stood up and started to pace the room.

Tyler looked at Derek and said, "Can you call Xander? He would want to be here."

Derek nodded and walked outside to make the call.

When the doctor arrived in the waiting room a couple hours later, he looked around and asked for Zoey's family. Derek stood up and put his hand on Tyler's shoulder and said, "Tyler is her fiancé."

Grateful for Derek, Tyler nodded to the doctor. "Anything you have to tell me you can tell all of us."

The doctor looked around the room and then continued, "Zoey had a bullet wound in her chest that we were able to remove. It missed her heart. She has fractured ribs and a punctured lung. She also has a concussion and swelling on her brain. She is unconscious. The operation went well but the next twenty-four hours are critical."

All the air in Tyler's lungs were gone. He couldn't breathe. "Can we go see her?"

"Yes, but only two at a time for now. I can take you back to her room."

After trying to take in a breath and gain some oxygen, Tyler and Derek followed down the corridor to her open door. Tyler entered first and sat in the chair next to her. Derek stood solemnly by her other side. Tyler's stomach dropped as he looked at the tubes and wires all connected to her. She looked so pale, and her face was bruised. The blood had been cleaned from her face and hair for which he was thankful.

"Sweetness you are going to have to wake up for me. We have a life to begin together."

From behind him he heard Chase's voice, "Yes, you do." Chase then walked up to Tyler and held out his hand. "My deputies found this on the ground in the kitchen. You'll still need this."

He placed a small box in Tyler's hand, and it was the engagement ring he was supposed to give to Zoey. "Thanks Chase."

"I am going to wait out with everyone else and give you some time."

"Thanks." Tyler set the ring down on the bed.

He continued to watch Zoey, hold her hand and listen to the beeps of the monitor. He rested his head on the side of the bed kissing her on her palm. Soon he found himself falling asleep slumped on the side of her bed. He wasn't sure how much time had gone by when he felt a hand combing through his hair. He brought his head up to see Zoey looking down at him.

"Zoey, God, you're awake," he said and for the first time since he saw the strobe light flash, he felt like he could get air back in his lungs.

Zoey attempted a smile. "I am."

Tyler stood up and leaned over and began to kiss her gently all over her face. Her lips, her cheeks, her eyes. He didn't want to leave any part of her neglected. "I love you so much. I thought I was going to lose you. I can't believe you took that bullet. You stupid amazing woman. Don't you know I can't live without you?"

Zoey had tears falling and said, "And I couldn't live without you."

Tyler sat back down and took her hand.

Zoey brought her other hand from the side of the bed and it held the ring box. "What's this?"

Tyler felt his face flush and started to grin. "Oh Sweetness, this is definitely not what I had planned, but here goes."

Zoey looked back at him in confusion but was joining him in a slight smile.

"Zoey, finding you on my couch has been the best thing to ever happen to me. I wasn't really living until you found me. It was as if you breathed new life into me from the second I saw you. I know I have told you this before, but you amaze me. You are so open in so many ways despite everything from your past, and I am honored that you have let me into your heart. And it is such an incredible heart. I want to start a life together and to have you be mine always. Will you marry me?"

Tears streamed down Zoey's face and she hoarsely whispered, "Yes."

Tyler put the ring on her finger and kissed her with every ounce of desperation and passion that the night had brought forth. Tyler knew that he had found his forever and he would never be the same again. They would always be surrounded by friends, family and their love building a future together.

Epilogue

It was nearly eight weeks later when Zoey and Tyler were at his parents with all of their friends celebrating their engagement. Zoey had finally been given the clearance to return to work by the doctor and couldn't wait to get back. She watched over her friends as they laughed and danced on the makeshift dancefloor that was Tyler's parents back yard.

Xander had made the trip to Blossom Hills for now the third time. He was sitting next to Zoey on the bench swing. He made his second trip after the attack. He arrived at the hospital several hours after Tyler proposed. He was visibly shaken and didn't want to leave her side for almost two days. Zoey had to kick him out and threatened to never give him another baked treat if he didn't go back to her place to get a shower and some rest. Tyler wasn't much better about leaving her side, but she was able to convince him to check up on things at home and the bakery for her. She thought he may have only gotten four hours of sleep that first week.

Xander gave his sister a side hug and said, "I am so happy for you. Tyler is a good guy and the people you have here are great."

Zoey beamed. "Yes, they are. You sure I can't convince you to move out here?"

Xander shook his head. "Nah. I still have a good job and a girl back home."

Zoey sighed. "Okay, but just know that I won't ever stop asking you to move out here."

Laughing he said, "I would be disappointed if you gave up easily."

TYLER WAS TALKING TO Chase and watching Zoey from across the yard as she talked to her brother. His life couldn't be more complete. Each time he thought back to the night he almost lost her he felt a sense of panic, but with each day it grew less and less.

Shane had survived his gunshot wound. He got off easy considering the long road to recovery that Zoey and Roberta had. Roberta had a longer recovery and had suffered more injuries. Shane was still being held without bail while waiting for trial on two charges of attempted murder, aggravated assault, and embezzlement.

When Chase talked to Tyler at the hospital, he explained that they were lucky he was so close to the bakery when the alarm went off. He had been called by Detective Buxton just minutes before to alert him about Shane's attack on Roberta and that he was armed and missing.

The group of friends had worked alongside of Dana and Phil to make sure the bakery stayed open. Tyler ordered each of them an apron that matched Zoey's black, white and pink ruffled one. To cheer her up one day the entire group posed for a picture holding a cupcake while they each wore their apron. Zoey loved the picture and had Tyler hang it up by the front counter.

Once Zoey was released from the hospital it took nearly all of them to convince her not to go back to work too soon. The townspeople were also very supportive and kind. Many residents dropped off casseroles and dinners so that Tyler and Zoey didn't have to cook.

Chase slapped his hand on Tyler's back and said, "You are a lucky guy. Just don't screw it up."

Tyler shook his head. "Never." Tyler looked over at the far side of the yard where Kyle, Ariel, Dixie and Jay were talking under a tree. "Now, when exactly are you going to stop screwing it up?"

Chase looked over at his friends and grabbed a wing. After taking a bite he said, "Don't know what you are talking about."

"Okay then."

Tyler smiled as Zoey and Xander joined them. Zoey tucked herself under Tyler's arm.

Chase took another bite of wings and said, "So when is the wedding."

Zoey said, "We are going to have it this fall. I love the idea of the changing leaves and we decided to have it at the grand hall at the orchards."

"You going to bake your own wedding cake?"

"Nope. Dana said she wants to do it. Her skills have grown so much, and she is excited to do it, and I am more than happy to let her take care of it."

The remainder of the group joined them, and Zoey turned to Derek while the others talked amongst each other.

She gave him a big hug and quietly said, "Thank you for saving me and bringing me here."

Derek gave a long exhale as he carefully embraced his friend. "Anytime Zoe. I missed my best friend, and I am so happy you are here. Even if you are marrying the nerd."

Zoey released from his hug and gave a friendly slap to him on the chest. She looked around at her friends who she now knew as her family and stopped at Tyler's warm gaze. Tyler wrapped his arms around her again, as he had done so many times now and she smiled as she said, "He is my nerd. Forever and always."